"Are you going to answer me?"

Morgan wanted to reach over and haul Tara close. He knew he had to resist, but what a temptation she was. He ached. He knew he had to face her, had to look at her, had to tell her the truth and risk—no, probably guarantee—it would push her away.

"Go home, Tara. Or back to the diner," he said softly, slowly turning his head to look at her, clenching the steering wheel in a death grip.

"Not until you answer me." She settled into the truck's seat. "Are you coming back?"

The silence was thick. "No. Coming back would be a mistake."

It took her a while to digest that. "Why?" she finally whispered.

Morgan's heart sank to somewhere deep in his gut. He paused, not wanting to see the reaction on her face, not wanting to see her hurt, anger or disappointment. He squared his shoulders. The words sat bitter in his stomach before he let them go.

"Tara. I'm...married."

Dear Reader,

The A Chair at the Hawkins Table series continues with Tara and Morgan's story. If you've read my other books, you've met Tara. Her talent and desire to cook great meals for the people she loves is a big part of what defines her.

When I sat down to figure out her story, I struggled with what kind of man would be her forever love.

At that time, I'd reconnected with a childhood friend on social media and we were revisiting a ton of memories from the old neighborhood. My friend was the youngest child in her family, just like Tara, and her father was a trucker who was often gone for long stretches at a time.

It occurred to me that the man for Tara would come into her life through her cooking. The Someday Café and Morgan were born with that realization. I saw him in my imagination sitting on that stool at the end of the counter—just like where Tara first meets him.

I hope you enjoy Tara and Morgan's story, and visit the rest of her extended family, here and in their respective books. They really are quite a family.

Please feel free to contact me at angel@angelsmits.com, www.angelsmits.com or at 5740 N Carefree Circle, Suite 120-4, Colorado Springs, CO 80917.

Angel Smits

ANGEL SMITS

—

Last Chance at the Someday Café

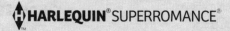
HARLEQUIN® SUPERROMANCE®

Recycling programs for this product may not exist in your area.

ISBN-13: 978-0-373-64052-2

Last Chance at the Someday Café

Copyright © 2017 by Angel Smits

This edition published by arrangement with Harlequin Books S.A.

For questions and comments about the quality of this book, please contact us at CustomerService@Harlequin.com.

Printed in U.S.A.

www.Harlequin.com

Angel Smits shares a big yellow house, complete with gingerbread and a porch swing, in Colorado with her husband, daughter and Maggie, their border collie mix. Winning the Romance Writers of America's Golden Heart® Award was the highlight of her writing career, until her first Harlequin book hit the shelves. Her social work background inspires her characters while improv writing allows her to torture them. It's a rough job, but someone's got to do it.

Books by Angel Smits

HARLEQUIN SUPERROMANCE

A Chair at the Hawkins Table

The Ballerina's Stand
The Marine Finds His Family
A Family for Tyler

Seeking Shelter
A Message for Julia

Other titles by this author available in ebook format.

This is for all the kids who grew up with me in the old neighborhood. Lisa, Barry, Larry, Greg, Debbie, Matt, Dan, Julie, Steve, Janet, Jamie, Colleen, Betty and April. Riding bikes, running the streets, climbing trees, shooting fireworks and trick-or-treating were that much more fun with all of you. Thanks for the memories.

And to Ron, for making being a grown-up just as much fun!

CHAPTER ONE

TARA HAWKINS WALKED in through the front door of her childhood home for the last time. She'd only been here a couple times since Mom's funeral, and now the house had sold. Tomorrow, someone else would start a new life here.

But tonight, one last time, it was theirs.

The foyer was empty. No coats on the hall tree. No shoes distractedly kicked off. The living room beyond was just as empty. Everything was stripped from the walls. No pictures. No furniture. Only the curtains at the front window fluttering in the breeze. It looked abandoned.

Her running shoes slapped against the newly polished wood floor. She kept moving, hurrying down the hall to escape the emptiness that threatened to reach out and suck her in.

Tonight, everyone was supposed to be here—all five of her siblings, maybe a couple in-laws and at least one nephew, possibly two. She was the last to arrive—again. They'd all give her a rough time about it. As usual. But this time, she had an excuse. She didn't want to be here. But then, neither did they. Not really.

They'd gather in the kitchen. The big kitchen had always represented home to Tara. She heard their voices in a harmonic flow that reached to her and soothed her grief.

Wyatt's deep growl. Mandy's high-pitched voice cooing to little Lucas. DJ's laughter mingled with Jason's soft chuckles. She didn't hear Addie, which meant… Tara hustled down the hall.

Addie stood at the counter, a big glass bowl of cookie dough in front of her, and scattered tools that she'd obviously brought with her at her elbow. Addie made *the* best cookies. Looked like there would be one last batch made here in Mom's kitchen.

Playful cheers went up as Tara entered. "About time," DJ teased.

"I was hoping to get her share of the cookies," Wyatt added with mock disappointment.

"Very funny." Tara rolled her eyes as she snagged one of the folding chairs. The dining table was staying with the house, too big and heavy to move, and the new owner, according to Addie, was happy to have it. All the chairs, however, were gone. When Mom had passed away, the chairs had been precious reminders of home. They'd each taken theirs with them. Tara's was in the spare bedroom of her apartment.

But she had plans for it. Such big plans. Her stomach flipped as she settled next to DJ. They didn't know. Well, most of them didn't know. Jason, her older brother and one of the smartest attorneys she'd ever met—and she was only slightly biased—knew. She'd consulted him and sworn him to secrecy. He'd never violate lawyer-client privilege—even for family.

He winked at her, and she mentally grinned. She sat back and watched Addie work, enthralled with her sister's confident actions. Was that what Tara looked like in her own kitchen? She hoped so.

She'd grown up helping their mother cook, and it had been the one thing she'd shared with Mom. Her sisters helped with big meals like holidays, but mostly it had been just Tara and Mom. The ache in her chest eased just a bit as she watched her big sister step into Mom's role.

"I've never asked you where you got that recipe." It hadn't been Mom's.

Addie shrugged. "I made it up."

"You what?"

"Yeah." Addie looked over her shoulder and smiled at Tara's surprise. "You're not the only cook in the family."

"I know that." Tara tried to dismiss her sister's teasing, accusatory comment.

"Oh, that reminds me." Addie shoved a cookie sheet into the heated oven and set the timer before turning around. "I found this." She pulled open the pantry door, lifted out a box that had definitely seen better days, then set it on the table.

"What's that?" Tara and the others stared at the battered cardboard box.

"Open it." Addie returned to the cookies.

Tara pushed the chair back as she stood and opened the flaps. Book spines. A rubber-banded stack of cards. Recipe cards. She gasped. "Where did you find them?" She pulled out the stack of stained, tattered cards. When was the last time she'd seen them? "Mom's and Grandma's?" She shuffled through them slowly, carefully—reverently.

"I think so." Addie looked up with a smile. "You'd know better than I would. They were in the back of the pantry."

Tara's throat ached as memories bloomed in her mind. Of Mom shuffling through these same cards. Sticking the needed card in between the loose frame of a cabinet door. Her gaze turned to that familiar cupboard door next to Addie now. It had never been repaired. Her vision blurred.

She swiped at her eyes and looked at Jason. She frowned. Why give her these today? "Did you tell them?"

He shook his head. "No, I didn't say a thing."

"Tell us what?" Wyatt asked. Seconds ticked by as Tara's gaze locked with Jason's. He simply shrugged. He wasn't helping. It was up to her.

"I—" Her excitement grew and with an emerging smile that suddenly made it all feel real, she finished, "I bought the diner in Haskins Corners." She hugged the precious recipe cards to her chest. "We closed the deal today."

Tara looked around, hoping for smiles and congratulations. The silent stares were not what she'd expected. She knew she'd shocked them all, but this silence was heavy. The buzz of the timer going off was especially loud.

"Oh." Addie broke the trance and pulled the cookie sheet out of the oven. The scent of chocolatey, peanut buttery deliciousness wound through the room, nudging everyone to awareness. They didn't, however, smile.

She hadn't expected total excitement from them, but neither had she expected this—what did she even call it—lack of support? Surprise?

"That's an awfully big commitment." DJ was frowning. "Especially for someone so—"

"Don't say it." She hated when they pointed out her faults.

"Young." He leaned closer, his frown deepening, if that were possible. "Not saying it doesn't make you any older."

"Now, DJ." Mandy hoisted Lucas up on her shoulder and gently patted his back in a rhythmic caress. "She's always talked about this. That's not a huge surprise."

"But it is a bit of a surprise now." Addie slowly

scooped cookies off the sheet. "Why didn't you tell us before you committed to it?"

"Because I didn't need your help. Just Jason's legal advice."

"And *you* didn't tell us?" Addie shook her spatula at Jason.

"Client-lawyer privilege. Sorry, it's business."

"That's no excuse." Addie roughly scooped dough from the bowl and plopped it onto the cookie sheet with an uncharacteristic thunk. "This is family."

"Addie." Wyatt's voice filled with warning, and while Tara appreciated the support, his scowl told her he wasn't any happier.

"Hon, don't take this wrong." Mandy put her hand over Tara's. "We just care so much about you."

"You all know me." Tara's indignation rose and her throat ached. She was not going to cry or lose her temper. She'd expected congratulations, not— not this. "You know I've dreamed about this since I was a kid."

"Yes, but—" Addie wiped her hands on a towel. "This is such a big step. We expected you to work for someone else, in a fancy restaurant for a while. Learn about business before taking such a leap."

"You know I wouldn't let her go totally stupid, right?" Jason tried to reassure them, but that only made Tara angrier.

"It wasn't your choice. Any of you." She let her gaze move around the room, meeting everyone's stare until landing on Jason's. "I asked for your advice as a lawyer. That's all."

"And I gave it," he reminded her. "It's a good deal," he told the rest of them. "She got a bargain and the interest rate on the loan was excellent."

"Loan?" Wyatt snapped.

"Yes, loan." Tara knew Wyatt's philosophy on debt. Combine his overprotectiveness with his experience seeing his colleagues in the ranching industry fall under debt, and she knew she'd hit a nerve. "I used my inheritance for most of it, but it wasn't enough." She glared at Jason. They didn't need to know the details. That's why she hadn't told them in the first place.

"You let her go into debt for this?" Wyatt snatched one of Addie's fresh cookies and bit into it, hard. "What were you thinking?"

"She can handle it. It's a solid deal."

She didn't need Jason to defend her, and Wyatt needed to back off. "Hellooo…" She waved her hands. "I'm still here."

Addie put the second batch into the oven, then turned to lean against the counter, arms crossed in front of her. Her frown said more than Tara wanted to hear. She looked so much like Mom when she did that. Tara's heart hurt.

But Mom would have supported her. She wouldn't have gotten upset about this. *Oh, Mom.*

I miss you, she mentally whispered. Mom had always encouraged her to follow her dreams, like she had for all of them.

And Tara was not giving up on this dream.

DJ must have seen her stubbornness on her face. "We aren't angry with you. Do you really think you're ready for this?"

Tara knew she was ready, but damn it, they were making her doubt herself. As the youngest, she had always felt the weight of her siblings' shadows. She slowly looked around the room full of people she loved. Their frowns said it all.

Addie and Wyatt shared a glance. An all-too-familiar glance that spoke volumes. Tara's emotions bubbled to the surface. "You don't believe in me!"

They both actually had the nerve to look surprised. "We didn't say that," Addie said.

"You don't have to say it." Tara threw up her hands. "It's all in that look."

Tara marched to the door, wishing and praying someone would stop her and deny all her fears, reassure her that she'd misunderstood, that she was wrong, that they did have total faith in her.

No one spoke. The only sound was each of her steps through the empty rooms and finally the smack of the front door banging against its frame.

She kept walking across the yard. "Do not cry," she repeated half a dozen times before she reached her bright red Jeep and climbed in. She slammed the door and rammed her foot on the gas before tearing out of the drive.

"I'll show you," she said to the rearview mirror. "I'll show you all," she repeated to the dust cloud that rose up behind her as she headed toward the highway.

SILENCE SUDDENLY FILLED the room, telling Morgan Thane he wasn't alone. The driving rock beat had swiftly faded away as his younger brother, Jack, turned down the volume on the stereo.

The weights in Morgan's fists still moved rhythmically, the soft clink of metal on metal now the only sound left.

"Do you even know what silence sounds like?" Jack asked, pulling his own earbuds free.

"You're listening to your own tunes." Morgan pointed at the earbuds Jack never went anywhere without.

"This is white noise to drown out your racket. That stuff gives me hives."

"Stuff?" Morgan tried to look insulted. "*Stuff*? College-educated guy like yourself can't come up with a better word than *stuff*?"

"Nope." Jack stepped farther into the room, leaving his phone on the table while he went to the fridge.

Morgan watched Jack move across the apartment. It wasn't big, so it didn't take him long. He knew his brother. He knew that body language.

Trouble. Something was wrong. "You going to tell me what's up, or am I supposed to guess?"

Jack yanked open the refrigerator. "You got any more of those energy drinks?"

"Yeah. Back of the second shelf." Morgan knew where every single item he owned was located. He'd always been that way, and after having so little as a kid—and with his soon-to-be-ex, Sylvie, taking off with everything else—he'd become a bit obsessed about it.

Jack reached in for a can, then popped the top. After he'd downed half the drink, he walked over to the computer to boot it up. He set down the drink, then settled in the old kitchen chair that doubled as a desk chair. He didn't say a word.

Morgan didn't stop. He was only three quarters of the way through his workout. So, the only sounds that broke the apartment's quiet were the hum of the computer fan and the easy rhythm of the weights against the bar as Morgan worked on curls.

Finally done, Morgan set down the weights. "Okay, spit it out." He grabbed the towel and his water bottle, letting himself cool down before diving into whatever Jack was working on.

"I'm looking for a load for you so this trip won't be a complete waste."

That quieted Morgan's next comments. Their company had several over-the-road hauling contracts. But what Jack was best at, and what had made them successful, was his brokering skills. The rest of the crew worked on everyday loads. But Morgan had a mission that had nothing to do with their regular customers, and if Jack could get him one-time loads, it paid well. As long as you weren't picky about what was riding behind you.

And Morgan wasn't. Morgan was freestyling as he hunted for his ex, who'd taken off with their daughter before the divorce and custody agreement had been finalized.

Nearly a year had passed since Morgan had seen his daughter, Brooke. She was supposed to start school this fall, and Morgan refused to think about her doing so anywhere but home, refused to even entertain the idea that she might actually not start school at all. Sylvie wasn't that organized or dedicated to anything.

Despite finishing his workout, Morgan nearly started lifting the weights again. Frustrated energy was the worst to burn off.

"So where you headed next?" Jack asked, without looking up from the computer screen.

When Sylvie had first disappeared, and Morgan had decided to hunt for her and Brooke, Jack had bought him a map of the entire United States that dominated one wall.

They both knew Sylvie well enough to know she wasn't going to take Brooke out of the States, but there were forty-eight of them and he'd driven through most of them trying to find her.

That US map had eventually been covered up by a new one of just the western states. It had taken only a couple months to narrow down where she'd gone. The network of truckers Morgan and his crew knew had provided a lot of the early information. Following the trail of credit cards had also helped—until Sylvie apparently realized she was leaving a trail. Now it was a map of just Texas. At least she'd stayed in the same state.

"Here." Morgan swept his hand over the western part of the state, waving his hand over the area west of Austin. "There was a charge on one of her old cards last week."

"It could have been stolen," Jack suggested.

"Yeah. Or she could be just passing through." But he couldn't ignore even the smallest clue. The small bedroom communities he was heading to were kitschy tourist towns with streets lined with old junkshops, eclectic restaurants and run-down motels. Sylvie territory.

No place for a child. Especially his child.

His frustration at not having found her, and at being stupid enough to get involved with someone like Sylvie in the first place, bubbled to the surface in the form of guilt. His protective streak was too ingrained, but she hadn't wanted his protection, hadn't ever planned to stay.

What if he never saw Brooke again? Or worse, what if the next time he saw his daughter, she was an adult who came to find *him* and wanted to know why he'd never looked for her, never found her? He swallowed the panic and resisted the urge to smash something.

"Get out of your head, Morgan." Jack's voice broke into his thoughts.

"And you wonder why I listen to the music?"

"No, I don't wonder." Jack did look at Morgan this time. "Let's get you a load, if we can. Hopefully, we can at least cover the fuel."

"Hey." Morgan pulled out a chair, spinning, then straddling it, stacking his thick arms on top of the back. "How much is this straining the business? Is it making it too rough on you?"

Jack didn't stop typing, his fingers smacking the keys loud and hard. "No. We're tight, like we always are, but we're good."

"Are you sure?" The tension Morgan could see in his brother's shoulders denied the reassurances.

"Even if we aren't?" Jack stopped typing and looked up. "She's important to me, too. She's my niece, Morgan. This is my mission, too. So get to work. I'll get you a load." He went back to typing.

"Thanks." Morgan stood and carefully put the chair back. "I'm taking the truck for a bath. I'll start my checks after we grab dinner."

Jack nodded. "I'll have your route mapped out by then."

Outside, the afternoon sun was bright, but the wind was cold, cutting through him. He'd left his jacket in the truck, not needing it this morning. He smelled damp in the air. Sucky start of a run.

There'd been way too much rain this year. And the season wasn't over yet. The last time he'd gone out, he'd been stuck in El Paso for two days, unable to get back because of the flooding. This time, if he got stuck, maybe it'd be closer to either Sylvie and Brooke, or home.

The big Peterbilt roared to life, purring beneath his hands, rumbling as he pulled across the yard. Nearly a dozen trailers sat parked inside the fence. These were empty right now, but by tomorrow, Jack would work his magic and the trailers would be out of here, on their way to being loaded, then delivered.

Two men headed toward the office. Phil and Brian—good men. Jack knew the crew better than he did these days. When was the last time Morgan had taken the chance to chat with them? He missed that. Missed time with his brother. He closed his eyes for an instant. He just missed downtime.

But finding Brooke was more important.

And if he missed anything, it was her.

He drove out of the yard, under the big steel sign he'd been so proud to hang—Thane Brothers Trucking. He'd worked damned hard to build this company. Hell, he still did, but what good was it doing any of them?

Damn Sylvie. He sighed and flipped on the

stereo. Blaring the hard rock forced the emotions out of his head. He steered to the truck wash, not letting himself dwell on what did—or did not—lay ahead on this trip. He wasn't sure how much longer he could do this, how much longer he could ask Jack and the others to shoulder his share of the load.

Sitting there, waiting for the attendant to guide him into place, Morgan wrestled with his indecision.

This run had to be a success. He had to find Brooke. When he'd first reported them missing, the authorities had done what they could. They kept him informed. But it wasn't fast enough. Yesterday wasn't soon enough to have his daughter back.

Morgan was running out of time. He knew it. He'd never stop looking, never stop searching for her. But he also knew Jack was lying to him. Things were tight, too tight. Jack needed him to get back in the office, to help run the company they'd built together. Morgan needed to do his job. He owed Jack and his crew that.

Damn it.

He couldn't ask his brother or his men to sacrifice anything more. This had to be his last run. Either he found them and came home—or he didn't and he gave up on this quest.

It was the right decision.

So why did it make his heart ache?

TIRED BEYOND BELIEF, Tara brushed the soft blue paint around the last doorframe. Doing the painting herself was one way she could save money on this venture. Over halfway done, she smiled. *Done.* What a lovely word.

Once these two walls were finished—and the furniture brought in—the Someday Café would be one step closer to reality. She'd be one step closer to true independence.

"Hello?" A woman's voice came across the empty dining room, startling Tara. She'd thought she was alone. Her arms ached, and she hoped to finish soon. She didn't have time for interruptions.

Still, she settled the brush on top of the paint can and turned. She knew she didn't look her best. A shadow of blue teased at the corner of her eye. Honestly? She had paint in her hair? Again?

The woman standing in the doorway wasn't anyone Tara knew. "Can I help you?" She wiped her hands on the tail of her paint shirt.

"Uh, yeah." The woman stepped forward, extending a hand tipped with black-lacquered fingernails. "I'm Sylvie." Her smile didn't quite reach her eyes. "I thought you might be hiring."

She was, but something about the woman jarred Tara. Maybe it was the black nails? Or maybe the pink-and-blue spiked hair? No. She squinted, trying to figure it out. The midnight blue lipstick on the lips that sported two metal rings? What'd they call those things? Snake bites? *Ouch.*

The youngest of six kids whose father had died when she was two, Tara had been coddled and nearly spoiled by her family—which sometimes left her ill-prepared for a world beyond their loving arms.

And leery of strangers. Like this Sylvie. But Tara knew it wasn't the woman's outer appearance that made her pause. No, it was the bloodshot eyes that lacked any warmth or caring.

"We won't be open for a few more weeks."

"Oh, that's okay. I have a job at the T-shirt shop—my real one—so I'm not in any big rush."

"Uh-huh." Tara bit her tongue, holding back the question she knew she couldn't utter. This wasn't a *real* job? This place that had taken every dime of her savings and inheritance and then some? This restaurant that was her dream, and yet the hardest thing she'd ever done, wasn't a "real" business?

Tell her aching muscles that.

Tara racked her brain for an excuse to end this conversation and get back to work. "Well, as you can see, I'm busy right now." She gestured at the paint and drop cloths. "Maybe in a week or so I can get started on the applicants." She'd already scheduled two interviews, but something told her she shouldn't tell this woman that.

"Sure. I'll come back." Sylvie smiled and spun

on her heel. At the doorway, she stopped and looked back. "This will look really cool when you're done. But that old blue is awful. White'll really brighten up the place."

"Really?" Tara couldn't hide her sarcasm. Keeping her mouth shut had never been a strength.

"Definitely. I studied design in school for a while. White is like a blank canvas." She spread her arms wide. "I could help you design a whole new place."

Tara didn't want a whole new place. "Uh, thanks. I'll let you know." Tara could only stare, hoping the woman wouldn't return. She left the way she'd come, the door slamming closed behind her.

Tara looked at the light blue paint she'd agonized over choosing and had spent the better part of a week putting on the walls. It was perfect and would look beautiful—she hoped—with the lace curtains she'd ordered.

The old-fashioned, homey, wood furniture was in storage until she finished painting, and the oak floor was scheduled to be refinished later this week.

Picturing those black fingernails putting out the lace doilies she'd bought at the flea market last week made Tara cringe.

No, Sylvie wasn't a good match for this place. She was too rough. Too edgy. This place had no edge. It was about comfort food and relaxation.

Turning to her work, Tara forced herself to slow down and not slap the paintbrush against the wall. *Old blue? Really?* She reached for the long-handled roller and started on the next wall, all thoughts of taking a break gone.

As she worked, her brain kept time with the rhythm of the roller. Was she doing the right thing? *Up.* She'd worked too hard to have doubts now. *Down.* What if everyone thought like Sylvie? *Up.* Not everyone had blue hair. *Down.*

The light shifted and the streak of blue in her own blond hair caught her eye again. Present company excepted. "I am *not* like her," she said aloud.

"Not like who?"

Startling her worse than Sylvie had, DJ came into the room. Tara dropped the paint roller, which landed with a sloppy plop on the wood floor, flinging more paint in the air—most likely adding to her hair.

"Good thing you're refinishing that," he said, unruffled as usual. He carefully made his way across the room. His back must be bothering him today since he moved slowly. Though he was healed, DJ would never be a hundred percent like he was before he'd been wounded in Afghanistan.

"Why are you here?" She bent to pick up the roller and wiped up as much of the paint as she could.

"Grumpy today?" He lifted a white bag with

a familiar logo on it. Her favorite burger joint. "Is that any way to greet the person saving you from starvation?"

"I'm fine." Her stomach rumbled just to make a liar out of her.

"Uh-huh."

He carried the bag over to the diner's long counter. She'd covered it with an old sheet while she worked, and he pushed it away, exposing the beautiful hand-carved surface.

Seeing it went a long way toward reassuring her that buying this place was a good idea. She'd fallen in love with the counter the first time she'd seen it, and it still amazed her it was now hers.

The scent of her favorite burger made her mouth water. "What's this?" She climbed up on one of the low vinyl stools that were anchored on chrome pedestals to the floor. "Bribery?"

"A peace offering." He had the grace to look chagrined. "We weren't very supportive the other day."

"You think?" She stared at him.

"Here." He fished a burger out of the bag and put it on the counter. On the tail of that delicious aroma, the container of fries emitted a wonderful smell of grease and heat.

Tara bit into the luscious burger, savoring the warm juices that exploded in her mouth. She loved to cook, but years ago, she'd learned the value of letting someone else cook sometimes.

This was one of those times. She did have a danged good burger on the menu, but this one she didn't have to make herself.

And it tasted like heaven.

"If you love these burgers so much," DJ said around a mouthful, "why don't you make them yourself? Heck, I like yours better."

"I could. But where's the fun in that?"

"It's looking good in here." DJ nodded to the mostly blue walls.

"Yeah," she agreed.

"Hey!" Another voice interrupted them. They both turned to find Addie standing there, a box in her arms, on top of which was an identical white bag emblazoned with the same logo.

"Beat you to it, sis." DJ grinned, barely taking a break from his meal.

Addie came over and settled beside Tara. "Here I thought I had a good idea."

"It is a good idea." Tara reached for the new bag. "At least you all know my favorite junk food." She grinned at Addie. "And she…" Tara nodded toward her sister with a pointed glance at DJ. "She remembered I like chocolate shakes with my fries." She pulled out the tall cup and shoved the straw through the lid. "Yum!"

"I brought this, too." Addie's voice was nearly a whisper. The box from the night at Mom's. The recipes. "Thought you might need it."

"Thanks." Tara ducked her head, concentrating

on her food instead of the warm emotion flowing inside her.

They ate until the door opened again. Wyatt came in and froze halfway across the room. His frown made them all laugh.

"Hey, big brother," Tara greeted him. "Come join us." Looking at the size of the white bag in his hands, she said, "Hope you're hungry, since there's going to be a lot left. Is Emily with you?" She didn't see his wife anywhere.

"No," he growled as he settled next to Addie. "DJ, the leftovers are yours." He shoved the bag down the counter.

"Was I just insulted?" DJ nabbed a spare pack of fries from the new bag with a wide grin. "Thanks for the fries."

"Anytime."

DJ shrugged. "What we don't want, I can take home to Pork Chop and Hamlet." His son's pet pigs were going to feast tonight.

Tara smiled, enjoying the food and the company. "We've got enough for Mandy and Jason, too. Too bad they aren't here."

"Yeah." Addie sat back, her eyes distant as she enjoyed her own shake. Strawberry—Tara knew without even looking—Addie's favorite since they were kids. "I miss us all being together." There was sadness in her voice.

"They aren't missing us." DJ laughed and they all joined in. Jason was in Europe on his belated honeymoon with his new bride, who was touring with a ballet company. And Mandy was with her fiancé, Lane, fighting a wildfire in Canada. Tara whispered a simple prayer that they all came home safe and sound.

"Are you going to be ready to open in time?" Addie started to gather the trash, always busy taking care of everyone.

"Relax, Ad." Tara reached out to grasp her sister's arm. "Just toss everything the pigs aren't getting in that barrel." The trash can was filled with a variety of boards, paintbrushes, plastic and everything she'd swept up. "Not like there's anything to really clean yet."

"You don't need any more work," Addie admonished. "Gentlemen, clean up after yourselves."

The look that passed between DJ and Wyatt made Tara laugh. They looked more like the kids they used to be than the men they were. It was nice.

Tara loved these people. Her family. Her siblings. She was proud of them, proud to be one of them.

Wyatt owned and operated one of Texas's most successful cattle ranches. DJ helped him, though her brother was still a soldier at heart despite his injuries. Addie was a teacher who focused on tough kids. Her other siblings, who weren't here—though they would be if they were in the state—were just as successful.

She was determined to be successful, too.

She looked around at the half-done diner she was trying to turn into a popular, busy restaurant. Their comments and reactions from the other night returned and sparked her feeling of inadequacy again.

What if their concerns were proven right and she failed? What if no one came here to eat? What if that Sylvie woman was right and it was an ugly mistake? The delicious burger turned to dust in her mouth.

Tara felt an arm slip around her. "Do what you always do," Addie said softly.

"What's that?"

"Ignore us completely."

CHAPTER TWO

TARA'S INSPIRATION FOR the Someday Café had come from the kitchen where she'd grown up. Mom's kitchen had been the warmest, most wondrous place in all the world—the center of the house and the center of Tara's life. When Mom had died, Tara had grieved nearly as much about losing her safe place as she had about losing the woman she'd loved.

Now, with the café's walls painted the soft, robin's-egg blue, the wood floor newly refinished and all the counters and appliances fixed and cleaned, the large room sat empty.

Not for long.

She'd spent the past few months—in between meetings with Jason about the legalities, real estate and staff—roaming yard sales and flea markets to find the perfect things to decorate her new space. Now all those things were coming out of storage.

First, though, she purposefully went out to the truck and gently lifted the dining room chair that she'd taken from Mom's place the day after the funeral.

Each of her siblings had the chair that meant the most to them. None of them matched, actually. Mom and Dad had bought the dining room set, the thick table and six chairs, at a garage sale when they were newlyweds. Six kids had done a number on nearly every chair in the house.

Tara wasn't even sure if any of the ones they had taken were originals. The final set was a mismatched bunch of wooden chairs. Some with ladder backs. Some with straight backs. Some with curved wooden arms. Some without.

All precious and familiar.

Wyatt had the big captain's chair with its curved arms and sturdy back that had been Dad's. The finish on both arms was thin from Dad's movements, rubbing the wood when he was deep in thought, and later from when DJ had had to use the arms to stand after he'd come home injured.

This one had always been hers. As the youngest, she'd been the smallest, so the Jenny Lind style had fit her best. She'd loved it. Still did.

Carrying it in, she set it near the long diner counter that was lined with the only seating places at the moment. Perfect.

"Where do you want this?" DJ's voice echoed in the empty space. He easily carried the square wood table over his broad shoulders. She smiled and pointed to the corner.

She'd planned where every single piece was going to go. She'd imagined it all.

Wyatt and Lane came in with an oval dining table. "Right here." Smack in the middle of the room. The biggest table, it would be the centerpiece for larger parties and events.

"I got this one, Aunt Tara." Tyler had a lone chair—his enthusiasm warmed her. He had the same determined look as his father had carrying the table.

"Put that by the table your dad just set down."

For the next hour, they all carried furniture and arranged to her directions the assorted, mismatched tables and chairs. Then finally, once the room was full, they brought in the boxes of knickknacks and decorations.

DJ started hanging pictures where she indicated. Tyler watched and handed him nails from a bucket.

Finally, as the sun slanted through the French doors that looked out over the wide stone patio she hadn't even started on yet, she stepped back and admired their handiwork. She smiled with pride and anticipation. Things were finally coming together.

Wyatt came to stand beside her and slipped his arm around her shoulders. "You did good. It looks great. Mom would love it."

For the first time since Mom had passed away, Tara felt at home. She smiled at her brother and hugged him. "Thanks for helping."

"Anytime."

Tyler walked over and grinned. "So, when do we get to eat?"

The room filled with laughter and Tara couldn't resist joining in. Everything was falling into place, just as she planned, just as it was supposed to be.

MORGAN CRANKED THE stereo in the semi's cab. The windows practically rattled, and he was certain he'd lost at least a couple years of hearing in his old age. He didn't care. He needed something to get this anger and frustration out of his system. Geddy Lee's voice with a screaming guitar at full volume was the perfect solution.

Outside the windshield, the sun fell behind the horizon, a fiery ball of light that painted the west Texas hills with a wide, red brush. This was normally what he loved about driving. But tonight? He just wanted this trip to end. He wanted this chapter of his life done. He was ready to move on.

The past week had brought nothing. No new info. No more sightings. Nothing. Damn it, Sylvie was still screwing up things.

Was he a bad father for even wondering if he should quit looking for her and Brooke? He wouldn't, and he couldn't, but some days he flirted with the idea of letting go. Of just giving up.

He didn't think Sylvie would ever really hurt Brooke. In her way, she loved their daughter. But

Sylvie thought of the girl as a mini-adult, expecting her to do things a kid had no clue about. Brooke took care of Sylvie more than Sylvie took care of Brooke.

No, Sylvie wouldn't ever intentionally physically hurt her, but she'd easily neglect and emotionally scar Brooke with her expectations.

That was worse—if there was such a thing as worse—abuse.

He'd promised himself this was his last serious run. Didn't mean he would stop looking, he just had to do it differently. Despite good intentions, the police were too overwhelmed to focus on a year-old case. He'd already talked to a private investigator who could take on the search. But Morgan knew no one would put the heart and energy into the hunt like he had.

Like that had gotten him anywhere. Sylvie and Brooke were still missing. Maybe it was time to hire someone who actually knew how to do this. All he needed was the money to pay for it.

Morgan didn't hear his phone ring, but the lit-up screen caught his eye. He didn't want to talk to anyone, but Jack rarely called. And when he did, it was usually business-related.

Pausing the pounding beat, Morgan answered, "Yeah?"

"Hey." Jack's voice was soft. Strange.

"What's the matter?"

Silence. Heavy and thick. "Nothing's the matter." Another long pause. "We got a lead on Sylvie."

"What?" Big rigs did *not* stop on a dime, but Morgan couldn't drive. Not now. He wanted to hear every nuance of this conversation. "Let me pull over."

Time stretched out as Morgan slowed and eased the eighteen-wheeler to a safe place along the side of the road, a spot barely wide enough for the trailer, but enough for him to feel safe on this deserted highway should anyone drive by. When he geared down the big engine, the empty countryside moved in close.

"Tell me," he finally demanded.

"We got a call from one of Ben Walker's drivers. He said there was a woman matching Sylvie's description at a street fair over in Haskins Corners last week."

"That's it?" Why did that fill him with disappointment? Because a week had passed, and she could be anywhere by now. "Does he know for sure it was her?"

"No." Jack was silent for a moment. "She had a little girl with her." Another painful pause. "A girl carrying a purple dragon."

Jack's voice faded into the approaching night. Morgan stared at the emerging stars just above the hills and vaguely wondered why they blurred. He scrubbed a hand down his face. He wanted to scream and cry and curse all at the same time.

He'd been in Haskins Corners yesterday.

Close. So, close. He stared at the clock in the dashboard. Only a few hours away. In the opposite direction of where he was headed. Pulling a U-turn was a bitch, but doable.

"I know what you're thinking," Jack said. "Deliver that load, Morgan. Leave the trailer. I'll get Kyle to pick it up. Then you can head back to Haskins Corners in the morning after you've slept. You're gonna need a clear head."

"I'm going now." He had to.

"It'll be nearly midnight before you get there. You won't find them. And if Sylvie sees that truck? She'll get spooked. You could lose them again."

Morgan hated it when his younger brother was right. He pounded his fist against the oversize steering wheel. "I know you're right. But—" Why hadn't he seen them? Why hadn't *he* found them? "Okay," he reluctantly agreed.

Jack ended the call, and Morgan turned the rig onto the highway, forcing himself not to floor the gas pedal, his heart and mind screaming for him to follow them instead of Jack's common sense. But Jack was right. Morgan had to be smart about it. This time.

How many times had he driven all these small towns scattered around the Texas countryside? Dozens? Felt like hundreds. He knew the locals as well as if he was one of them.

He didn't think Sylvie would immediately recognize *this* rig. They'd bought it after she'd taken off, and he'd purposefully not put the company logo on it. But she'd be suspicious of any eighteen-wheeler since he'd always driven.

And that was part of why they'd grown apart. The steering wheel survived another pounding—barely.

TARA GREW UP in a house full of brothers and sisters. One of six. As the youngest, she'd been the "cute" little sister. From the moment at Dad's funeral where everyone looked at her with that "poor little baby" look, clear up until last week when she'd gotten her final permit from the city for this restaurant, she'd struggled to be taken seriously.

Now, standing in the center of the unoccupied dining room, she wondered if she wasn't making the biggest mistake of her life. Every penny, every drop of sweat and several drops of blood were invested in this place.

She'd finally sent everyone home. She'd hired a good crew and they'd all worked hard to put in the final touches and last-minute cleaning.

She loved the result. Loved just standing here, soaking up the sense of homecoming this place exuded.

Tomorrow, she and her staff would return and

start on what they all *wanted* to do. Cook and serve amazing food.

Slowly, Tara walked behind the counter, through the prep area, then through the big, metal swinging doors into the spacious industrial kitchen. She turned and frowned at the nondescript door at the back of the kitchen. The door led to the tiny closet she'd converted into an office. An office that held a small desk, just big enough for her computer and printer, a small two-drawer file cabinet and her chair. The chair from her mother's house.

Tara had been only two when their dad died, so her memories of him were vague and little more than flashes. Her brother, Wyatt, was more dad to her in her mind, though he'd been only fifteen when he'd stepped into that role.

Mom, however, was strong in her memory. Tara had been the last to leave home and had gotten the most time alone with their mother after the others had left the nest. She hadn't realized how precious that time was until Mom was gone.

Tara walked to the door and opened it. The desk lamp lit up the room, barely. Pulling out the chair, she settled in the well-worn wooden seat. It felt so good. "I think you'd like this place, Mom," she whispered.

She often talked to her mom's spirit, feeling, like now, that her mother was nearby. Hoping so anyway. "I'm going to use most of your reci-

pes." She knew her mother wouldn't mind. Helen
Hawkins had loved to cook, loved making big
batches of food. Tara had inherited that love, and
Helen had been more than willing to share the
kitchen with her youngest child.

Tara remembered standing on this very chair,
its back pushed against the counter, to stir a mix-
ing bowl of something with a big wooden spoon.
Those had been the happiest times of her life.

For a while, she sat there, letting the content-
ment and sense of accomplishment settle over
her. She'd done it. She'd finally done it.

Tomorrow, the doors would open and peace
and quiet would vanish. Tara stood, flipped off
the light and turned to leave. Closing the office
door, she headed across the kitchen toward her
purse and the jacket she'd draped over the rack
by the door.

Her fingers curled around the fabric the same
instant a horrendous crash broke the quiet of the
peaceful night.

"What the—" After she'd jumped nearly a foot,
she yanked open the back door, realizing too late
how stupid that was. It could be anything—or
anyone—out there in the darkness.

The megawatt spotlight above the door shone
bright as daylight, and she blinked to adjust to
the glare. One large trash can was on its side.
The lid was open, half the contents scattered on
the pavement.

Great, just great. Now she had a mess to clean up before she could go home. Hopefully, the new Dumpsters would be delivered soon so this wouldn't be a common occurrence.

Sounds of something moving near the trash can made her pause. What was it? The idea of being bitten or attacked by an animal did not thrill her. "Okay, whatever you are, come out and shoo." More rustling inside the trash can.

Whatever it was didn't seem too scared of her. She moved closer and tried to peer inside. "Hey. Scat!" There was no way she was reaching inside. She looked around for a stick or a broom or something to use to poke at it. Nothing.

"That's what I get for making everyone clean so thoroughly," she mumbled. "Okay, whatever you are, go away so I can clean up and go home." More rustling but nothing came out. Now what?

"Okay, buddy." She stomped back into the kitchen. Maybe by the time she returned, the stupid thing would be gone. Mop in hand, she shoved open the door again, making as much noise as she could to hopefully scare the thing away. She approached the spilled trash can.

When she stopped, everything was silent. No rustling. No little feet scratching against the plastic can. Nothing but the normal night sounds that came from a distance. She smiled. It was gone.

"Hello?" Another step. "Yoo-hoo, little critter." Another step. "Are you gone?" Nothing but silence. Slowly, she pushed the end of the broom handle into the dark interior of the trash can.

The animal came out with a screech and something furry and disgustingly wet flew past her bare legs. She screamed. She couldn't help it. It was done before she could stop it.

Her heart pounded so hard against her ribs, it hurt. She hadn't realized she'd been holding her breath. "Damn it!" was the first thing she managed to say. "Ewww," was the second. She did not want to know what was now drying on her leg. She'd find out when she got home and showered. Besides, she still had to clean up everything scattered on the new asphalt.

At least once she righted the trash can, she could see what she was doing. She did peer inside carefully, just in case. No beady little eyes looked up at her, thank goodness—just smelly, slimy trash. Finally, she had everything cleaned up and the lid securely in place.

After closing the diner's back door, she headed to her car. As she walked across the parking lot, she swore she could feel eyes staring at her. Beady little eyes giving her the stink eye. "Sorry, no free meals," she called into the night, laughing. "I'm tougher than I look, you know. I've got three older brothers."

Climbing into her car, she flipped on the headlights, and the beam found a small furry form at the edge of the lot, near the creek that meandered past the property. A fat raccoon glared at her.

Tara laughed. She was exhausted. And punchy. And dirty. But she'd survived. Tomorrow—she glanced at her watch—today was going to be a piece of cake.

MORGAN'S STOMACH RUMBLED as he hit the outskirts of Haskins Corners just after dawn. He needed to find a safe place to park, grab some grub and figure out his next move.

It was early. Nothing much was open. But a familiar, ancient diner came to mind.

The parking lot was big enough to park the truck now that he was bobtailing. This time of day there would be plenty of room, even if he'd had the trailer.

Except, this morning the parking lot was more than half-full. He pulled to a halt. What the heck? Dozens of cars filled the upper half of the lot, though there was still room in the lower.

What was going on? He'd never seen this much traffic here, even at breakfast time.

Slowly, he turned the rig into the lot, stopping at the outer edge along the creek side, underneath the trees. The silence of the air when he shut off the engine still amazed him. He climbed out and made his way across the newly paved parking lot. Nice. Smooth. There wasn't even the hint of a pothole in sight.

And landscaping? Bushes and trees in the median? Daisy was moving up in the world. The now-elderly woman who'd run the joint since the 1970s must have come into some money.

Approaching the front door, however, Morgan paused. This couldn't be Daisy's domain any longer. A menu was posted in a fancy metal box on the wall. Different, but if the scents coming out of the kitchen were any indication, good. His stomach rumbled again in response.

Inside he froze. The layout of the place was the same, but run-down had given way to kitsch, and utilitarian to almost pretty. The clunky vinyl booths and Formica tables were gone. In their place sat tables and chairs that looked better suited for a dollhouse than a diner.

He wasn't especially tall, but his years of bodybuilding workouts had made that type of furniture totally off-limits. He knew better than to sit on any of those chairs. He'd probably end up on his ass with splinters beneath his butt.

Morgan frowned. He was here and he was hungry. The perky little hostess was new, too. Since when did diners have hostesses?

"Just one?" she asked.

"Uh, yeah." Where exactly would she put him? He resisted the urge to retreat instead of following her. The lace curtains and tablecloths didn't help with the feeling he had of stepping into a woman's boudoir.

"I'll just sit at the counter." It was still there, still the same, but cleaner. Much cleaner. With a shrug, she dismissed him as easily as he did her.

"What can I get ya?" Another young woman with bright, albeit tired eyes and a name tag that read Wendy stood on the other side of the counter, a carafe of coffee in one hand.

"A whole lot of that."

She poured a big mugful, then slid it toward him. "I hear ya." She stifled a yawn. "Here's our brand-spanking new menu." She pulled a laminated folder from between the napkin holder and saltshaker. "Take a look at it, and I'll be right back." She hustled away, the coffeepot landing smoothly on the burner as he opened the menu.

Omelets? He'd made the mistake once of ordering an omelet from Daisy. He should have known to change the order when she'd said, "A what?" Her omelet had consisted of scrambled eggs with bits of meat mixed in.

Now there was a full page of them. Egg whites? Mushrooms? Holy cow. This was different. His mouth watered.

BREAKFAST WAS TARA'S favorite meal of the day. The warm, rich, sweet scents of baking, hot grease and coffee were a unique perfume. Nothing better in the world. That was part of why she'd decided to offer the breakfast menu all day long. That, and competing with the big boys—she had to play their games.

The kitchen was full of aromatic food, pots, pans and noise. Tara tried to shut it all out and focus. Robbie was her lead chef for mornings. But while he was the best at what he did, he was also the most easily distracted. And the past few days had been full of distractions.

She'd decided to do a soft opening the week before the official grand opening. This was their first day and the place was over half-full. First impressions were vital and so far so good.

She had to trust Robbie and Wendy and everyone else she'd hired. She had to. It was now or never.

Already a couple dozen people had come in this morning, and she was busy whipping up another batch of biscuits. Mom's recipe was a favorite, and Tara had to remind herself that she couldn't eat the profits. But oh, she loved Mom's biscuits.

"Oh, my." Wendy rushed through the door, her arms full of dirty dishes. She wound her way through the controlled mess and deposited everything in the sink.

"Oh, my, what?" Gabe, the busboy/dishwasher

said as he lifted the sprayer and proceeded to blast off what food residue he could from the plates.

"Hunk alert," Wendy called out in a pseudo-whisper.

Tara wasn't sure when the staff had started this ridiculous behavior. Whenever a good-looking guy came in, one of the waitresses would make this announcement. She knew she should stop it, but with a brand-new staff, she was going to allow anything that helped them become a cohesive team.

Besides, the guys had come up with their own balance. *Bombshell* was the term her evening cook, Wade, had used. The gray-haired cook wasn't interested in the modern vernacular, much to the younger guys' displeasure. He reasoned that they needed an education. Still, the term had stuck.

And so the descriptions of customers flew around the kitchen. Tara focused on the biscuits.

"You really should see this guy." Wendy passed Tara and whispered in her ear, "He's perfect for you."

Not only was her staff getting involved in the life of the diner, they'd started to make their feelings known about her life—specifically, her lack of a love life. It didn't help that her brothers, DJ and Jason, had both gotten married and Wyatt and Emily had eloped in the past few months.

Her sister, Mandy, talked about dresses and bouquets every time she came in with little Lucas for lunch. Love was in the air everywhere—and her staff thought she should join in.

"Not interested," she said, focusing on the biscuit dough. "Told you that already."

"This one might make you change your mind." Wendy's voice came out all singsongy as she wiggled her eyebrows. "You never know." She'd filled a tray as she'd talked, then hefted the thing up on her shoulder.

"Just focus and don't spill that."

"Yes, boss."

Wendy disappeared out into the dining room as Lindy, the hostess, came in. "You gotta see this guy," Lindy said as she carried a stack of dishes to the sink. The girl was a ditz at times, but she knew when to chip in and help.

"You girls need cooling off." Gabe lifted the water spray and sent a brief blast of water at Lindy, who squealed.

"All right." Tara needed to stop them now. "Everyone get to work." Her voice was soft, though, so while they stilled the horseplay, the glances and snickers continued.

Shoving the tray of biscuits into the oven, she stepped back and dusted off her hands. Her mouth watered at the sight of the previous batch she'd baked and, mentally promising her mom, "just one," she reached out.

Suddenly, hands cupped her elbows, and she found her waitresses on either side of her. "Hey!"

"You'll thank us later." Wendy laughed.

The laughing trio had to angle awkwardly through the swinging doors, and the thump of the doors closing barely broke the din of the dining room. Nearly all the tables were full and even the counter had only a few empty stools.

Tara didn't have to ask. The man at the counter, on the end. Blond, short-cropped hair. Broad, bodybuilder shoulders. And muscles. His arms were huge, stretching the fabric of his black T-shirt tight. She didn't dare look in the direction of his faded blue jeans.

"See?" Wendy didn't even bother to try to hide her pointing hand.

Tara stared. "Oh. My," she whispered, then spun on her heel. She scurried into the kitchen before he could look up and see them all gawking at him.

Robbie looked through the order window. "What's wrong with you?"

She stared at her cook, the only apparently sane person in her kitchen. There was no way she was telling him anything.

But that man… He was exactly what she'd normally be attracted to. He was the opposite of her brothers, so different from her normal reality.

Which was why she'd turned around. She'd made more than her fair share of bad choices in men. She did not have time for any kind of relationship right now. None whatsoever. Not even a wishful one.

Even if those arms could make any girl feel safe.

CHAPTER THREE

MORGAN STARED AT the menu, peering over it as two waitresses dragged a woman dressed in chef garb out of the kitchen. *That was an interesting little display.*

As soon as they let go of her arms, she turned through the diner doors, like the bird in the cuckoo clock his grandmother used to have.

Morgan smiled. He hadn't thought about Gran in ages. She'd been the closest thing he and Jack had had to a real family. He missed her, wishing he could give Brooke someone special like that in her life.

The waitress who'd originally handed him the menu returned. "So, have you made up your mind?" The grin on her face said there had definitely been an inside joke involved with the chef coming through those swinging doors.

"Uh, yeah." He ordered the Denver omelet, hoping it was as good as it sounded. He'd caught a whiff of several dishes that passed by and was already salivating.

"Anything else?"

"Yeah, leave the chef in the kitchen to cook it,

okay?" He winked at her, and she had the grace to blush even as she laughed.

"I think we can arrange that. Tara isn't fond of coming out of her cave anyway."

"Tara?"

"Yeah, the owner. And chef." She nodded at the dining room behind him. "She bought this place and has been pushing us for a month to open this week."

He glanced over his shoulder and nodded. "Just this week?" He was impressed. For a brand-new place, it was pretty busy. "Hopefully, nothing happened to Daisy." He recalled the elderly woman who'd previously run the old diner.

"Nope. She's alive and well." Wendy refilled his cup. "Retirement will be good for her."

He wondered if Daisy agreed with that. She'd always given him the impression she'd die before she'd retire.

"Let me put in your order." The waitress stepped away and Morgan looked around again.

Even this early in the day, there was a crowd. He'd come here knowing Daisy had been a fixture in town her whole life. He'd hoped to ask if she'd seen Sylvie. Disappointment settled close. He wondered if there was any way to contact her.

It wasn't long before his plate appeared, and the meal looked as good as it smelled. He glanced at the waitress. "Hey," he said.

"Do you need something else?"

"No. Just a curious question. Who does the hiring here?"

"You looking for a job?" She looked hopeful, almost eager.

"Uh, no." He laughed. "But I know someone who might." Sylvie had been working as a waitress when they'd met. Did the fact that a new restaurant had appeared in town have anything to do with someone sighting her? Was she working here, maybe on another shift? He tried not to get his hopes up.

"That'd be Tara. Don't know if we're looking for anyone else, though."

"If she has a minute, I'd like to chat with her."

For the first time since she'd warmly greeted him, the girl looked reluctant. "I'll see if she can break away."

"No hurry." He dug into the omelet and stifled a groan of pleasure. It tasted even better than it smelled or looked.

TARA KNEW HER staff meant well, but she needed to make them understand that she could *not* afford *any* distractions right now. Not with her track record. She busied herself putting the finishing touches on the lunch prep.

She'd nearly flunked out of high school because she'd thought boys were more important than homework. When Wyatt had caught her sneaking out of the house one night, it'd been the final straw. From then on, he'd made sure she didn't go anywhere until her homework was done.

She'd resented him then, but now appreciated how hard that must have been for him. He'd been young and single, an older brother who took his responsibilities very seriously. Her behavior had probably put a serious cramp in his social life.

In college, she'd nearly screwed up again. She'd met Travis and thought he was "the one." He'd been the one all right, the one for Cheryl and Lisa and Julie and who knew how many others. Looking back now, Tara wasn't sure which had been worse—the distraction of the pursuit or the heartache afterward.

DJ had been the one to save her then, listening to all her wailing and tears, never once letting on that his baby sister was being a pain in the neck.

Even recently, she'd met that cute firefighter after the fire that had nearly destroyed the county. A hotshot on the crew that had come to town, he'd definitely turned her head. And turned right around and left as quickly as he'd come.

No, she didn't have time to get involved with anyone. She couldn't afford the distraction if she was going to make this place a success. And that man at the counter? Oh, yeah, he'd definitely be a distraction.

He already was, if her staff's reaction to him was any indication.

"Hey, Tara." Wendy came through the doors.

"Our hunky customer wants to talk to you to see if we're hiring."

"What?" She whipped around, staring at Wendy, who nearly doubled over in laughter.

"I take it you wouldn't want him working here?"

Dear Lord, that would be the end of her. "No. Certainly not." Sweat broke out as she imagined the big man lumbering through the kitchen, brushing past her, easily lifting the heavy trays with those big, strong arms.

"Just tell him we're not hiring." She didn't dare talk to him, not with those images swimming in her head.

"Sure you don't want to take the time to visit?" Wendy moved close. "He's even better looking up close. Nice green eyes."

"Yeah, I'm sure his eyes are what you're looking at."

"Maybe." Wendy headed toward the door. "Well, if you're not going to take advantage, I'm certainly going to enjoy."

"I'm too busy anyway. I'm off to the fair." She tried to look nonchalant as she grabbed the bag of flyers and headed out. It wasn't like she was running away or anything.

AFTER FINISHING HIS delicious breakfast, Morgan left to walk around town. He found himself looking at every person he passed with a suspicious eye. At every glimpse of purple, which was oddly frequent, he nearly gave himself whiplash trying to see if it was Brooke or Sylvie.

It never was.

He'd gone up and down the narrow main street three times. He was pushing his luck. He fought the urge to go into every store to question the staff. He had a faded picture, but from what little he'd gathered about Sylvie, she looked different than she used to.

Her blond hair was now dark, not brown or black, but blue apparently. Or it had been a couple months ago. He had no idea what color it was now.

She'd gotten tattoos and piercings, which, while they weren't that odd these days, they weren't something she'd had before. They disguised her, making her look nothing like the pictures he had of her. Would he even recognize her?

Was he ever going to find them?

He grabbed a soda from a street vendor and settled under a big cottonwood tree in the center of the park. Maybe if he sat here and watched he'd see something.

The sun moved slowly across the sky, and he fought the growing disappointment. Other than going door-to-door, what was he supposed to do? He glanced wistfully at the playground. Had Brooke ever played there? She'd always loved to swing.

If he hung out here, would he find her or just get himself arrested for stalking little kids? As a dad, he knew he'd be suspicious of some guy hanging out at a playground.

A woman came down the sidewalk, a big bag hanging off her shoulder, the sun glinting in her bright golden hair. The curls rippled in the breeze as she walked, and he couldn't tear his gaze away. She turned around, and for an instant, a flash of recognition shot through him. He didn't know her, but she looked familiar. Where had he seen her before?

At the diner this morning. With her hair down, she looked different. She'd come and gone so quickly, he was surprised he recognized her now.

What had the waitress said her name was? Tina? No. Trudy? No, definitely not. Tara? That was it.

He watched her move. She went from booth to booth, looking at the items displayed, and, after she'd picked up something small and paid, she handed the clerk a piece of paper. A flyer? What was she doing? She moved easily through the crowd, passing out the flyers from her bag and sharing a smile with nearly everyone. Good advertising. He hoped it worked.

Just then, she looked at him. Their gazes met, held for an instant, then she looked away. Did she recognize him, too?

Something about the woman intrigued him.

Rising, he followed her, her interactions amusing him. How long had the waitress said the restaurant had been open? A week? Before opening, had Tara been doing this? If she'd been running around glad-handing for the past month, especially during the busy weekends, had she seen Sylvie? Had she seen Brooke? His heart sped up, and so did he.

EVERY DAY, ESPECIALLY on the busy weekends and hopefully between the morning rush and lunch—before the day grew too unbearably hot—Tara planned to visit the street fair that was a staple in town.

Tara loved the fair and could easily spend the entire day shopping, as she had in years past with her sisters. Artists, jewelers, seamstresses and food vendors of all kinds sold their goods. But her purpose now was to advertise the café, not spend her meager profits.

She'd printed flyers with coupons and handed them out to the vendors and anyone who'd take one. It was working—already her staff said people had brought the flyers in.

Today was no different, and she made her way down the street, taking her time and doing a little shopping along the way.

She noticed that the hunk from the diner this morning was sitting under the cottonwoods in the park. Those broad shoulders made the massive trunk of the old tree actually look small. One leg stretched out across the grass, and he'd bent one knee to rest his forearm on. The soda can looked minuscule in his big hand.

He looked up then, catching her watching him. She glanced away, feeling her cheeks warm. She moved on to the next stall.

Visitors and locals mingled in the square, and it was the perfect place to spread the word about her café. She'd actually toyed with the idea of renting one of the outdoor booths to give away food samples.

But she couldn't afford to be away from the café for the entire day, and neither could any of the staff. Not yet anyway.

Maybe she should give Mr. Hunk a coupon to get him to return. That would make her staff— especially Wendy—happy. And that was the only reason it crossed her mind, she told herself.

Really.

Glancing over at the trees, she realized he'd left and before she could stop herself, she scanned around, wondering where he'd gone. She didn't see him. Why did that realization dim the bright day? Shaking her head, she dismissed the man and her silly thoughts.

"Hey, Dave," she greeted the older man who made beautiful tin sculptures. She'd already commissioned one of a squirrel in a chef hat to go in the entry of the diner. "How's Mr. Squirrel coming?"

"Looking good. I'll be done early, I think."

"Great." He'd already sent business her way, and she left another stack of flyers.

With similar interactions, she moved along the line, realizing how many of these people she'd come to know and now considered friends.

Halfway down the block, she stopped at the T-shirt vendor and recalled the woman who'd come in to apply for a waitress job, the one who'd insulted her, unintentionally, but the woman's rudeness still stuck in Tara's mind. Relieved the woman wasn't there, she was glad to find a man behind the wide table.

She didn't remember seeing him before. Was folding something people who sold T-shirts did in their sleep? They always seemed to be doing it.

"Hello," she greeted him with a smile. He looked up, but rather than smiling, he frowned, then seemed to force his lips into a stiff grin.

"Hi!" She tried again. He kept folding.

"Let me know if there's anything you'd like me to ring up." He moved to sit in a chair beside an ancient cash register. He picked up a magazine and focused on it, ignoring her.

"I'd like to introduce myself," she said. He looked up and fake-smiled again.

"Yeah, I know who you are. You bought the diner from Daisy."

"Yes, I did."

"I ain't giving out any of yer flyers," he grumbled. "It's hard enough makin' a livin' doing my own business." He went back to his magazine. "You wanna buy something?"

She stared at him, surprised. Not now, she didn't. Everyone else was very open and helpful, friendly. What was wrong with this guy?

"Sorry. I didn't mean to upset you." She wasn't giving up. "I'm offering a discount. If nothing else, you and your family might enjoy coming by for a meal." Did she really say that without gritting her teeth? She was fairly impressed with herself.

"No, thanks."

"You haven't even tried."

"Lady makes a mean omelet," another voice said beside her, and Tara turned to see The Hunk standing there, pawing at T-shirts. He wasn't even looking at the T-shirts he was unfolding. He was looking at her instead. And smiling. Another T-shirt returned to the pile, rumpled and unviewed.

"You want to buy something?" The man behind the counter looked up from the magazine only long enough to glare at the growing pile of messy shirts.

"Not sure yet." Hunk continued to smile, his expression more mischief than mirth. "I'll let you know."

She couldn't ignore him. He'd complimented

her, for one thing. "Glad you enjoyed your meal. I hope you'll return."

"Plan to." He faced her, leaving the T-shirts for the other man to refold. "I'm Morgan Thane." He stuck out a hand, a beefy hand that matched the rest of him, muscular, strong and intimidating. A total contradiction to the smile on his face and the curiosity in his eyes. "My truck is parked in your back lot. Hope that's okay."

She took a step away, reluctant to touch him. "Tara Hawkins." She didn't want to be rude, so she finally took his hand, feeling her fingers engulfed but thankfully not crushed. His palm was rough and warm.

Wendy was right. His eyes were green—a deep, dark green. Like the underside of those cottonwood leaves he'd been sitting beneath. *This is ridiculous.* Tara forced herself to slip her hand from his. "You're welcome to park there, yes. Daisy said lots of truckers come by. Are…are you here job hunting, Mr. Thane?" That didn't make sense, unless he was tired of driving truck. "Or just here to mess up the displays?"

"Uh—no?" He looked puzzled, then glanced at the piles of T-shirts and laughed. "I'm just keeping him on his toes." His expression faded and grew distant. "You ignore a business and it'll fail. Miserably." He tilted his head toward the man still focused on his magazine instead of them. "I see it as doing him a favor."

"Uh-huh." Somehow that didn't totally ring true, though it did make sense. "My waitress said you were asking about hiring." *Yes. Keep this on a business level.*

His eyes widened and he stepped closer. "Oh, yeah. No, I'm actually, uh, looking for a friend." Even in the middle of the day's heat, his body's warmth reached out to her.

"Does your friend have experience as a cook or a waitress?" She might not need anyone now, but she knew turnover would be an issue. It always was in the food industry.

He stared at her, and Tara struggled to keep from falling under the spell of those eyes.

"Actually, yeah. I was wondering if she'd already applied."

Why did he look around then, as if someone might be watching them? Something seemed off, and she frowned.

A group of girls came over to the table then and the distracted clerk hurried over, busying himself refolding the shirts Morgan had messed up.

Morgan looked at the man and gently grabbed Tara's elbow to guide her away from the table. She barely resisted the urge to pull her arm from his grasp, but before she could, he let her go.

"Did anyone named Sylvie come in and apply?"

Surprised, Tara stared at him. "Uh, yes. Why?" She was a friend of his? What kind of friend? She mentally rolled her eyes. What business of hers was it? What did it matter? But somehow it did.

"When?" The urgency in his voice startled her. He looked ready to pounce. "When did you last see her?" His words came out in a rush.

"It's been almost a month ago. That was the only time I've ever seen her. I don't know her." She wasn't really someone Tara could see herself being friends with, that's for sure.

His expression fell, and she saw the disappointment cover his face. "Damn."

"What's going on?"

He paced, running his fingers over his close-cropped hair, as if forgetting he didn't have long hair to shove them through. She watched that big hand, fascinated.

"I've been looking for her for some time and every time I get close, I miss her."

"What do you mean, miss her?"

"Hey, do you work here?" One of the girls who had been looking at the T-shirts came over to them.

"Uh, no." Tara frowned, looking around for the man who'd been behind the table. "He was here a minute ago."

"There isn't anyone." The girl actually pouted. "Darn, I wanted this one." She held up a black

T-shirt with a ghastly skeleton on it. Maybe it was a blessing the man wasn't here.

"Morgan did you see…?" She turned to find Morgan gone. In the distance, just this side of the park, she saw him jogging down an alley that led away from the street fair. The T-shirt salesman was a short distance ahead of him, hurrying away.

CHAPTER FOUR

MORGAN'S CURSES FILLED the air. Where the hell had the guy gone? As he'd talked to Tara, he'd watched the vendor behind her react. Something—recognition or realization—had dawned on the man's face. Looking up the side street now, Morgan didn't see a trace of him.

Half a dozen people came and went around him. A couple women stood on the corner, chatting in the sunlight. A boy played in the dirt with one of those yellow toy trucks Morgan had wished for as a kid.

But no shaggy-haired T-shirt vendor in sight. Morgan walked for a couple blocks, looking down alleys and casually glancing into whatever window he could without turning into a Peeping Tom. Nothing. Nowhere. It was as if the guy had vanished into thin air.

Finally, resigned, Morgan headed to the street fair. If nothing else, the guy had to come back and get his merchandise. But when Morgan returned to the booth, an older, worn-out-looking woman was there. He tried to question her, but she was too busy to talk.

"You wanna buy a shirt? I got customers." She held up one of the rumpled garments. To any other questions, she just shook her head, focusing on the seemingly endless line of customers.

"Then tell me where the man went. Your partner?"

"I don't keep track of no one but me." She turned to a couple women on the other side of the booth. With a sigh, Morgan settled under the oak to wait, though he wasn't really sure what he was waiting for.

Sitting there in the mottled sunlight, with nothing to do but think, Morgan wondered why he was even here. Was he just wasting his time? No. This was the best lead he had, and he couldn't walk away. The idea of leaving wasn't even an option. He had to find Sylvie and Brooke.

He had no choice.

As he watched people moving around the spacious park and shopping at the varied booths, it was with a calculated eye. He was studying. Looking—but not hoping. He never let himself go there.

He'd given up on hope a long time ago. Losing it was too painful. But where else could he look? Who else should he talk to? He thought about calling Jack, but he was tired of calling his brother with no news. Tired of failing.

Tara Hawkins must have gone to the diner. Despite himself, he looked around for her. Damn it.

He didn't see her anywhere. Maybe she'd know more. Should he go back there?

Turning toward the T-shirt stand, he forced himself to focus. This was his mission—Brooke was his responsibility.

Throughout the rest of the day, the woman at the booth did a brisk business. Nothing unusual. Just busy. She cast Morgan several furtive glances, which made him more determined to stay put. The man didn't return.

Finally, as the sun set low, the woman pulled boxes from under the table and packed the remaining stock. No one came to help, and she glared at Morgan.

If he didn't want to have an up-close-and-personal meeting with the sheriff, he knew he had to be careful about how he approached her.

When she taped the last box closed, Morgan moved closer for one last try. He didn't say anything at first, simply stood, watching, trying not to intimidate her too much. She, on the other hand, had no hesitancy in glaring at him.

Slowly, deliberately, Morgan pulled out his wallet. Not to get money, but to slip out the familiar, worn picture. He hesitated. Was this a good idea? He had no clue, but he didn't know what else to do. Praying he was making the right choice, Morgan put the picture on top of the last box. "She's mine," he whispered around the lump in his throat. "She's a year older than that picture."

The woman paused and looked at Brooke's grin. Recognition flashed in her eyes an instant before she shut the reaction down.

"Yeah?" She hefted a box onto a metal dolly. "Cute kid."

"She is. I haven't seen her in a year."

The silence hung thick in the twilight. "Whatcha want me to do 'bout it?" The woman moved another box, more slowly this time.

"Have you seen her?"

"Maybe." Another box moved. It barely fit on the dolly, but she put it there anyway. It'd be awkward as heck to move, but he doubted that would stop her. And it didn't.

"Can I help you with that?" He reached for the handle and the woman lifted an elbow to push him away.

"I got it. Thanks." She stepped behind the dolly, shoving her foot against the bottom rail and tilting it. She grunted briefly as the big box fell onto the rail and her shoulder.

"Do you know her?" Morgan asked.

The woman met his gaze, and the sadness in her eyes surprised him. "Don't know her. I seen her, I think, but lots of people come through here." She tilted her head toward the now-empty booth.

"If you see her again, would you let me know?" He tried to tamp down the emotion flaring annoyingly to life in his chest. He pulled a busi-

ness card out of his wallet and put it on top of the
boxes as he retrieved the precious photo.

"Maybe." She took a couple of steps, struggling with the weight.

Midway through the gate to a dirt parking lot,
she stopped and looked over her shoulder at him.
She reached out awkwardly over the carefully
balanced boxes and picked up the business card.
She stared at it in the fading light. Morgan half
expected her to toss it to the wind.

Instead, she slipped it into her back pocket,
and he finally remembered to breathe. He stood
there, watching her load her car, then climb in.
Before she turned the corner, he snapped a quick
photo of the license plate and car with his phone.

She hadn't done anything wrong—that he
knew of—but the information might be useful.
If not now, maybe later. Who knew what a private detective could do with something like that?
If television was to be believed, a lot.

Slowly, Morgan walked toward his truck. The
streets were empty now, a few vendors still pack-
ing up, but no customers left.

Streetlights had come on and squares of gold
fell out of the glass windows of houses he passed.
He saw families sitting down to dinner. Couples
in homey kitchens putting meals together. Something shifted in his chest. Envy. Longing.

If he walked these streets, glancing in windows, would he find Sylvie? Not likely. Sylvie

had tried to cook a few times, and she'd been getting better, but she'd never liked it. There wouldn't be any homey warm scene to watch. Or any chance to find them that way.

Loneliness settled in close, and he shivered to push it away. He didn't have time to feel. He had too much to do. He headed toward the diner, telling himself it was only because that's where his truck was parked.

It had nothing to do with the fact that Tara would be serving up warmth.

And maybe a little bit of belonging.

DESPITE THE HEAVY RAIN, the Saturday morning rush was in full swing. Tara stood on tiptoe to peer out the round window in the doors that separated the kitchen from the dining room. Nearly all the tables were full and her staff hustled back and forth.

She couldn't help smiling. Just then, a customer gave Wendy one of the coupon flyers. *Yes*. Her work was paying off. She glanced around, hoping to see more.

Her gaze found the French doors to the patio where raindrops hit, then slid down the panes. The street fair would be hurt by the rain, but some of today's crowd was likely due to the weather.

She wasn't about to complain.

Then she glanced at the long counter and froze. Morgan sat at the far end. A newspaper was spread out in front of him as he absently sipped from a mug and read.

She should be surprised he was here after his abrupt departure from the park the other day. But she wasn't. Not really. Briefly, she wondered what had happened at the fair. Not that he owed her an explanation, but she couldn't help being curious about where the two men had gone.

For a brief instant, she watched him. Any moment, one of the waitstaff would come through the doors, but until then, she didn't move. He really was something.

Most of the men in her life were like her brothers. Tall, rangy cowboys. Muscular, yes, but not like this. Their physique came from working with the cattle and riding horses; Morgan's seemed more deliberate. More defined. Purposeful.

He had to work out. Suddenly, an image of him, sweat glistening on the hard curves of his bare chest, his arms straining as he lifted a bar with black weights on each end, leaped to mind. If her arms hadn't been full of fresh linens, she'd have reached up to fan herself.

Forcing herself to stop this nonsense and get back to work, she stepped out of the kitchen, hugging the linens tight. She took her time putting them away in the antique wooden cabinet nestled in the corner.

She did *not* have time for this. Hadn't she

learned her lesson? Men—good-looking men—
were a distraction she couldn't afford right now.

Once the linens were settled, she headed to the
cash register and pulled out the day's receipts to
prep the deposit. Robbie was here handling the
kitchen, so she had a couple hours to get paperwork done.

"Mornin', Morgan. Can I get you a warm-up?"
Wendy's voice, friendly, inviting and warm, came
across the dining room, and Tara looked up again.
A twinge of jealousy surprised her. The waitress
stood across the counter from the burly truck
driver, holding the carafe.

He didn't respond at first and Tara paused, just
as Wendy did, waiting.

"You okay?" Wendy touched his arm, giving
him a tiny shake. "Morgan?"

He shook his head. "Guess I'm tired." He
rubbed his eyes. "I need to get some shut-eye."
Then he smiled. His eyes sparkled and a tiny dim-
ple grew in his left cheek. Tara stared, frozen by
the sight of him. What would it feel like to have
that smile aimed at her?

Wendy repeated her offer.

"No, thanks." Morgan set down the cup. "I've
gotta run. Good breakfast. Thanks." He nodded,
tossing the folded newspaper onto the counter for
someone else to read. A ball cap sat at his elbow.
He settled it over his close-cropped hair, the wide

brim hiding his eyes from Tara's view and shadowing the rest of his face.

Before turning to leave, he flipped a couple bills on the counter, then stood and shoved his wallet into the back pocket of a worn pair of jeans. Her gaze followed.

Tara watched every move. Moments ticked by until she realized she was staring openly at his backside. Shaking her head, she forced herself to look away. *Focus on something—anything—else.*

"See you tomorrow?" the waitress asked hopefully, her gaze darting meaningfully to Tara.

Tara tore her gaze away from them, forcing herself to focus on the deposits. And to try to control her breathing. It should be against the law for a man to wear a T-shirt that fit so well. Wasn't there some kind of ordinance?

"Maybe. Depends on my load." His voice dipped low. How the hell did he make it reach deep inside her?

He looked up then, his gaze reaching out beyond the shadowed hat brim and finding hers. Tara stared back, knowing she should look away, but unable to do so.

Her breath caught, and she tried to release it.

Then he was gone, the glass door closing quietly in his wake.

"Wonder why he's in such a toot?" Wendy asked, sidling up to Tara, as if she knew more than she was saying.

Tara shrugged, forcing her face not to show her own curiosity. Wendy didn't need any more encouragement.

"He doesn't owe us any explanations." Tara cringed at the breathy sound of her own voice.

"Maybe not you." Wendy grinned. "*I* need to know."

"Why is that, exactly?"

"I'm determined to fix him up with you. It won't work if he's not here."

"Oh, for heaven's sake." Tara turned away, her hands full of receipts, her cheeks warm for a reason she refused to identify. "Don't start that. We've been over this. I'm not interested." She headed into the kitchen.

Wendy followed her. "Your words say that, but I saw the way you looked at him."

"You're imagining things." Tara shoved open the office door with her hip, hoping Morgan hadn't seen her gawking at him. Which she hadn't been doing. Not really. It was her job, after all, to keep an eye on things. "We've got work to do." She set the papers on the desk, ignoring the raised eyebrow from her waitress.

Thankfully, Wendy took the hint—this time—and went back to work.

It was easy to decide to focus on work, but while her hands separated the receipts into neat little stacks, Tara's mind wasn't as easily distracted. Where was he going? What was he doing here? She'd noticed on her walk back from the street fair that his truck didn't have a logo that told her where he was based. That wasn't unusual. Lots of the truckers who came in were independents. But none of them came in more than a day at a time.

Truckers didn't stay in one place for long, always on the way to or from someplace else. He'd been here the last couple days and spent time at the street fair. Why was he sticking around?

"You're thinking about him," Wendy said softly from the doorway.

Besides being startled, Tara was irritated with her employee. "Cut it out. And stop pushing me at him. I'm. Not. Interested."

Not sure who she was trying to convince more, she booted up the computer and stared at the spreadsheet. That would surely keep her busy for the next hour or more. She had to do something.

The loud crash in the alley sent both of them rushing to the back door.

"Ricky's back," Wendy said unnecessarily. The staff had christened the pesky raccoon, and the name had stuck.

"In the middle of the day?" She and Wendy stepped into the alley. Raccoons were nocturnal animals. "Not likely."

"Then what?"

"Meoooooww!" A big gray tomcat, its fur matted, dirty and soaking wet, sat on the top of the brand-new, tipped-over trash can, pawing on the—thankfully—still-latched lid.

This was not happening again. What was with all these animals?

Tara rubbed her forehead. At this rate, she was never going to get the bills paid.

MORGAN LEFT THE diner before he ended up staying there all day. He couldn't. It would be a mistake.

He walked slowly through the rain, across the worn flagstones of Tara's patio. Even though he knew the stones had been there since well before Tara had bought this place, he thought of them as hers.

Today they were washed clean by the raindrops, but a year ago? An article in this morning's paper had commemorated the wildfire that had raged through this valley last year.

He remembered hearing about the damage and the efforts that had gone into helping the people who'd lost so much. Some of his crew had trucked in loads of relief supplies. He'd been too distracted with his own loss to be any good to anyone.

Had these stones been blackened with smoke and ash? Had they escaped damage simply because they were stone that couldn't burn?

Looking up at the rooflines of the buildings

along the street, he realized they were old, as well, so perhaps the fire hadn't touched this area.

A year. So much had changed in that year. The fire. Tara buying this place. Sylvie stealing Brooke away. The knot in his chest that never seemed to go away grew just a little bit tighter.

Time had dulled the pain, but nothing would erase it, not until he found Brooke.

Brooke.

She'd had another birthday since he'd last seen her. Surely last year's gift, the purple dragon, was worn out by now. He'd bought her another gift, which was nestled in the lower cabinet in his truck. He carried it everywhere, just in case he found her.

So close. He was *so* close. He could feel it. The jerk at the street fair yesterday had led Morgan on a merry chase through town. Twice he'd thought the guy was going to stop and lead him to Sylvie or Brooke. Instead, it had been nothing more than a wild-goose chase.

Cold rain slipped down the back of his collar, reminding him that he didn't have time to slide down this rabbit hole. Morgan glanced at his watch. He had a phone conference with Jack in an hour. He might be on the road, but he needed to do what he could to help the business, if nothing else to make sure he still had a livelihood to return to once he found Brooke. He needed to get to the truck, get online and work.

As he hustled across the parking lot, Morgan thought about his brother doing the majority of the office work. Morgan tried to step up and do his own work when he could, but his mind was elsewhere.

In this weather, there wouldn't be many people out anyway. Even Sylvie was smart enough to get in out of the rain. He glanced down the street toward the park. At least, he hoped so. The idea of Brooke out in this made him shiver.

Maybe the woman from the T-shirt booth would call him today. He'd gladly stop by the booth again, but what good would that do? Frustration made him edgy. He kept walking to burn off energy.

He could go back and talk to Tara. Maybe she had more info about Sylvie from her application? An address maybe? But then she'd wonder why he needed it. Friends kept in contact.

He wasn't going to explain to anyone here about Sylvie. He couldn't risk it. He'd trusted before and been betrayed when they'd tipped Sylvie off. She'd run, and he'd had to start his search all over. He wasn't sure he could go through that again.

He certainly couldn't afford to.

Inside the cab, Morgan booted up his laptop and used the diner's Wi-Fi to get online. He had nearly a hundred emails to get through; instead, he did a quick search that resulted in nothing.

Who was that guy at the T-shirt stand? There was something there. He just didn't know what it was.

Rubbing his eyes in tired frustration, Morgan sat back on the bunk, pulling the laptop with him.

The article about last year's fire still stuck in his mind. Curious, he did another search. The Someday Café had a fairly good internet presence. The pretty owner, Tara, had paid decent money for the website. Hmm…they had takeout. He'd have to remember that.

Might be safer than sitting at that counter watching her move around…

There were promo photos of the diner, one of her in full chef regalia. She smiled at the camera, stirring a big pot in an obviously posed photo. A pretty picture.

Who was she? Really?

She hadn't grown up in Haskins Corners, but a good chunk of the inhabitants knew her. He stumbled across an article from a small, regional culinary magazine. It referred to the fire and talked about how the volunteers had created meals for the fire crews in a school kitchen.

There, in the middle of the group, laughing in pure abandon was Tara Hawkins. She wasn't dressed to cook, but in shorts and a tank top that left her arms and legs bare. Tanned and bare.

He liked the way she looked in this picture. At the diner, she'd looked pretty but stressed. In this picture, her hair hung loose and wavy past her shoulders. Not pulled tight against her scalp.

Reading on, he found her connection to this community. Her brother owned a ranch nearby. Had it been damaged in the fire? That wasn't the focus of the article, so Morgan didn't learn any more. If nothing else, it made him more curious about her.

His phone rang then, and after saving the picture to his hard drive, he answered.

"Any luck?" Jack didn't bother with the niceties.

Neither did Morgan as he explained yesterday's events. "Nothing great. I did find a place where she applied for a job. They didn't hire her."

"Damn. That would've made life easier."

"Yeah."

"What next?"

"I'm going to stick around for a couple days. But I gotta look like I'm here for a reason. Anything local I can do?" If he could do short hauls in the area, maybe that would buy him more time.

"I can see. I'll call if I find anything." The sound of rustling papers came through the line. "Anyplace else she might have applied for a job?"

"There's not much here. Retail. The diner. That's about all she's qualified for." He tried to envision the small town in his mind. "Maybe a couple of bars."

"Check 'em out." Jack's voice was tinny all of a sudden.

"Did you put me on speaker?" Morgan hated not knowing who could hear him.

"Yeah." Jack laughed. "One-handed typing sucks, so get over it, bro. I need your help with these numbers."

For the next few hours, they worked on financials and tried to figure out budgets for the next six months. The places Morgan was going to check would be open well into the night, so he could afford to give Jack the time.

The rain was relenting and letting the clouds temporarily part when he finally stumbled out of the cab. He needed to find something to eat before he continued his search. Morgan thought about going to the diner, but besides the distraction it would prove, he did need to look elsewhere. While the sidewalks in this town practically rolled up at night, there were a couple bars.

Sylvie had been a party girl when they'd met, and settling down hadn't agreed with her. Was she back to her old habits?

He'd just rounded the corner when the wind picked up and raindrops fell again. With a muttered curse, Morgan turned up his collar as he headed toward the flashing neon lights.

Suddenly, something—someone—plowed into him. He found his arms full of soft, damp, sweet-smelling woman.

CHAPTER FIVE

TARA GASPED, STRUGGLING not to drop everything in her arms. No such luck, as her purse and groceries tumbled to the ground. She didn't suffer a similar fate only because Morgan caught her.

Morgan.

"You okay?" His voice was deep, his arms warm, solid bands through her jacket. His breath brushed her cheek and she wasn't sure how long his gaze held hers.

"Uh, yeah." She hastily pulled away once her brain kicked into gear. Cold replaced the warmth of his arms. Trying not to look at him or think about how close they were, she bent to gather her groceries. They'd scattered clear across the wet sidewalk. One of the plastic bags had torn.

"Let me help." Morgan crouched beside her, and Tara couldn't help noticing his thick, muscular thighs right there in front of her—or the enticing curve of his biceps as he easily took on the weight of the canned goods. What items she could grab, she shoved into the remaining bag before facing him again.

His arms were full of her groceries. And he

was smiling at her. Damn. She'd wondered earlier what that smile would do to her. Now she knew. Her stomach did one of those annoying little backflips. Karma was a bitch. Hastily, she reached for the last few items and shot to her feet, berating herself for letting him distract her. She'd sworn she wouldn't let that happen again.

When she'd bought the diner, she'd also found a sweet little apartment within walking distance of both work and downtown. What she hadn't taken into consideration tonight—besides slamming into a solid, brick wall of a man coming around a corner—was weather. The fact that it had been raining on and off all day had made the trek long and cold. And wet. Very wet.

She knew her hair was plastered to her head, and she was sure she looked like a drowned rat. Maybe the late-day shadows would disguise her at least a little. Self-conscious, she tried to deflect the focus away from herself. "I—I thought you'd be leaving town."

"Still working on that. Good thing, too. Looks like you need my help." He winked.

He seemed entirely too happy about that fact. She scowled and fought the answering smile. "I can take—" Glancing down, she realized she couldn't take any of it. The other bag was ripped beyond salvaging, and she only had two arms. Surely, there was a way to stack it, cram everything into the one bag.

"Where you headed?" he asked, settling the canned goods more solidly in his arms.

"Home."

"Point me in the right direction." He was still smiling. "I'll help."

Tara shivered, as much from the cold of the rain as the realization that she had no choice but to show this veritable stranger her home. Either that or leave her groceries sitting here on the curb.

"Come on." She headed toward her apartment building, knowing that at least some of her neighbors were home. Mrs. Walton across the hall was *always* home. If Tara screamed, someone would hear her. But would they do anything?

She mentally rolled her eyes. She was being ridiculous.

Morgan walked beside her, his height and bulk blocking some of the rain, and Tara gave up resisting the urge to look at him. He was as soaked as she was, but why didn't he look like a drowned rat? If anything, he looked better all wet.

His jeans drew her gaze. The damp denim plastered to the hard contours of his leg muscles. Definitely a bodybuilder, he had a grace most hulking guys didn't. The T-shirt he wore was a dark color, so the damp didn't look as obvious, except to make the definition of those muscles clear. Six-pack abs. Pecs that were solidly defined and wide shoulders that flexed with the flow of muscle, broad and strong.

Tara doubted she could circle those biceps with both hands... The idea of touching him so intimately sent a flush from her head to her toes and back again.

Thankfully, they reached their destination, and she hurried to the protection of the porch. The rain intensified, and she dodged the cold drops falling down her neck. The patter of the raindrops on the veranda's roof seemed loud and insistent.

"Nice place." He looked around with interest when he joined her. "How many apartments?"

"Six," she explained as she opened the door of what had once been a great Victorian house. Much of the grandeur still clung to the facade, but the inviting hominess of the place had long faded. "I'm upstairs."

Stepping inside the foyer, she gulped as his size overwhelmed the tiny space. His broad shoulders nearly brushed the sides of the narrow doorway.

Once the door was closed and the patter of the falling rain muffled, silence pressed in on her, making her question again the sanity of bringing him to her home.

"If you'd feel better, I'll just leave these things here. They should be safe enough. You can come back and get them."

She stared. "How did you know?"

"That you're nervous about bringing me here?" Morgan laughed, but it wasn't a teasing laugh or a laugh that mocked her. It was almost self-deprecating. "You're not stupid, Tara. You should be cautious. I appreciate that."

Carefully, he stacked the cans on the small side table by the metal mailboxes in the wall. He'd wrapped a couple pasta boxes in the torn plastic bag, and, pulling them out now, he examined them to make sure they were dry. One looked the worse for the wear. "Sorry about that."

He turned to go, nodding at her as his hand curled around the old-fashioned door handle. "I'll be on my way."

He'd almost reached the other side of the porch before she broke out of her stupor and called after him. "Wait!"

Morgan looked over his shoulder at her.

He stood on the edge of the rain, the streetlight's bright glow falling over him the same way the raindrops did. So close. He was so close. Body-heat-sharing distance. Tasting the scent of him, she almost sighed at the rawness of him mingling with the damp night. She didn't want him to leave. There was so much more to him, and she was intrigued.

"The least I can do to thank you is let you dry off." This was ridiculous. She'd never been paranoid, never been inhospitable before. Why start now?

He turned around fully.

"I really do appreciate your help," she added.

"You're welcome," he said softly, though the depth of his voice echoed around the empty foyer.

"Come on." Reaching into her pocket, Tara pulled out her keys, then headed up the stairs.

MORGAN FOLLOWED TARA through the front door of the big, old house. He could see where it had been a grand place in its day, but where the foyer would have opened to several rooms, it was now a lobby of sorts, closed off and small. A door to the right had a brass A on it. B was across the hall, and straight ahead beyond the stairway was a door with C sitting a bit sideways.

A curved set of stairs led up, the carved handrail and delicate spindles showing definite signs of wear. As she stepped on the runner that ran up the center, each stair gave off a deep groan. He didn't hesitate to grab the groceries he'd just set down and followed her.

Three more doors branched off the upper landing. She stuck a key in the door straight ahead. Apartment E. It opened soundlessly, and she led him inside. She tossed her purse on a small table and shucked her jacket, putting it on an old-fashioned coat tree a few inches beyond.

Fading daylight and the streetlight's glow flooded the room through a turret-shaped alcove on the opposite wall. It looked inviting, and he took several steps before realizing he'd moved. He stood in the center of the room where he could easily turn and see everything. A small kitchen. The main room. Two wooden doors, both ajar. A bathroom with a claw-foot tub and a bedroom beyond. His gaze clung to that shadowed view. Rumpled bed, covers tossed up but not made.

Tara frowned but didn't argue or try to stop his perusal. "Just put those on the kitchen table," she directed, and he stepped into what seemed like a simple kitchen. Not what he expected in the home of a chef.

He continued to look around with growing interest. The pale green wall color and white subway tile fit her, though the regular stove and small counters did not.

He didn't say anything, and he didn't think he made any noise, but she turned her head. Their gazes met and held. Her eyes were pale blue, a color that fit with the light tone of her blond hair. Wisps fluttered in the air that wafted from the heat vent.

The image he'd seen of her on his computer where she'd been wearing the tank top and shorts flashed in his mind, reminding him that beneath that damp sweater were sweet curves and pretty, smooth skin.

Look somewhere else. He yanked his gaze to the surroundings, forcing his mind to think mundane thoughts.

This place told him more than he'd expected.

He felt welcome here. She was relaxed and made her way around the kitchen table with ease.

"Can I get you something to drink?" she asked as she put the groceries away.

"Nah, I'm good." Morgan shoved his hands into his pockets to keep himself from reaching out. He'd always learned by touching and feeling, not just looking. And this place was filled with things he was sorely tempted to pick up and feel, experience. Including her.

"Well, I'm cold." She rubbed her arms, and he couldn't tear his gaze away from her movements. "I'm making some coffee." Her smile reached out to him. "I'll share."

Stretching, she opened some upper cabinets and pulled out a canister. He stood there staring like a fool when her shirt rode up, just a little, to expose her sweet, flat abdomen. He tore his gaze away from her again. The scent of fresh-ground coffee wafted in the air as she busied herself making a pot. What was wrong with him? He had to get out of here before he said or did something stupid. He looked around for an escape.

As he turned, nearly bolting for the door, a shelf above the kitchen table caught his eye. Polished wood, it overflowed with books. Cookbooks. These weren't fancy, gourmet books. No, these were old, tattered—the kind he remembered seeing in his grandmother's house. That woman could cook.

"You get ideas for your menu from those?" He tipped his head toward the shelf.

Tara looked up. "From…?" She followed his gaze and smiled as if she didn't notice the tension thick in the air. "Some, yes." She took a step toward the shelf. "Some I can't use since they don't even make the ingredients anymore. But I was able to modify a few of them."

She pulled down an especially tattered book and flipped through the yellowed pages. Finally, she found what she was looking for and pointed to a spot on the page. "This is the recipe I started with to make my turnovers." She looked at him and smiled. "The ones you liked so much last night."

Morgan smiled back, and the sound of the clock ticking over their heads was loud in the stillness between them.

His mind wound around itself. She'd noticed how much he'd liked the turnovers? She paid attention. To him.

"Do you know all your customers so well?" Damn. His voice broke on the third word. He cleared his throat.

"Some." She stepped back and, with deliberate movements, pulled thick coffee mugs from the cupboard. "Sugar, right?"

"Uh, yeah."

She grabbed a sugar bowl, a dainty cup with the same green color as the walls in the design on the sides. He focused on that, trying and failing to not focus on her movements.

Filling both cups, Tara took her time preparing them, his with sugar, hers with a touch of cream and sweetener. Her hands were delicate, the nails trimmed short and even. She didn't wear any jewelry—no ring, no bracelet or watch. None of the glitz other women wore, but she didn't need it.

He almost didn't take the cup when she extended it to him. Almost.

Their fingers brushed. Where her skin was soft, the cup was solid. Both were warm. The scent of the coffee and something else—perfume—wafted between them.

Morgan leaned against the counter and cradled the cup. He had to do something with his hands or he'd try to touch her.

"So, tell me about Morgan Thane." She leaned on the opposite counter and faced him. She took a deep drink from her mug and waited.

"Not much to tell. My brother, Jack, and I run our trucking company. I drive. He's the office. Nothing fancy. What about you? Wendy says you just bought the diner." He wasn't into sharing anything about his past with her. Not yet, and certainly not now. Discussing Sylvie was off the table here in Tara's pretty little kitchen.

"Yeah." She smiled and he knew he'd found her soft spot. He focused on his cup, wishing instead that he could taste the excited blush that swept up her cheeks.

"I've been working on the diner for a couple months. Daisy wanted to keep going, but she just couldn't do it anymore."

"The diner looks different but—" He frowned, looking for the best way to explain his thoughts. "Feels the same."

"Thanks. That's a compliment. I always loved Daisy's place. I tried to keep some of it."

Tara grinned and he felt a responding warmth in his chest. He laughed, surprising himself with how good it felt. He couldn't remember the last time he'd enjoyed a woman's company.

Not since long before Sylvie left.

TARA KNEW HER apartment was small, and this kitchen even smaller. She should have felt cramped here with him. But she didn't. She liked the closeness, and despite all her good intentions, she wanted to be closer. Much closer.

Morgan Thane attracted her. And despite her denials to Wendy, he was most certainly her type. He was a good-looking, apparently decent guy. Yep, her type.

"Where are you from, originally?" Not from here. She might have grown up in Austin, but the ranch down the road where her brother now lived had belonged to her grandparents. She'd spent plenty of time here. She knew most of the locals.

"Dallas," he said with a definite grimace in his voice. "The business is based there."

She nodded, taking in the information—the safe, untempting information. She tried to formulate safe, intelligent questions. "You said you have a brother. Older or younger?"

He laughed. "Younger by three years."

Ah, the older brother. She tried not to compare him to her own three brothers.

"You have brothers and sisters?"

She grimaced. "Five. Three brothers. Two sisters. All older."

"That was a houseful." He almost sounded wistful.

"Definitely. Crowded." She ignored his reaction.

Morgan finished his coffee and moved to the sink to rinse the cup. She didn't move, and his arm brushed hers. Heat shot up Tara's arm and her heart picked up pace.

Despite a faint voice in the back of her mind trying to warn her, she couldn't resist. Her curiosity, among other things, was piqued.

Time stretched and somehow the voice grew a bit louder—her earlier misgiving about bringing him here returned. Not because she feared him. No, she was the problem. She had too much to lose by letting another man disrupt her plans.

She forced herself to step back—mentally, as

the kitchen was too small to physically do so—
from the temptation he provided.

The clatter of the cup against the sink startled
her and she jumped, coming into even closer contact with him.

He'd definitely warmed up. And his T-shirt
was dry.

Neither of them moved.

She dared to look at him. He was so close, and
she could see the texture of his day's whiskers
and the fan of his eyelashes around his green
eyes.

"Thanks for helping," she whispered, staring
at him over her cup's rim. Her fingers gripped
the handle for dear life.

For an instant, he didn't respond, and she worried he hadn't heard her over the patter of the
raindrops against the windowpane.

Slowly, Morgan took a step toward her and
plucked the cup from her hand. He set it on the
counter. Then, he moved his hand upward, slowly,
his palm cupping her chin, his thumb making a
featherlight swipe over her lips.

She caught herself before she licked her lips,
hoping to taste anything his touch left behind.

"I should go." His voice was soft, but she definitely heard the heat in it. He didn't move away.

"I—" She swallowed. "I'm glad you came by. I
enjoy your company." What was wrong with her?
Why had she said that? Though she had thought

it dozens of times since he walked into her diner that first day.

He chuckled softly but didn't say anything more. Instead he used those articulate lips for something better. He tasted of the rain, of the coffee he'd just finished and something else. Something warm, something—tender.

Tara stopped thinking. Only feeling—the solid bands of his arms around her waist, his fingers splayed across her back, the warm wall of his chest beneath her palms and the full length of her forearms.

When had she closed her eyes? She couldn't recall, she didn't care and she reveled in the darkness, tasting, touching—feeling this wonder.

Slowly, Morgan slid the tip of his tongue across the seam of her lips, hinting, asking for entry, seeking more of her. And she wanted more of him, too. Much, much more.

Hesitantly at first, Tara slipped her arms over the hard contours of his chest to loop over his shoulders and around his neck. She held on tight, her fingers brushed the close-trimmed hair at the nape of his neck.

Was that sound her sigh or his? "Again?" his touch silently asked, and she leaned closer, if that were possible, and let him in.

Everything about the man was solid and warm. Hot. She leaned into him, and he took the full weight of her against him. Angling his head, his lips found more of hers, drinking her in. His hands curled around her, the heat of his palms burning through her clothing, making her feel as if she'd been branded by his touch.

They couldn't get much closer, but she ached to be much, much closer. Ached to feel him against her skin.

As if he had some type of psychic power, his hand slid beneath the fabric of her sweater, brushing her skin like a match touching kindling. She trembled.

"Morgan," she whispered against his lips, needing to say something but unable to form a sentence.

He didn't move. He didn't breathe, it seemed. Then he withdrew his hand from her skin. "No," Morgan whispered, surprising her as he put his hands on her shoulders. "This…" Shaking his head, Morgan stepped back, those warm fingers lingering, then leaving a trail down her arm, before he abruptly turned away. "Thanks for the coffee. I'll let myself out."

He couldn't seem to get away fast enough. Before Tara could move, she heard the door open, then close. Morgan's footsteps were loud and hurried down the stairs. The front door opened, then closed. After that, she couldn't hear anything more. Only the patter of the rain on the window broke the silence he left behind.

He was gone.

She was happy. Relieved. He'd saved her from herself, from her own weakness. She stared at the closed door, hearing the rain beating on the roof.

He'd be soaked in seconds. She shivered, recalling how he looked in his damp clothes. Was he right? Was their kiss really a mistake? Why did he think that? The speed of his escape said so much and didn't tell her a blessed thing.

STUPID. STUPID. STUPID. Morgan called himself every kind of fool as he stomped down the sidewalk. He could still taste her, still feel the soft, giving warmth of her lips under his. Every muscle in his body, save for the one thumping deep in his chest, screamed to turn back and pick up where he'd left off.

When he'd left his truck earlier, all he'd planned to do was go downtown and ask some questions. He hadn't intended on meeting Tara. Hadn't planned to follow her home like a sad puppy dog. And he certainly hadn't planned to kiss her.

That had been the stupidest piece of all.

But oh, so worth it. His memory filled with the images and sensations of her so close, so sweet and warm.

He cursed and resumed stomping across the damp pavement.

Soon, he was at the diner and he climbed into the cab of his truck. He was soaked through again, and the rain still pounded, loud and tinny against the truck's metal roof and the windshield. It was deafening. He sat in the bucket seat and stared at the storm, understanding its fury completely.

His phone rang, and he almost missed answering Jack's call because digging it out of his sodden jeans pocket took effort. "What?" he barked into the phone.

"Well, aren't you cheery," Jack snapped. "What the hell happened to you?"

"Nothing."

"Yeah. Sure."

Morgan could almost hear Jack rolling his eyes. It was Jack's favorite expression when he was frustrated with him, which had been quite often when they were growing up.

"Look," Jack started over, ignoring Morgan's mood. "I got you a load. It's from here in Dallas and back to Haskins Corners by tomorrow night. It's doable, if you aren't in the middle of something."

The middle of something? Morgan thought about Tara and the mess he'd left at her apartment. Yeah. Not in the middle of anything really important. "I can leave now and get back here by tomorrow afternoon."

"That's what I told the client."

Good. That was solved. They talked details for a few more minutes, then, after the call ended,

Morgan slipped into the back. He hustled to change into dry clothes then settled behind the wheel.

He needed to get out of here. Going through his checks, he prepared to head out. Between now and the time he returned, he'd come up with a plan. He'd find another place to park. Maybe the woman from the T-shirt stand would call and he'd have another lead. Either way, returning to the diner was not in the cards.

Someone pounded on the side of the truck. Hard. Even fist beats against the metal door. Morgan frowned and reached over to open the passenger door.

Tara stood there, staring at him. She was soaking wet, her hair plastered to her head and around her face. Her eyes looked big and endearing, nearly dragging him in. Her damp clothes clung to places he tried really hard not to look at.

"Are you leaving?" she yelled over the roar of the engine and the pounding rain.

"Yeah." He wasn't saying anything else. That's what had gotten him in trouble earlier.

"Are you coming back?"

He still didn't speak, not for a long time. Instead, he shrugged and stared straight ahead through the windshield. She didn't leave. She didn't get in out of the rain. She simply stood there. He could feel her gaze on him. He was not going to give in, not going to turn and drink in the look of her.

Something must have made her change her mind. Instead of stepping away from the roar of the truck, she curled her hand around the thick, metal handrail and pulled herself up. Before he could think or say anything, she was there, inside the cab. The door slammed with a loud wham.

"Are you going to answer me?"

He clenched his teeth and had to actually fight with himself to stop from looking at her. God, he wanted to haul her close. He knew he had to resist, but what a temptation she was. He ached, resisting. He knew he had to face her, had to look at her, had to tell her the truth and risk—no, probably guarantee—he'd push her away.

"Go home, Tara. Or inside the diner," he said softly, slowly turning his head to look at her, not moving another muscle of his body except to clench the steering wheel with a death grip. "Just…go inside."

"Not until you answer me." She settled into the seat. "Are you coming back?"

The silence was thick. "No. Coming back would be a mistake."

It took her a while to digest that. "Why?" she finally whispered.

Morgan's heart sank to somewhere deep in his gut. "That kiss—" He gulped. "Can't happen again."

"Why?" she repeated.

He swallowed, not wanting to see the reaction on her face, not wanting to see her hurt, anger or disappointment. He squared his shoulders. The words sat bitter in his stomach before he let them go. "Tara. I'm…married."

CHAPTER SIX

TARA STARED. At the rain on the side window.
At the silhouette of the big man who'd touched
her so gently a short while ago. The anguish on
Morgan's face cut through the growing shadows.

She curled her hand into a fist. *How dare he?*
The fingers of her other hand closed around the
door handle. Icy, cold rain splashed in as she
shoved the heavy door open. She didn't say anything. Neither did he. Climbing down, Tara closed
the door, though she wanted to slam it to ease the
pain slicing through her entire body.

She ran. Dodging the fat, wet drops as well as
the mortification snapping at her heels. After he'd
left her apartment, she'd run after him, through
the rain, not caring that she was soaked, not caring that she shivered, only needing to catch up to
him. Needing to understand what had just happened.

What had she been thinking? She hadn't. She'd
simply reacted, the very thing she'd promised
herself she would not do anymore.

But now she knew. Nothing. Nothing at all was going on between them.

She needed to get away. From him. Very far away.

Reaching the rear door of the diner, Tara yanked it open and hustled through the kitchen. The lights and clatter of cookware were painful contrasts to the quiet night.

She wasn't supposed to be here. She'd taken tonight off—a first in the weeks since she'd bought the place. That's why she'd gone grocery shopping, why she'd been heading to her apartment when she'd run into Morgan.

The idea of being home alone made her stomach twist. But facing anyone—her staff, customers—was not an option. She had plenty of bookwork to do. And recipes to work on. More than enough to distract her.

Her tiny office sat open and dark, nearly deterring her. No, she was stronger than some lying, no-good, married jerk...

Who tasted of damp and coffee...

She closed and locked the door, sinking into the much-loved wooden chair. She booted up the computer, trying to focus.

How could he? He didn't wear a ring. He didn't act like a married man, though what did a married man who was always on the road act like? Tara didn't know. She'd never had any experiences like this.

The damp on her cheeks from the rain warmed. Or were those tears? She pounded the desktop. "Damn him."

"Tara?" Wendy asked through the closed door. "Is that you?"

She did *not* want to talk to, or see, anyone right now. Maybe never again. She felt so stupid. So betrayed. So—disappointed. It hurt. Damn, it hurt. And that just added to her anger.

"I'm…I'm busy right now." She tried to make her voice sound as normal as possible.

"I need to talk to you."

"Not right now." She couldn't face anyone. "I'll come find you. Later." She glanced at the clock. Wendy's shift didn't end for a couple hours. "Before you leave."

"Okay." Wendy's voice faded and only silence followed.

The deep rumble of an engine shook the entire building. Despite herself, Tara listened to Morgan drive away, listened until the roar faded into the night, the ache in her chest growing as the quiet returned.

Fool.

The rhythm of the rain taunted her, trying to mask the sound of his retreat, and failing. At the last minute, she shot to her feet and stared out the tiny window. Red taillights shone on the damp pavement, brightening at the stop sign, then fading again as Morgan accelerated and slowly turned the corner. The night settled in dark.

And cold. Tara suddenly felt cold. So very cold.

Two HOURS HAD passed and still Tara was angry with herself for letting Morgan get to her, and just as angry for reacting so emotionally to his revelations.

She'd holed up in her office for those hours, pretending to work on bills, making little headway and wallowing a bit too much. Another demerit in the Morgan Thane column.

But it was getting late. Wendy would be leaving soon, the night shift arriving at about the same time. She found Wendy watching a little girl seated, alone, in booth five.

"That's what I needed to talk to you about earlier." Wendy's words came out only slightly accusing as she whispered.

"How long has she been here?" Tara whispered back.

"Almost three hours."

The little girl sat in the corner of the booth with a ratty, stuffed purple dragon in her arms. She held it in her lap, talking to it as if she expected the toy to understand.

Most kids her age, which Tara guessed to be about six, had been asleep for hours.

Her uneven, dingy blond ponytails bobbed as she spoke. When she finished speaking, she hugged the dragon, burying her face in the matted fur.

Tara recalled seeing her in here a couple times before. She came in with a young woman who was usually more interested in the guy across the table or with her phone than the little girl. Was that why the girl was talking to the toy? A wave of painful empathy washed over Tara at the loneliness the girl must feel.

Where was the woman now? Tara looked around, but didn't see her. She moved closer to the table. "Hello," she greeted the girl, smiling, not wanting to upset or scare her. While the girl looked up at her with big brown eyes, she didn't smile back.

"Are you here with someone, sweetie?"

The girl only nodded in response.

"Who?" Tara stalled by checking the sugar dispenser and the salt and pepper shakers. The girl was too young to be here on her own. An adult had to be here someplace. The restroom perhaps?

Finally, the girl pointed. Tara looked over her shoulder. The twentysomething who was normally with the girl sat at another table back in the corner behind the small room divider, flirting with a man. She looked like she'd been there awhile if the lipstick stains on the coffee mug were any indication.

"You're with her?"

The girl nodded.

"Why are you sitting over here?"

The girl shook her head and shrugged. "She told me to stay over here."

Tara frowned. It wasn't a big deal to have the girl taking the table since it was late, and there were only a couple tables full. But the girl was by herself. Well, except for the dragon.

"Why?"

"She said to leave her alone."

"Is she your mom?" Why did that idea bother Tara? She thought of her own mother, who'd had six kids and still managed to make them each feel special. Mom never ignored them. Ever.

The girl shook her head. "No. She's the baby-sitter. But I'm not a baby." The protest seemed tired and worn-out, even coming from the child.

"Where's your mother?"

"At work."

"What about your father?"

"I dunno." The girl hugged the dragon tight. "Mama says I have to be good and not upset the sitter cuz she can't find nobody else."

Tara slowly wiped off the table, wondering what she should do. Thankfully, someone *was* here with the girl, though she wasn't doing a very good job of watching her.

"She don't like me being around," the girl whispered into the fur.

"Who? The babysitter?"

"No. Mama." The sadness in the girl's voice

tore at Tara's heart. She almost hated to ask the next question.

"Why?"

"She's trying to find me a new daddy," the girl whispered, leaning toward Tara. "I don't know why." The girl wrapped her arms tighter around the dragon. "Me and Lanara both like my real dad just fine."

Whoa. Tara stared at the girl. She had to remind herself that this wasn't really her business. But the girl looked so lost and distressed.

Not sure what to do and even less willing to upset her any more, Tara decided to tread on safer, less emotionally charged ground for now. "Is that your dragon's name? Lanara?" she asked.

"Yep. Daddy read it in a book." The girl turned the battered animal around so Tara could see its worn face. "Daddy gave her to me for my birthday."

Interesting. Tara nodded. "She's lovely. Did you have anything to eat?"

The girl shook her head. She sat up straighter, looking beyond Tara.

"Come on, kiddo." A woman's voice came from behind Tara. "We're going with Jake." She reached past the girl and pulled out a small purse from behind the girl's back. A tall, dark-haired man stood at the door, waiting impatiently.

There wasn't any bill on either table, and only

the cup that had lipstick on one edge to even indicate they'd been there.

"Would you like something to go? A cookie?" Tara offered.

"No, thanks," the woman said. At the same time, the girl said, "Yes, please," and looked up hopefully.

The girl jumped down from the booth, her ratty tennis shoes slapping against the wood floor. The woman grabbed the girl's arm, and together they wound their way through the tables to where the man waited.

Tara hurried to the glass container on the counter and hastily grabbed a handful of cookies. "Take these with you." She put them into a bag.

"We didn't order those," the babysitter snapped.

"I know." Tara smiled. "It's a gift." She winked at the girl and extended the bag to her. "You come back anytime, okay?"

The girl smiled and nodded, using her free hand to wave the dragon's floppy arm.

Tara forced herself to smile and wave back, struggling not to frown. That whole interaction felt weird, though despite the late hour, she couldn't put her finger on why. She cleared off the table and headed into the kitchen. Robbie was cleaning up his last order and preparing to hand the kitchen over to the night cook. He didn't see customers, so it was doubtful he even knew about the girl. Wendy didn't remember her before tonight.

Tara planned to ask the rest of the staff about the girl, to see if they recognized her, too, and ask them to let her know if she came in again. She didn't look in imminent danger, but something didn't feel right. She wasn't happy, like a kid should be.

Tara wasn't sure what she should do, if anything, but she couldn't totally dismiss the situation.

Or maybe she was looking for a distraction. Tara forced herself to focus on clearing tables and not worry about everyone else's problems.

Though she doubted she'd forget the girl or the rest of today's events anytime soon.

MORGAN HAD DRIVEN straight to Dallas, whittling away at the night. He'd expected to sleep the couple hours it would take to prep the load and get everything ready once he reached his apartment. But sleep eluded him.

Damn.

Frustration of all types created energy, and the only way Morgan knew to burn off excess energy was by working out. He'd outfitted his apartment to accommodate his exercise routine. The bar suspended from the bedroom doorframe had seen many a pull-up session. Today, it would see more.

"What's eating you?" Jack didn't bother to

knock. Morgan made a mental note to get that key back.

"Nothing." He counted to focus on his progress. *Eleven.* "Just my workout."

"They don't have gyms in...where the hell were you? Corners something?" Jack headed to the fridge to stare into the depths.

"Haskins." *Fifteen.* "It's on the paperwork. I know you read it."

"Read, but I didn't commit it to memory."

"Might be a useful skill to develop." *Eighteen.*

"Waste of brain cells." Jack yanked out a beer and actually seemed to consider it.

"Before noon?"

Jack shrugged. "Maybe not." He put it back somewhat reluctantly. "Truck'll be ready to go by two. Will you?"

"Sure." *Twenty.*

"Uh-huh. You sleep yet?"

"No." *Twenty-two.* "I'll catch a catnap after this." *Twenty-four.*

"I'll hold the load if you're not awake." Jack glared at him. "I'm serious. You aren't driving tired or hyped-up on caffeine. Remember, I know you. What's eating you? Start talking or I'll send Gary or Phil instead of you."

The expletive that filled the room would have gotten Morgan backhanded as a kid. Jack just laughed. *Twenty-seven.*

Three more pull-ups strained his arms, the

burn reminding him why he did this. He jumped to the ground and grabbed the towel and wiped his face. "I didn't find a damned thing. The leads are dead ends."

Even he heard the defeat in his voice.

"Then other than this delivery, why are you going back? It's an easy swap to send one of the guys. Kyle's been asking for extra hours now that his wife is expecting."

"Again?"

Jack laughed. "Yeah. Guess absence makes the heart grow fonder?"

Morgan glared at him.

"Sorry." Jack turned back to the fridge. "Where to next?"

Guilt swept through Morgan. He'd thought a lot about his situation as he'd driven last night, about all the hours he spent on the road, alone, accomplishing nothing. Of the burden Jack took on at the office.

About Tara and the mess he could get into without much effort. "Nowhere."

Silence followed his statement. Jack slowly rose, staring over the fridge door at Morgan.

"You giving up?"

"Maybe." Why did that idea make his chest hurt? Morgan shook his head. "No. But I think it's time to give the PI a try." Instead of continuing with his workout, he grabbed his water bottle and downed nearly half of it.

Jack closed the fridge, a water bottle in his hand, as well. "Really? You got enough cash together for that?"

"No." Morgan did not want to have this conversation. "I just feel like it's time. I'll…I'll figure out something."

Jack didn't ask anything for a long time, the look of confusion on his face telling Morgan he'd have questions soon.

"Feel? Since when are you a touchy-feely kinda guy?"

"Funny. Real funny, dumbass. You learn anything more about the schools?"

Jack and he had created a list of all the schools Sylvie might have enrolled Brooke in, even the fancy, expensive ones. Jack was working on contacting them all.

"No." Jack grabbed a chair and sat, propping his feet up on the other one.

"What about day care?"

"Sylvie isn't going to put Brooke in day care. Too expensive and visible."

"She might not have a choice." Why, Morgan didn't know, but anything was possible. She had to support them somehow. She had to have some type of job, didn't she?

Jack was silent, staring at the toes of his battered running shoes for a long time. Finally, he looked up, frowning. "So, you're planning to come back to the office?" he asked softly.

Morgan straddled the bench for sit-ups and focused on that. "Yeah, I guess. Maybe you can take some time off."

Jack glared at him. Morgan had never shrunk away from his brother's intense anger, and he wasn't about to now.

Unfortunately, when Jack got that look in his eye, it reminded Morgan too much of Dad. Of that mean, angry drunk who came home half-toasted and finished off the task in front of the TV with *Monday Night Football* and a twelve-pack. "Back off, Jack."

"Why?"

Morgan didn't move, didn't dare. As a kid, he'd been the older brother, the one who had to be stronger, in control. Not that he'd always accomplished it. There'd been plenty of black eyes inflicted between them.

"Just like that, you're giving up?"

"Did I say that?" Morgan glared back. "I'm just letting someone else take the lead. I'm not going to argue with you."

"Maybe you should."

"Why in the world would I?"

"Shit, Morgan." Jack took a step toward him. "You're a shadow of yourself. Since Sylvie left, you're a closed, shut-off ass."

"A what?"

"You heard me."

Morgan actually felt laughter bubble inside his

chest. "Name-calling, really?" He picked up the towel from the workout bench and after wiping the sweat off his face, looped it around his neck and fisted the ends. "Nice try."

Jack laughed, too. But it wasn't as filled with mirth as it should be. "Don't let Sylvie do this to you, Morgan." Jack's voice was deceptively soft. "She's done enough damage. You'll never forgive yourself if you quit now."

"What exactly do you mean by that?" Now he didn't feel like laughing—he felt his anger rising, that ever-present sense that he should protect her, even if she didn't want that protection—or him—anymore.

"Oh, come on." Jack was in his face. "Do you even feel anything anymore except that damned need to chase her? How are you going to turn that off and focus on office work when she's still out there?" He pointed at the door.

Morgan's knuckles went white. "What do you suggest I do?" His voice was loud now. "I've spent a year hunting for her. A year. I've accomplished nothing."

"You said yesterday you had a good feeling about the leads. You were heading to the bars to ask questions. What happened with that?"

"Nothing." Morgan should get up and move. He needed to shower before he did anything.

"You've driven every flippin' highway in this state, as well as half a dozen others. You don't come home. You sit in that damned truck and drive until you can't stay awake anymore. You're no quitter, so why are you stopping now?"

Morgan speared Jack with a look he knew was as cold and mean as Dad's had ever been. "Didn't I tell you to back off?"

Jack didn't move. They were silent for a long minute, both men finishing bottles of water before speaking. Jack crushed his with a loud crunch and pitched it into the trash.

"Forget I asked. What about the place where Sylvie applied to work? They might be a big help. Guess the PI will just take care of it all, right?" Jack glared but didn't say any more. He stalked to the door and slammed it behind him so hard the entire apartment shook. The tenants upstairs probably felt the impact.

Silence settled around Morgan. Empty silence that didn't sit well on his shoulders.

Seated on the workout bench, he stared down, not at the steel and lead of the dumbbells that made up the next part of his routine, but at his hands. His calloused, scarred hands.

He'd earned every one of those calluses with good honest work. The scars? Not so much. The white line across the knuckles of his left hand was from the left hook where he'd connected with Big Ken's jaw—and split his hand wide open.

The white line up his forearm had faded, but it was a cleaner cut. A scalpel when he'd busted his arm in the battle with The Mauler. His pinkie finger on his right hand wasn't quite straight. Who was he kidding? It'd been broken three times, never quite healing right.

But those scars represented money that got him and Jack out of Dad's reach, put Jack through college and gave them a chance to survive.

He wasn't proud of how he'd gotten them.

Sylvie had been from that fringe world he'd slipped into when he'd first hit the road. She'd never asked where the scars came from. She'd probably already had an idea. And she'd have to actually care to ask about something like that.

Tara wasn't from that world. Did she even know about it? He curled his mangled fingers into a fist. A position he was more familiar with.

He'd dared to touch her. Dared to reach out for something he wanted. Was he crazy? He knew better than to reach too high. That had never gotten him anything but pain.

Morgan didn't have room for regret.

But it knocked on the door of his conscience now. He hadn't lied to Tara, not really. He should have kept his distance, should have kept his libido under control. No, this was all on him.

How would she know he was married? There wasn't any sign of a wedding band—now or past—on his left hand. Hadn't been since Sylvie had taken off.

Oh, he'd filed for divorce. He'd done everything he was supposed to—except make it final. He had to find her to do that, but when he did... And not because he was pining away for Sylvie. No, mostly because he didn't want to traumatize Brooke. His lawyer had assured him that he'd get custody of his daughter with little question from the courts.

Especially after Sylvie had taken Brooke away like she had. The lawyer had gone on to explain that they could put a warrant out for Sylvie for violating the provisions of any custody agreement.

Morgan could turn Sylvie into a criminal in a heartbeat—and terrorize his daughter when the cops swooped in and arrested her mother. His soon-to-be-ex-wife wasn't smart enough to keep her temper under control. She'd make a scene. It would work in his favor.

But Brooke would be the one to pay the price, and Morgan wasn't willing to take that risk. Or give Sylvie any weapons against him. He'd stay married and alone if he had to, if that were the case.

He'd stay away from Tara and the temptation she represented.

And there she was, back again, front and center in his thoughts. *Tara.* He could almost feel her, almost taste her sweet kiss. Taunting him with what he couldn't have.

His curses flew around the room, filling the air with a deep blue. He tossed his drink at the trash and, missing, he returned to the pull-up bar.

One.

CHAPTER SEVEN

THE STREET FAIR was in full swing. With a break in the constant rain the past few days, the vendors, visitors and Tara were taking advantage of the opportunity to get outside.

"Hi, Tara," rang out from several booths as she walked along, perusing the offerings at each one. She liked this town, these people, and on the whole they supported her business. So she tried to support them and theirs.

Today she'd brought a basket of Addie's amazing cookies, each wrapped up so she could hand them out as thanks. She stopped at the tin sculptor's booth first.

Dave was doing a brisk business today. He looked up as she approached and smiled. "I'll deliver your sculpture the first of next week if you'd like."

"That would be wonderful." She'd already cleared a spot by the door for Mr. Squirrel. "I wanted to bring by a gift for you, to thank you for all your support." She pulled out a package of cookies that she'd wrapped in a ribbon. His eyes lit up.

"Are those the famous Hawkins cookies I've heard about?" He rubbed his hands together in anticipation.

"They are Addie's specialty. Enjoy!" She set them on the table and he whisked them underneath with a flourish. She moved on to the next booth, smiling and anticipating the new addition to her decor.

She was inspecting a bracelet in the next booth, thinking it would be a great birthday gift for her sister Mandy, when she felt a tug on the hem of her shirt. Surprised, she looked down, thinking she'd caught it on something.

Instead she found herself staring into the wide eyes of the little girl who'd been in the diner with her babysitter a few nights ago. "Oh, hello." She smiled and knelt to be at eye level with her.

"Can I have one of those?" the girl whispered, pointing at the basket of cookies. Her eyes were wide, and she didn't return Tara's smile. Tara noticed she didn't have the purple dragon with her, and there were smudges of dirt on her face and hands.

"Of course, you can." She reached for the cookie and watched the girl lick her lips. "Did you have breakfast, sweetie?" It was still early in the day.

The girl shook her head.

Tara looked around. "Are you with the babysitter?"

"No." Her ponytails bobbed. "Mama's at work

for only a little bit. Her boss is there so I'm not 'posed to be there." She was still staring at the cookies. "Mama told me to stay out of the way."

And this was her staying out of the way? Granted, Haskins Corners was a small town and kids often ran around in the park and playground. And the townspeople kept an eye on each other's kids like it was second nature. But little ones like this were seldom far from a watchful set of eyes. Tara looked around to see who was looking toward them. She saw no one.

"Where does your mom work?" Tara had half a mind to go have a chat with the woman. The girl must have sensed her intent, as she shook her head slowly and started to back away.

Tara frowned and lightly put her hand on her shoulder. "I'll gladly give you the cookie, but how about we get breakfast first? There are some really good waffles at one of the booths." She didn't dare take her away from the fair in case her mother came looking for her.

"Might serve her right," Tara whispered to herself. To the girl she said, "Come on." She extended her hand, just as she would to her nephew Tyler if he were here. The girl took it more readily than Tyler did now that he was a grown-up nine-year-old.

"Do you like bacon?" Tara asked, planning a complete meal.

"Ever'body likes bacon." The girl rolled her big, brown eyes.

"Most people do, you're right." They reached the booth and Tara ordered them each a waffle with bacon and a cup of orange juice. She wasn't hungry, but she didn't want the girl to eat alone.

She led her to a picnic table near the playground and set their meal on the worn wood. "Hop up." Tara lifted her, noticing as she did how thin and tiny she was.

"Do you need help cutting that?" Tara asked as she took her seat across from the girl.

"It's big. Yes, please," the girl whispered and Tara gladly took on the task, soon handing her the fork. It only took an instant for a bite of waffle to disappear.

"You know, I'm not sure I know your name." Tara made conversation, hoping to learn something to help this sweet child. "I feel like I know you. I'd like us to be friends." She nibbled on the crispy bacon. "I'm Tara."

"I'm Brooke," the girl said around another bite of waffle. "I'm gonna go to school soon. Mama says that'll make her life easier."

Tara bet it would. No need to find childcare if the school system was taking care of them. Tara had heard Addie talk about the number of kids who really struggled because their parents weren't involved. The topic was definitely a hot button for her sister who taught in Austin.

"There you are."

Tara looked up to see the babysitter from the other night stalking toward them. She stopped at the edge of the table, her hands on her hips. "What are you doin'?" she asked Brooke.

"Eating." Brooke shoved another bite in, not having finished chewing the other one.

"Slow down, sweetie." Tara reached over and patted her arm. "There's no rush."

"We gotta go. Your mom called, and she ain't getting off like she thought. You're coming with me." Brooke's face fell, and she slowly set down her fork, turning to climb down.

"Please, let her stay and at least finish her breakfast," Tara said in what she hoped was an authoritative voice that the babysitter would follow. Looking closer now, Tara realized she was a kid herself, a teen with an attitude to match.

"Make it quick, kid." She sat beside Brooke with a thud. "I'm meeting Jake in five minutes. He's my boyfriend," she told Tara.

Slowly, Brooke put her legs under the table and picked up her fork. She finished half the waffle and all the bacon before she spoke again. "I'm full."

Tara smiled. "Good. You don't have to eat any more."

"Can we keep it so I can have some tomorrow?" Brooke looked at Tara, pleading in her eyes.

"Waffles don't keep," the babysitter offered.

"It'll be gross by tomorrow. Come on, we gotta go." She stood, impatiently.

"Tell you what." Tara leaned toward Brooke. "You know where I work, right?" Brook nodded. "I own the diner, so I can make you a new waffle anytime you like."

"Anytime?"

"Yep."

"Even for supper?"

"Even for supper. Anytime you're hungry, you come see me. We're friends, remember?"

"Come on." The teen had already walked several yards away.

Brooke hastily climbed down, then instead of hurrying to catch up, she looked at Tara. "I like being your friend," she said, then turned and ran behind the other girl. The crowd quickly swallowed them up, but not before Brooke looked back one last time and waved.

Tara tried not to worry about the little girl, but she did feel better now. It was a start.

BEING IN THE office was strange. The floor beneath Morgan's feet didn't move, and the view outside the window stayed the same.

"For gawdsake, sit down," Jack grumbled from his desk. "You're driving me nuts."

Morgan planted his backside in the desk chair—that he'd had to dust off this morning—and stared at the computer monitor. He'd never taken any classes in accounting, but he understood it. He recognized the columns, knew what they were doing with all the numbers.

Except his brain wasn't on work today. He fought the urge to get up and walk to the window again.

A short while later, the rumble of a truck's engine drew his wandering attention. A black behemoth came slowly through the arched gate. Morgan stared. That rig. He'd recognize Dewey's setup anywhere. The shiny black paint provided a vivid background for the bright orange flames on the sides. On the front grill of the Peterbilt, evil-looking teeth grinned maniacally at traffic. "What the—?"

"What?" Jack frowned, frustration on his brow. "Problem?"

"What's Dewey Franklin doing here?"

"Probably showing up for work."

"Since when?"

"Since last fall. He's a good hauler." Jack shook his head, then with a shrug, turned to his own computer. "He takes most of the high-risk jobs. Makes us a good buck."

"I'll just bet he does." Morgan slammed his teeth together and stalked to the door. He didn't care how much money the asshole made for them, he didn't want him here. Dewey—and the world Dewey represented—had no place in this business.

"Where you going?" Jack called after him.

When Morgan didn't answer, and kept going, Jack must have thought—rightfully so—that there was trouble. "Hey!"

Morgan heard Jack's footsteps behind him but didn't stop.

"Wondered when you were gonna come back." Dewey's gravelly voice, laced with laughter, came around the open door of the truck's cab.

Morgan stopped. Not for any other reason than the smidgen of sanity he'd developed over the years. "You're not welcome here," Morgan ground out between his tight teeth. "Keep moving."

"Sorry, Morgan. No can do." The big man lumbered out of the cab, his wide grin cutting across his face. "I got a contract."

Morgan slowly pivoted on his heel and pinned Jack with one of his nastiest glares.

Jack didn't flinch. "He's right."

Frustration bubbled inside Morgan. First, he'd lost contact with his men. Now, he'd apparently also lost complete say in who even worked for them.

It was his own damned fault. Turning, Morgan decided the office might be a better place for him. He needed to learn his own business from square one, it seemed.

"Hey, Morgan," Dewey called.

When Morgan turned around to look at him, Dewey did a few punches in the air, his battered fists flying and missing Morgan's chin—barely. "Thought maybe you were going back on the circuit." There was an ornery glint in Dewey's eyes.

"What the hell *are* you doing here, Dewey?" Morgan stepped closer, pushing into the man's personal space. "I thought you were here to work." He looked pointedly at Jack again, too.

"Ah, come on, man. You know why I'm here. Money. Ain't that why we do anything?" He nudged Morgan with a hard elbow. "Nice gig you got here. Almost said somethin' when I saw you in Haskins Corners the other day." His grin grew wider, if that was possible.

Haskins Corners immediately brought Tara's image to mind. What was Dewey doing there? Morgan frowned. "Keepin' tabs on me?" Not even Jack knew Morgan's actions with any regularity.

"Ah, lighten up." There was an edge to Dewey's voice.

Morgan stared at Dewey. The man hadn't changed in the—what?—five years since their paths had crossed. "You been fighting this whole time?" He almost couldn't believe anyone would take the abuse that long.

"Yeah, some. Though I do a lot of other stuff nowadays." The beefy trucker puffed up his chest. "I do some managing."

Managing? What the…? "Like who?" As Dewey talked about names and faces Morgan had left behind when he'd ditched living danger-ously, it dawned on him that Dewey might be just the break he'd been looking for. Had Sylvie left it all behind, as well? Or not? The questions he'd had a couple days ago, when he'd been headed to the bars in Haskins Corners but got distracted by Tara, returned. Was Sylvie still haunting the back roads of the fights? That *had* been where he'd first met her.

Morgan leaned against the warm metal of the truck's frame. Casual. Seemingly uncaring, as his heart pounded in his chest. "You seen anyone else from back in the day?"

"Back in the day?" Dewey cackled. "You act like it's school. Though that last one, I guess you got a heck of a schooling."

Morgan's joints still ached from that beat-ing. Mack had been one of the roughest, mean-est fighters in the ring. No mercy in that man's eyes. No compromise in his soul.

"Mack still fighting?"

Another laugh. "Hell, no. He went even further the next fight. Near killed Jacob. No one wanted that. Tate called the authorities. Shoulda seen ev-eryone scrambling to get out before the cops got there. Hauled all of 'em away. Tate's got a good attorney, but Mack's ass is in the state pen for a mighty long time." Dewey's voice faded, and he stared into the blue sky. "Least, I hope he's still there. I might retire if he ever comes back."

Morgan thought that was probably a good idea for them all.

"'Course you, that's a whole 'nother story. You got potential, Morgan. I'd back you."

That almost surprised Morgan. He hadn't fought in over five years. He wasn't going to start now. Not unless... The idea of going back to that life, even temporarily, left a bad taste in his mouth.

"Now, Morgan—" Jack stepped forward, almost in between him and Dewey. "You quit all that for a reason."

Morgan had nearly forgotten Jack was there. "I know." He wasn't going to explain now what he was thinking to Jack. Not in front of Dewey. "Just wonderin' about some of the people I used to know." He turned to Dewey. "There still a horde of followers?"

"Followers? You mean the women?" He elbowed Morgan again. "You lookin' for some action, my friend? I can get you some of that, too. Though I saw that little gal you're so hot on in Haskins Corners last week."

"Who?" he asked cautiously, not wanting Dewey to know about Tara if he didn't already. Sylvie on the other hand... "You've seen Sylvie?"

Dewey's laugh was nearly a cackle. "She's kinda tough to miss. You lose her?"

Morgan nearly went after the man and his insinuation right there in the yard. He'd fought

Dewey a few times, enough to know it wasn't an easy slam dunk to beat the man. But Morgan hadn't been thinking straight for weeks. Why start now?

When Morgan leaned in closer, Dewey lifted his hands in the sign of surrender. "I'm just sayin', I got an in, man." Dewey grew quiet. "What's the point if you're not gonna step into a ring?" He turned away, pulling paperwork out. "I'd like to get some of my money back, but I ain't gonna beg. You change your mind, your brother knows how to reach me."

"You know where Sylvie is?" Morgan asked, his voice low and menacing.

"Maybe. You fight. Maybe I'll get the information for you. I can get you in next weekend."

Was this the last puzzle piece? Was he finally going to find Sylvie—and Brooke? Morgan stepped into Dewey's personal space, real close, real tight. "Prove to me you know where she's at, and you bet your ass I'll fight." Morgan stalked away, glaring at Jack, who, slack-jawed, stared at him. "I'm taking lunch," he told Jack and headed to his pickup. His concentration was shot. Dread threatened to overwhelm the flicker of hope he felt.

The old Chevy was as small a vehicle as he could stand to drive after sitting in the big rig for so long. He revved the engine and took off through the lot like a bat out of hell. He didn't have to crank the radio. It was already on full blast, heavy guitars blaring in the close confines of the cab.

Driving past Dewey, Morgan thought about flipping the guy off but knew Jack wouldn't like it. And whether Morgan liked it or not, this was Jack's haven now. Morgan felt as out of place in the office as ever.

TARA STARED AT her brother. DJ had come in for lunch again, and she couldn't help wondering what was going on. It was Saturday and Tammie was home. Surely he'd want to spend time with his wife instead of his sister.

"What?" he asked around the bite of his thick burger.

Tara crossed her arms and tried to judge his mood. "Why are you here? Why aren't you at home with Tammie and Tyler?" Was there trouble in their new marriage?

DJ looked at his plate and slowly dragged a fry through the ketchup. "Tyler's at a fair at the school with his buddy. And uh, well, Tammie's, uh, having a difficult time right now."

"And you left her alone? DJ—"

"Now hold on." He lifted a hand. He actually looked angry.

She remembered the dark, withdrawn man he'd been when he'd first come home from Afghanistan. It hurt to see that man return.

"It's not what you think."

"Then you'd better start explaining."

DJ took his time eating the rest of his food. She tried to wait patiently, cleaning the counters around him.

Finally, he pushed his empty plate away and wiped the grease from his lips with the napkin. Tossing it on top of the plate, he met her gaze.

What she saw in his eyes wasn't anger or sorrow or pain, but fear and happiness all mixed up. What the heck?

"Tammie sent me here because she knows I'm dying for a good burger." He tucked his hands under his arms, leaning back in the chair. "But whenever I eat one around her now, she gets nauseous."

That didn't make sense. Tammie loved burgers. She came in sometimes specifically for one of Tara's special ones. "I don't—" She stared at the shit-eating grin on her brother's face.

Nausea. No. "Is she? Are we going to have—" Another little Hawkins to spoil? "Really?"

DJ laughed and nodded. "She's pregnant." The wonder in his voice nearly overshadowed the tinge of worry in his eyes. "But she's having a rough time." Now the happiness faded.

"Oh, dear. Is everything okay? No problems?" The idea of anyone suffering bothered her, especially someone she cared about, like her sister-in-law.

"She says she went through this when she was carrying Tyler." Guilt washed over his face. "I hate thinking of her going through all this alone," he said softly.

Was that what was bothering him? "You can't change the past." He'd struggled with Tammie not telling him about Tyler's existence years ago, but they'd gotten past that and had a great life. "You can't let it mess up what you've got now."

"Oh, I'm not." He seemed to give himself a mental shake. "But, dear Lord, having a baby scares the crap out of me."

This soldier—who'd deployed to Afghanistan, who'd been injured there and spent months in the hospital fighting to learn to walk again—was afraid of a little, tiny baby?

Tara stared at her big brother and did what any good, red-blooded little sister would do. She laughed. "Really?"

At his glare, she sobered—incredulous. "You're serious. Oh, DJ." She walked around the counter and plopped down next to him. "I'm sorry." She still felt that ornery little-sister urge to tease him but squashed it into oblivion as his hand clenched into a frustrated fist. "I guess...I'm surprised. You're such a great dad to Tyler."

The anguish in his eyes hurt her. "I didn't even know he existed until he was eight."

"I guess..." It was hard to remember that. The boy had become such a big part of their lives. "It's hard to even remember what it was like without him around."

"Yeah. Don't get me wrong. I love being his dad. But I don't know what to do with a baby. And what if it's a...a girl?"

This time her laughter was warm. "You can handle it. You helped with me, remember? I'm sure Tammie was just as scared when she had Ty. She'll show you. You can do this."

"Glad you think so."

"I do." Tara went back to work. "You didn't screw me up too badly." She laughed again and this time he joined her.

"I wouldn't go that far."

"Okay, all bets are off now." She swatted him with a towel.

"Does that mean I don't get any pie?" He looked hopeful now, more like the man she was used to.

She rolled her eyes. "Sucker," she mumbled to herself and grabbed a plate. "Berry or apple?"

"One of each? I'm eating for two now."

"Oh, stop it!"

"Make the apple to go. I'll see if Tammie can keep that down."

Tara smiled, pleased for her brother. And herself. She loved being an aunt to Mandy's little Lucas and DJ's Tyler. A girl, all sweet and soft, might be nice to have around. The idea of how a baby girl would wrap DJ around her little finger made Tara smile.

"If it's a girl, you are *so* in trouble," she teased, handing him the plate. "What does Tyler think?"

DJ's full-throated laughter sounded good. "We haven't told him yet. We're going to tonight. I don't think he'll want a little sister." DJ winked at her and focused on his pie.

Another little girl's face floated through Tara's mind. The one who'd been in the diner the other night. Sadness for the girl took the edge off her happiness.

She'd said she didn't know where her dad was. Did she have an aunt or uncles who would want her if her parents didn't? What about grandparents?

"What's the matter?" DJ stood, gathering the dirty dishes and putting them in the bus tub. Addie would be proud.

"Nothing." Tara didn't look up at him, focusing instead on the collection of recipe cards on the counter. They were the ones Addie had given her at Mom's house.

"Missing Mom?" he whispered.

"A little. These help, actually."

"Looking for something specific?" He looked over her shoulder. "Oh, you should make this one." He tapped a stained card. "Mom's fruit salad was the best."

"It was good. Maybe." She faced him. "Do you ever remember Mom making those cookies Addie makes?"

"Nope." He stared at her. "That's bugging you, isn't it?" He looked almost ready to smile, then forced his lips not to. "Why is it so hard to believe she made it up?"

"Just…'cause." She gathered the cards, leaving the fruit salad on top. Might be a good suggestion to add to the menu.

"Why do you even care? You want to add it to the menu or something?"

"I've thought about it." The idea of cookies reminded Tara of the little girl again. Was she getting food? Attention? Her hair combed?

"You're worrying about something more than cookies."

"Not really. Here." She grabbed the take-out container. "Take your wife her pie."

"That's not going to get you off the hook." He took the container. "And if you're that interested in having the cookies here, ask Addie. I'll bet she'd share."

"Maybe." Tara wasn't nearly as convinced Addie would share. Their older sister—the control freak of all control freaks—would have to think it was her idea. And Tara hadn't been able to pull that off with Addie in…well, ever.

CALMER NOW, MORGAN settled at his desk, determined to get his work done. He would succeed at this, even if it killed him.

Jack was silent for most of the afternoon, typing away at his computer as if Morgan wasn't even there. He barely bothered to look over.

"Okay, I'm sorry I blew my stack with Dewey."

"Yeah, that was pretty stupid." Jack still didn't look away from his computer, typing for some time. Finally, the clock hit 5:00 p.m. and Jack started clearing off his desk and shutting his computer down.

"You got plans tonight?" Morgan asked. Jack seldom didn't have plans.

"Nothing tonight. Want to grab dinner? Catch up?"

"Sure." Morgan wasn't cleaning his desk. He didn't have to. He knew exactly where everything was. "What do you have in mind?" He didn't know of any diners nearby with amazing food and a pretty owner.

"Mexican sounds good." Jack grabbed his jacket. "I'll drive."

"What's with you?" Jack never volunteered to drive.

He didn't respond until they'd reached his SUV and Jack had climbed behind the wheel. He hit the brakes at the stop sign on the edge of the lot. "So." Jack looked both ways and slowly edged out into traffic. "You going to fight again?"

Morgan didn't look over. "Not if I can help it."

"Damn it, Morgan. You heard Dewey say that guy who hurt you so badly nearly killed someone else."

"He's in jail."

"Doesn't mean there isn't someone else out there just as bad, or worse."

They sat at the next red light in silence. Jack broke the quiet first. "I remember what you came home like. I—" His voice faded. "Don't do this."

There weren't many things Jack had asked Morgan for. Ever. As kids there hadn't been enough of anything, except whiskey for Dad. It wasn't much different now that they were adults. Torn, he looked for a response. "Do you think I want to?"

"No." Jack sighed. "There have to be other options."

"Like what?" Morgan's anger returned. "We've done what for a year, Jack? Chased shadows, that's what." His frustration at not finding Sylvie or Brooke nearly overwhelmed him. He closed his eyes, wishing his brother had turned on the music.

They drove another couple blocks, the only sound the hum of the engine. "I met someone," Morgan admitted.

Jack didn't say anything, but the look he threw Morgan was full of surprise.

"It's time to end this. If the only price I have to

pay to get my life back is a few bruises—I'm in."
Morgan watched the city pass by, and Dewey's
words came to him. Realization dawned. Dewey
had been in Haskins Corners last week. He'd said
he could get Morgan a spot this weekend.

Morgan knew where the fight was going to be.
"Turn around. Now!"

"Why? I'm hungry."

Dinner was going to wait. "Here's the deal.
What are the odds you get two loads to a small
place like Haskins Corners?"

Jack frowned. "Slim. Possible, but slim. I'd
bundle them."

"Yeah. So did Dewey have a load last week
there, same time as me?"

He shook his head.

"We need to get back to the yard. I need to
talk to Dewey."

Jack glanced at his watch. "He's already gone.
Loaded up an hour ago."

"Where's he headed?"

"I'd have to look on the manifest. I did fifteen loads today. I can't remember who got which
one."

"That's at the office?"

"Yeah. We could call him."

"He ain't going to talk on the phone. He only
told me what he did to taunt me."

"Yeah." Jack grinned. "He did get to you." At
Morgan's glare, the grin disappeared from Jack's

face. Instead of saying anything more, Jack pulled a smooth U-turn. "You owe me a pizza. A big one. Thick crust. The Works from Giovanni's."

"Yeah. Whatever."

The buildings whizzed by as Jack drove the way they'd come. "Who is she?" Jack asked softly.

"Tara?"

"That her name?"

"Yeah." Morgan pictured her in his mind, missing her more than he'd ever missed Sylvie. "I met her in Haskins Corners. I'm not going into details now, but—" He wasn't sure how to begin to explain. "But I'm not stupid. I can't get involved with her, or anyone, until I get Brooke back. Sylvie is screwing up enough for the both of us."

"How does this Tara feel about your situation?"

"She doesn't know." He speared Jack with a glare. "She's a good woman. Runs her own business. She's an amazing chef. She doesn't need any of my garbage messin' up her world."

Jack rolled his eyes but he didn't say anything. For once, Morgan didn't push him. They didn't have time.

The yard was dark except for the security lights that spilled pools of white light around the lot. Only two trucks were parked inside the chain-link-and-razor-wire fence. Jack's seldom-used white hauler and Morgan's blue baby. The rest of the team was on the road. Earning the money.

The gates pulled open once Jack hit the remote.

He parked, then hustled up the steps into the office. "Where is it?" Morgan asked as he flipped the light switch.

"Let me get it. You'll make a mess of my filing system."

"Thought it would be on the computer."

"It is. But I keep a paper backup."

"And you say I'm the old-fashioned one?"

"Funny." Jack pulled open the second drawer of the file cabinet and lifted out a binder. He set it on the desk and flipped pages. "Here it is." He read silently, Morgan trying to read over his shoulder.

"Where's he at?"

"Right now, between here and Austin. He's heading to Rose Creek."

"That's just past Haskins Corners. Is he going through there?"

"Yeah. Probably."

They looked at each other. "I'm going. Now."

Jack filed the book again, pausing before he faced Morgan. "Why? Are you going after Sylvie or to see this Tara?"

Morgan wanted to answer his brother honestly. They'd always been that way with each other, a bargain they'd made when they were kids in reaction to their father's endless lies. "I don't know." Morgan stared at his hands, clenching and unclenching his fists. "Both?"

"You taking the rig?"

"Yeah. Sylvie would know the pickup."

"Fair enough." Jack nodded. "I don't have a load, but if you can get Brooke, it's worth it."

"Thanks, bro." Morgan headed to the door. "If you get me one on the way back, I'll gladly take it." Morgan stepped out into the night, heading toward his truck.

"Hey, order my pizza," Jack called.

"Get whatever you want. On my account." Morgan jogged toward his truck.

"You have an account at the pizza joint?"

"Yeah. How do you think I keep my girlish figure?"

Jack's laughter faded as Morgan pulled open the door to his rig and climbed in.

CHAPTER EIGHT

MORGAN DROVE THROUGH the night. The truck's headlights cut through the dark, casting golden columns over the smooth blacktop. Raindrops fell like sparkling confetti. To the left, yellow lines flashed by, bisecting the road.

Every few miles, the circle of a white yard light announced the location of a ranch house. Some had a kitchen or living room light on, but mostly their inhabitants were already in bed.

He hadn't met another truck or car in nearly an hour. Had the world vanished? God, he'd never felt this alone.

The empty road had been his home since he was eighteen. Tonight—not for the first time—he didn't want to be here. Didn't want to keep searching. Didn't want to continue this damned quest. He wanted it done—wanted to have Brooke back and get on with his life.

It was worse, especially on nights like this, when the wind howled down the highway and his only company was late-night radio and a few stars. He could put in a CD or kick on the iPod, but music wasn't what he wanted. Not this time.

He needed voices. Human voices, even if they were saying inane things.

Who was he kidding? Tara's face flashed in his mind. He wanted to hear her. Jack's question rattled around in the darkness. Was he going back for Sylvie or Tara? For the past or his future? The only response to his questions was the hum of the tires on the pavement.

Leaning back in the driver's seat, Morgan stared out the windshield, seeing where he was going through each swipe of the wipers. Muscle memory steered the truck as his mind leaped ahead to the diner. What was Tara doing right now?

Pushing through the kitchen's swinging doors, carrying tantalizing dishes to hungry patrons? Joining in the camaraderie that wrapped around the staff as they teased each other?

She'd smile at everyone, even him, he hoped. How *would* she react when she saw him again after their last…meeting?

Morgan glanced at the dash clock. Ten fifteen. Dinner rush was long over. Maybe she was taking a break, climbing up on one of the counter stools. The one where he normally sat? On the end. The one with the view of the entire place.

His mind imagined her there. He wanted her to be there. And he wanted to be there with her. Wanted—

Damn. He'd outgrown adolescent crushes years

ago. So, why couldn't he get Tara Hawkins out of his head?

Rubbing his burning eyes, Morgan knew he needed to stop. Driving this rig into the ditch was not a good idea. But he was so close. He recognized the next exit. He'd park behind the diner just for tonight and maybe catch some z's. Another glance at the clock told him Tara wasn't on that counter stool. He couldn't remember the last time he'd had a full, good night's sleep.

Morgan knew that parking his truck in the diner's lot was a bad idea. A *really* bad idea. Only problem was, there wasn't anyplace else. Eighteen-wheelers weren't the easiest things to park. Most public places with lots that were big enough didn't allow it. Few streets did, either.

The Someday Café really was his best, and only, choice. Maybe some of Tara's apple pie first, though, and a cup of warm coffee. That sounded so good right about now. It was a safe bet she was home, getting ready for tomorrow's early shift. Living her life.

Steering his mind back to the road, Morgan headed down the ramp and onto the two-lane highway.

Finally, the lights of town loomed, curving around the horizon against the hills. None of the buildings were more than a couple stories, so everything was low to the ground. A sign welcomed him to town and told him how many people lived there.

Main Street was quiet and dark, with only the gas station and the diner giving off any light.

The lot was nearly empty this late at night, making parking easier—which was a good thing. Tonight, he'd sleep so tomorrow he'd be clearheaded. Maybe he'd go to the street fair to see if the T-shirt vendor was back. After that, he'd find Dewey.

His plans in place, Morgan climbed down from the cab. Rain landed cold on the back of his neck. That woke him up. A to-go order would be a good idea.

Halfway across the pavement, Morgan stopped. Through the glass panes in front, he saw her. There, behind the long counter, Tara frowned at the computer terminal that served as her cash register.

For a long minute, Morgan barely noticed the rain, watching her and wishing things were different. Wishing he was a different man. Wishing…

He cursed. If he were that different man, he would have kept on driving instead of taking the turnoff and driving here. He'd have found another parking place. Any other parking place. The shoulder of the road even. If he were a different man, he'd leave her alone.

But he wasn't that good a man. He started walking, then pushed open the diner's door, intending to savor the smile she gave, letting himself pretend it was for him, not the one she automatically graced every customer with.

THE DINER WAS QUIET. Not surprising, since it was nearly midnight. There wasn't much life in town after 10:00 p.m., but there was a late crowd that came in when the bars closed. Daisy had said she made a nice chunk of change with the late crowd.

Tara wasn't sure it was worth it. The two hours of dead time before the bars closed wasn't bringing in much traffic. At least she had caught up on the small tasks that got lost in the busy day—like rolling silverware in napkins. And checking on the computer the staff kept complaining about.

The soft squeal of the door opening sent a shiver up her spine. She tried not to worry about who might come in this late at night. Wade was working, but he sneaked out to the alley to grab a smoke whenever it was dead. No one was in the place right now. She was alone—

Except for Morgan in the doorway.

He froze, as if he was just as surprised to see her there as she was him. Or reluctant to face her. What was he doing sneaking in? And yes, he had the look of a man sneaking in.

"Oh, hey." He spoke softly, the growl in his voice deep as if he'd been quiet for too long. She got the impression he was considering turning around. He probably hadn't expected to see her here. Of course, she wasn't supposed to be here, but Wendy had gone home sick.

Tara would have suspected Wendy of trying to set her up with the man—as she kept threatening to do—if he hadn't been gone for several days and she hadn't seen how green Wendy looked before she left. Tara really needed to find time to talk to Wendy about Morgan and just how unavailable he was.

Tara put on her best hostess smile and grabbed a menu from the freshly cleaned stack. She focused on keeping it businesslike and professional—distant. "Booth or table?" she asked.

Morgan looked like he was resisting the urge to roll his eyes. "I'll sit at the counter. Like usual." He headed past her, taking the menu from her. He slapped it down in front of his seat. "I'll take coffee." He didn't look up, but sat and stared at the list of choices he'd looked intently at dozens of times before.

"Our special tonight is beef stew and homemade biscuits. Dessert is apple caramel cake." Tara waved her hand over the menu, pointing at the laminated pictures like she did for all new customers. "Our pastry chef just finished a fresh cake."

Morgan glared at her. "Aren't you the pastry chef?" he asked.

He knew what she was up to. She bit back her flippant comment about paybacks.

She pulled away, leaving him to make up his mind as she would any other customer. No staying to chat, no suggesting choices. None of that. She filled the coffee cup and set it in front of him with one of the freshly rolled sets of silverware. She knew he didn't take cream in his coffee, but she set one of her cute little silver pitchers in front of him anyway. "Just in case you'd like some." She walked away.

"Tara." His voice came out in a warning.

She tried not to sigh at the sound of her name on his lips, those lips that had… No, she would *not* think about that. She would not let him get into her head. She kept walking, moving into the kitchen, away from him. Leaning against the wall, she heaved a heavy sigh.

Maybe if she stayed here long enough, he'd get tired of waiting and go away. Or maybe not. He wasn't the kind to give up on anything. She shivered again. And this time, she refused to analyze why.

Maybe she should have turned the Open sign off. Pushing away from the wall, Tara forced herself to go through the swinging doors. She was not letting his presence intimidate her. Pulling her order pad from her pocket and her pencil from behind her ear, she headed toward him.

"Have you made up your mind?" She plastered a smile on her lips. The impact of his gaze made her heart stumble a little.

"Who's cooking?" he asked.

"Uh...Wade is. Why?" Then she remembered she was supposed to be keeping her distance, not treating him like she knew him well or as if he knew this place nearly as well as she did. She cleared her throat to get herself on track. "All our items are made by our cook staff to the same recipes." She'd been striving for consistency but hadn't quite made it yet.

"Then I'll take a bowl of the stew with an extra biscuit."

She scribbled on the notepad, fairly certain she'd never be able to read her handwriting. Thankfully, she wouldn't have to. "The special comes with the cake. Would you like that, too?"

"Yeah." He leaned forward on the counter, putting the menu behind the napkin holder, and Tara had to force herself to not step back.

"'Course, if *you* were cooking..." He paused for a long minute until she looked at him. "I'd take something...hotter."

His voice was deep and gravelly, yet soft— and she was almost sure he wasn't talking about food. She stared at him, met the heat in his stare, then finally looked away. She stepped backward.

"I can make you whatever you'd like." Why was she giving him special treatment? She wouldn't do that for anyone else, would she?

No, she was just giving good customer service, she assured herself.

Their gazes clashed again, and the world telescoped in to just them. Just him. Right there... inches away.

Tara turned away and was surprised, and shocked, when his rough hand closed gently around her wrist.

"What do *you* want?" Was he talking about food again? She took a step away, and he let her go.

"We can't have this conversation."

He was silent as if figuring out what to say next. "I'm sorry, Tara. I don't know what else to say."

"And I accept your apology. There's nothing else to say, you're right." Tara turned toward the kitchen. "I'll, uh, get started on your order."

"I'm sorry if my being here bothers you." He sounded disappointed. Sad. His voice slid over her nerve endings.

"It doesn't," she lied, because it did. It bothered her that he was the first man who'd attracted her in months, the first person who'd seemed to understand her in ages—if ever. And that attraction was returned. She knew it. He'd admitted it. He'd kissed her, for heaven's sake.

He, however, had commitments that she wasn't willing to ignore.

But the way he made her feel—like she was more alive, and warm, the sense of mattering to someone—made her want to—oh, how she wanted to...

Tara scurried into the kitchen. Leaning against the doorframe, trying to catch her breath, she prayed her heart would stop pounding.

Shoving her muddled thoughts aside, she headed to the stove. She'd start the order. The sooner she fed Morgan, the sooner he'd go away and leave her in peace.

Wade came in the back door just then, and she breathed a sigh of relief. She gave him the order. Now she was the one needing the break. The coolness outside beckoned, and she stepped through the back door.

MORGAN KNEW TARA was trying to ignore him. Not that he blamed her. She didn't return from the kitchen until his order was ready to deliver.

Two young men had come in while she was in the kitchen. They'd seated themselves at a booth near one end of the counter. Laughing and joking, they reminded Morgan of how he and Jack used to be. Back before they'd had to grow up.

Tara silently put Morgan's plate in front of him, then headed to the men's table, a coffeepot in one hand, her order pad in the other. Morgan knew better than to try to resist watching her. The entire restaurant was reflected in the chrome above his head. What the hell? He'd enjoy what he could.

"What can I get you, gentlemen?" She set the coffeepot on the table and pulled the pencil from her falling-down ponytail.

"Well, well, well." One man leaned forward. "How 'bout you sit down and keep us company, pretty lady?"

Morgan didn't roll his eyes. Much. Still, his attention riveted on the man.

"I don't think so." She stood there, poised and not at all ruffled.

"Come on, sweetheart." The other man leaned forward and Morgan saw his hand move toward her. He also saw her swiftly grab the coffeepot.

"These things aren't so expensive that I'd mind buying a new one," she said softly, lifting the pot. "Might fit just fine on your head." She smiled while she said it.

Too bad the lunkheads weren't smart enough to see she wasn't kidding. They laughed like the hyenas they were. "You don't look like the type to like it rough, honey," the first man said. "But we can oblige."

That was too much for Morgan. Slowly, he pivoted on the stool and aimed a glare at the men. He didn't move any more than that, and Tara didn't see him as her back was to him. At first, the two men didn't notice him, either. Finally, the first man looked at him, then away, then hastily returned his gaze to Morgan.

He saw the man swallow hard. He smacked

his friend, then pointed at Morgan. The second man turned. Together, they stared. One man's face washed white.

Tara saw the gesture and turned to see what he was pointing at. She glared at Morgan.

Morgan grinned. He couldn't help it. She looked so cute frowning at him, though she'd probably just as soon put the coffeepot over his head as the idiot's.

Slowly, Morgan spun and returned to his meal. He still watched them in the reflection. The men solemnly ordered their food and talked quietly when she left their table.

"That wasn't necessary."

Morgan hadn't heard her come up behind him. She was so close. He should have noticed her scent or heat or something. He certainly did now, and he had to fight the urge to reach for her.

"Maybe. Maybe not." He continued eating, not looking at her. The stew was really good.

"But thank you," she whispered before walking toward the kitchen.

He watched the swinging doors close behind her. "You're welcome."

Morgan guessed Tara was going to avoid him until he left. He wasn't sure what he should do about it.

TARA WAS DETERMINED to stay busy and distracted until Morgan returned to his truck. Not like she didn't have plenty to do. She glared at the computer screen that resembled an old test pattern jiggling across the screen. The guy on the phone earlier today had said something about a video card. He'd used the word *new*. More money was all she heard, and she didn't have any of that.

The waitstaff used this computer, and the one out front, to input and collect the payments. They needed it every day. She needed it fixed before the breakfast rush.

"Maybe just give it a smack on the side," Wade said through the pass-through widow. "That's what we used to do when I was a kid and the TV looked like that."

"I'm not smacking my two-thousand-dollar computer," she snapped.

Wade shook his head and returned to the bowels of the kitchen. Tara sighed. She didn't have time for this. She was tired and edgy as it was. She refused to think about what—or who— caused that edginess.

She'd have to stop by the office supply store to get some extra order pads—just in case. The old-fashioned paper and pen method didn't break down.

The swinging doors parted just then, and Morgan stepped through. Hastily, she returned her gaze to the monitor. "You're not supposed to be back here."

"Your fan club out there wants to pay their bill."

"That's what I'm working on," she snapped. "I'll be right out." She should have known better than to expect him to leave.

"Whoa. Remind me never to tick you off." He grinned at her. "That look could certainly kill."

She blew at the few strands of hair that had fallen in her face. "You've probably already survived it." She didn't look at him, though. She tried several keyboard commands. "It's this stupid computer."

"She won't smack it," Wade called from the kitchen. "Why don't you give it a try?"

"You have biscuits to cook," she called to her short-order cook. She didn't even listen to his grumbled response.

Morgan stood there grinning. "So, can I get coffee, or do I have to wait for IT to brew it?"

Scowling, she grabbed the carafe from the burner behind the counter and poured him a full-to-the-brim cup. No cream this time. "Here you go."

The nearly empty restaurant was filled with silence as he stayed there, sipping his coffee, making her conscious of his presence. She kept trying to focus on the computer. Morgan didn't move away. Slowly, the world around her filtered in— soft murmurs from the table where the men were finishing their meal, the clatter of metal on ceramic drifting out of the kitchen as Wade worked on his magical biscuits, the distant sounds of the passing traffic.

Morgan came to stand beside her. "Stop glaring at it. That won't help."

"Are you sure?" She knew he was right, and she was wasting her time, but it frustrated her too much. Giving in was not an option.

"Let me look at it."

"You're kidding, right?"

"Does this face look like I'm kidding?" He grinned at her.

"Yes."

"Move over."

Playfully, Morgan shoved her aside with his shoulder. His broad, solid shoulder. She stepped back, startled by the warmth of his body against her. His hands, wide and flat, looked huge against the tiny keys. But despite their size, they flew over the keyboard.

Suddenly, the screen stopped squiggling and the image she'd been trying to bring into focus—the quaint photo of the restaurant where they stood right now—filled the screen. Clear and as pretty as she'd hoped. Ready to take a new order.

"You did it. I thought it was impossible." She stepped closer to him and the computer. "That's perfect. How'd you do that?"

His smile was wide—and smug. "Magic."

Great, a smart-ass. She sighed. "How'd you know what to do?"

His left eyebrow lifted. "Just because I drive truck doesn't mean I'm an idiot." He stepped back, grabbed the coffee cup to take a healthy swig.

"I didn't say that," she called after him.

He pushed open one of the doors. "Where's Wendy anyway?"

"Home sick." She pulled the neatly printed bill from the printer and smiled. "Why? It's okay for her to take abuse from those types of moron customers, but not me?" She didn't bother looking up at him.

"Did I say that?" he growled. "No, I did not. Nor did I mean that."

"I know." She followed him, needing to get by but not wanting to step too close to him. "Go sit down, Morgan. Finish your dinner. I have work to do."

The big man didn't budge. He was so close that, even over the heat coming from the kitchen, she felt his body's warmth reaching out to caress her. Morgan faced her, blocking her escape. "Tara—I'm not here to hurt you or ignore you or any of those things. I just want—"

He fell silent. She could only stare. She swayed, her body reaching for him even as her mind screamed that she had to get away from him. "Morgan?"

He didn't answer.

"What do you want?" she asked. The instant the words left her mouth, she regretted them. Not because of the answer she knew she wouldn't get, but because of the anguish that filled his face.

"Don't ask me that," he said through clenched teeth. "I don't dare answer."

"Why?"

"Why? Because I'm—" He swallowed. "I'm this close to not giving a damn about what I'm *supposed* to do."

"What are you supposed to do?" Why did she continue to prod him, like picking at a sliver until it came out—except all she did was drive the hurt deeper?

"I'm supposed to be responsible. I'm supposed to behave." That last word held a note of disdain. "I'm not supposed to want…" He cupped her chin with his palm, dwarfing her jaw with his size. "This," he whispered. He dragged his thumb across her lips. On reflex, her tongue reached out and followed the path his thumb had taken. Could she taste him there?

Morgan groaned. "Don't do that."

"Don't do what? This?" She turned her head, just barely, just enough to put her lips in the center of his palm. She softly kissed his touch, letting her eyelids drift closed as his heat slipped along the length of her body. He'd leaned into her.

"Tara."

"Mmm?" Somewhere deep inside her head, she knew she should stop, knew this was wrong, but that voice was so faint it vanished as quickly as it came.

"I'm—"

"Don't say it." She put her finger over his lips. "I don't believe you. You don't act like your heart belongs to someone. You don't act like someone who's tied down."

"I didn't say that."

"Then what did you say?" She opened her eyes and glared at him. "Tell me the truth. Now."

Silence stretched out thick and heavy. "It's complicated."

"Uncomplicate it. Explain." She had to know what was going on, what she was really getting into, but the longer they stood like this, the further away her sanity slipped. "Morgan. Now." Sweat broke out all over her body at the unintended double entendre. Even she was turned on by her words. "Tell me now."

He was so close, she felt the friction of his body moving against hers as he took a deep breath. "Sylvie—"

"Sylvie? She's your wife? You said she was your friend." Tara knew she sounded bitchy, but she couldn't help it. This hurt.

Morgan frowned at her. "Okay, maybe I wasn't totally honest about our relationship. There wasn't any reason to explain to you then. Yes, Sylvie is who I'm looking for. Yes, we're married."

Tara stepped back, anger flooding through her. What did he see in her? Jealousy, and a mix of several other painful emotions, flared wild and green. "You're as bad as they are." She pointed at the doors, indicating the obnoxious diners. "At least their come-on was honest."

"That's low, Tara. I thought we were, at least, friends." He shoved open the doors, then headed to his seat, grabbed his jacket. Morgan angrily slipped it on before pitching several bills on the counter, then leaving.

She watched until he disappeared into the rainy night.

"No change needed." The two other diners got up and hustled out behind him, leaving another pile of cash on their table.

"There'd better be a good tip in there," she said to no one. Grumbling, she stomped over to count the payments. "You men all suck."

"You say somethin'?" Wade asked.

"No." No sense ticking him off, too. She still needed him to cook.

CHAPTER NINE

According to Jack's manifest, Dewey was picking up a load here in Haskins Corners this afternoon, then heading to Fort Worth. Dewey wouldn't arrive at the client's business for another couple hours, so Morgan would come back. Until then, this town wasn't that big, and he figured he could jog through most of it in a couple hours.

Running was about the only consistent workout he got on the road. Sometimes there was a gym nearby, but today the run gave him the opportunity to move around town, essentially unnoticed.

As well as burn off a mountain of Tara-induced frustration and energy.

Maybe he'd find Dewey sooner this way. How hard could it be to locate *that* truck?

He jogged past a tiny movie theater that still had one of those white marquees with the black plastic letters. A Disney logo told him this was one of those kid movies he'd probably know all about if Brooke was with him. Something, grief maybe, twisted in his gut. This was getting really, really old. But instead of the melancholia taking over, his anger grew.

Damn Sylvie.

He moved farther down the street, heading to the park. Today the street fair wasn't in business. Which might be a good thing with the thick, heavy clouds hanging overhead. It had rained most of yesterday, so business must have been slow.

The few semipermanent structures around the park were covered in tarps, and a light rain gently pattered on the vinyl. The empty spaces between, where the temporary setups would be tomorrow, were quickly growing into mud puddles.

It was almost eerie. Few people were out, and those he saw were all doing business at the bank, the post office and such, hurrying from one doorway to the next.

Turning down the main drag, Morgan decided to head toward the part of town Dewey was more likely to haunt.

The creek ran through town, meandering behind buildings that had been here for what looked like decades. Morgan didn't remember the water being so swift or high on the worn banks before, though. From here, looking across the flowing water, he could see the back of Tara's diner.

He'd had breakfast there sometime around dawn. Tara hadn't been there yet since she'd worked late last night. The back door was open at the moment. Sounds of pots and pans and cooking came across the water. It sounded homey and warm.

This morning, the diner had felt as empty as the streets did now. At the crosswalk, Morgan stopped, looking up and down the empty street, the back alley and at the assorted buildings.

A loud crack cut through the morning air. The big pine that sat among the stones on this side of the creek swayed precariously. The rocks were already loose from the past week's frequent downpours and the creek's swift current.

If that pine fell across the creek, it would reach the back of the diner. Nothing in its path was safe from harm.

He'd have to mention it to Tara. If—and that was a big *if*—she'd even talk to him.

Dread settled in close. This was not what he wanted his life to be. This was not who he wanted to be. Alone. Searching. Endlessly.

But right now, it didn't matter what he *wanted*. What he needed was to find Sylvie and get Brooke back. He headed along the creek's winding path away from the quaint diner and toward a very different part of town.

The rain fell in earnest now, in bigger drops that formed a curtain around him. With a curse, he picked up the pace, heading to the footbridge down the bank.

He'd just come around the corner of a body shop when he heard voices. He glanced back to see two twentysomething men huddling at the overhang of a rear doorway having a smoke.

"You going to the fight tonight?" one man asked the other. The voice was young and rough, cutting through the sound of the falling rain. Morgan slowed his pace.

"Nah. I gotta work."

"You're gonna miss a good one. I hear there're three different matches."

Morgan stopped, leaning against a brick wall, acting like he needed to rest instead of eavesdrop. This was exactly why he'd come down here. How many times had he heard this type of conversation? Some things never changed. A ball of dread filled his stomach.

"Anybody we know?"

"Yeah. Brawler's supposed to be there. And some guy from Houston that Tate says is a real powerhouse. Could make a nice chunk of change quick if you pick the right guy."

"I know. Probably make more than I'll get in my paycheck."

"Probably."

"Too bad there ain't a match every night. I'm tired of working this damned hard."

The men fell silent for a few minutes. Morgan stayed close enough to still hear anything else, hoping they'd say where the fights were going to be held.

Dewey had offered to come to Haskins Corners. He had to have known there was a fight scheduled. Morgan's memories rushed in of all the years he'd made ends meet by fighting, the years before he'd realized how far on the fringes of reality he'd gone.

Would Sylvie return to her old habits? he wondered again. He strained to hear the men talk as the rain pattered louder. He barely caught the rest of their words, but he did hear *railroad* and *barn*. That had to be where the fight would be. Tonight.

Like all the rest, it'd be late enough in the night that the normal world was settled in their quaint little houses, but not so late that the fringe elements were already drunk or stoned enough not to care.

Was this the break he'd been waiting for? Would he finally find Sylvie there? Was Brooke nearby? Or would he be totally disappointed?

Again?

He had to try.

"I CAN'T BELIEVE you said that to him." Wendy's voice carried clear across the dining room to Tara. It helped that the place was empty, but still.

"Shh. Apparently Wade has a big mouth." Tara glared in the general direction of the kitchen, knowing full well the cook couldn't see her.

"If you chased Morgan away, there'll be hell to pay." Wendy worked furiously, a bit too furiously, cleaning the back counter. That chrome was going to be real shiny when she got all her anger worked out.

"And why is that exactly?" Tara glared at Wendy, too. She was getting quite good at it. Rolling her eyes at herself, she finished putting the last of the catering orders into the system.

She'd always loved to cook, always dreamed of owning her own restaurant. As a kid, dreaming big, she hadn't known what a caterer was. Now she did. It was the part of the business that would keep the doors open, and the part she found the most challenging.

She rang in—to the newly fixed and well-behaved computer—and billed for two upcoming weddings and a retirement party for one of the teachers at the high school. She smiled despite Wendy's attitude. She might actually make a living at this someday.

"You owe that man an apology." Wendy had come up to stand beside her, hand on hip, tapping one foot impatiently.

"For what?" Tara knew why *she* thought she should apologize to Morgan, but she was curious why Wendy thought so.

"For insulting him." There was that. "And for not being willing to listen."

"Listen to what?"

Wendy threw her hands up in dramatic defeat. "You are so disconnected sometimes. Don't you realize he might need someone to talk to, someone to confide in? He's out on the road all alone."

Tara stared at her waitress and friend. "Confide in me? About what? How many men do you actually know?"

"Several." Wendy looked insulted. "I don't know. He just looks so sad sometimes."

"Look, I know you mean well. But I've got three older brothers and confiding secrets is *not* something they do."

She pictured Morgan, first as she'd last seen him, fuming and walking away. Then, that image morphed into the laughing, good-looking guy who was normally in here. Lastly, she saw him as he'd told her—what little he'd told her—about Sylvie.

None of those images was of a man wanting to spill his guts to her. If anything, he'd put considerable effort into covering the pain she saw flash in his eyes.

"Okay, I'll admit I insulted him, but the last thing Morgan wants is to tell me all about his life's secrets. And it's not really something I want to know about."

"You're hopeless." Wendy backed off finally as customers came through the door. A young couple with a toddler. Wendy grimaced at the little boy. High-chair duty meant floor mopping at some point in her near future. They all knew it.

With a sigh, Wendy seated them and even gave the boy's chubby little cheeks a soft pinch.

Tara laughed as Wendy walked past her toward the kitchen. "See what falling in love gets you?" she whispered just to irritate Wendy. "Floor duty."

Wendy stuck her tongue out at Tara just before she slipped through the swinging doors. Tara laughed. She enjoyed the friendly banter with all her employees, but more so with Wendy. It reminded Tara of growing up with her sisters.

For the next hour, they hustled to wait on several groups of customers.

Finally, the rush ended and they could take a break. Tara made herself and Wendy mocha lattes with the fancy espresso machine. They'd earned the treat.

She handed Wendy her cup. "Okay, I'll admit, I was a bit bitchy to Morgan last night." Had it really been just last night? Seemed like ages ago.

"A bit?"

"Yes, a bit." She slid onto one of the counter stools. The one on the end, where she could see the entire place, either straight on or reflected in the chrome decor in front of her. No wonder Morgan sat here.

She'd have to figure out a way to talk with him and hopefully not end up in another argument. His truck was still parked out back, but she'd seen him leave earlier—clad in sweats and a tank top. She hadn't seen him come back.

How far did he run to keep himself in such amazing shape? Shape she definitely appreciated. She couldn't help looking out the window to see if maybe he was out there.

The rain had quit for now, and the sun was trying to break through the thick cloud cover. The ground was wet, with puddles scattered over the parking lot and street. He'd be wet whether it rained any more or not.

Tara tapped her fingers on the counter. Wendy was right. She owed him an apology. But how would she start? What should she say? "I'm sorry I snapped at you" lost a bit of appeal when she followed it with the statement about how he started it.

She wasn't saying anything until she figured out *what* to say. Sitting here solved nothing. She headed back into the kitchen. Nervous energy made her pace.

"Just in time." Katie, her new pastry chef, put her hands on her ample hips. "I got bread dough that could use some kneading."

And Tara had energy to burn.

Kate Watson had taken the blue ribbon in baking the past five years at the county fair. The only reason she hadn't before that was because she hadn't entered. She'd started working here last week, and one of the first tasks Tara had asked her to take on was to figure out Addie's cookie recipe.

Addie wasn't sharing, but so far, Kate's attempts hadn't been right, either. She had given the customers plenty of delicious alternatives, though.

"That might be a good idea." Tara went to the metal counter where the bowls of dough sat, waiting. She pulled out the big ball of sweet-smelling, light gold dough and plopped it onto the floured surface.

Push. Pull. Repeat. She felt the resistance, felt the pressure in her shoulders as she continued the repetitive motion. The rhythm helped her focus, helped her think—smooth, even thoughts. She closed her eyes and let herself slip into the motion.

In the darkness behind her eyelids, images wavered. Images of him. Morgan. Last night. He'd yanked on that battered jacket, glaring at her with anger and something else, something she'd ignored, in his eyes.

Hurt? Pain? What had hurt him? Her comments? The men he'd had to confront to protect her? His past? Why hadn't she seen that?

She'd been angry at his comments, at his stepping in when she hadn't asked him to. But if he hadn't? If he hadn't been there, and she'd been alone with those jerks, what would have happened?

She shivered. She didn't want to think about

it. Didn't want to think about how he made her feel, made her want something she shouldn't. He wasn't hers to want.

And maybe it wasn't all his fault. She recalled the brief kiss she'd given him. Yep, she owed him an apology. She opened her eyes, seeing the bright white subway tile, nearly blinding from the fluorescent light's glare. The shelf over her head held flour and yeast. All the pieces that made up the bread she was now making.

The scent of all those particulars wafted around her and she savored the aroma, anticipating the sweet buns and loaves she'd have to serve her customers once this all came out of the oven.

Another scent shattered the sweetness. What—

The remnants of cologne and the scent of the damp outdoors. She frowned and turned her head. Morgan had come in the back door and stood there with a water bottle in his hand, his shoulder against the doorframe. How long had he been there? She hadn't heard any footsteps.

He smiled. "My grandmother used to make bread. I'd almost forgotten about that until now." He took a deep swig of water.

She'd worked enough. Quickly, she put portions of the big ball into the loaf pans to the side of the counter. She covered them with the damp cloth to rise again, then dusted off her hands. Finally, she turned to face him. He hadn't moved. Except to finish the water. He crushed the bottle, the crack of plastic overly loud in this quiet corner of the kitchen.

"My mom liked to bake more than she did cook." She untied her apron and lifted it over her head. She hung it on the hook by the table. "That's how I got the opportunity to do most of the cooking."

He nodded.

The air in the room felt thick and awkward. She wanted to say something, wanted to say the right thing this time and not make matters worse.

"You're thinking too hard," he said.

Tara laughed, at herself and at his ability to boil it all down. "Maybe. I do that when it's important."

"What's important?"

She looked up then. She'd moved closer to him than she'd at first thought. Or he'd moved… There were mere inches between them. Staring into his eyes, she tried to see the anger or the pain from last night. Neither was there. What was he thinking? What did he want from her?

"I owe you an apology," she finally said. "What I said was…inappropriate."

He laughed. "Maybe it sounded like that. But you were right."

"I was?" Did she look as shocked as she sounded?

MORGAN WAS A bad boy at heart. He knew that. When he'd gotten married, he'd wanted to be reformed, had actually let himself believe in the dream of happily-ever-after, two-point-five kids and picket fences. He'd told himself he'd accomplish what his old man had never managed.

But Morgan wasn't cut out for straitlaced. He never had been and knew he never would be. For the first time, looking at Tara now, disappointment accompanied that realization.

As a kid he'd thought about running away from home, but he'd felt an obligation to his little brother. He'd stayed and taken the whippings for them both, knowing he might deserve some of them.

He'd married Sylvie, not because he loved her—he'd never believed he was capable of the emotion—but because he was young and stupid, and she was pregnant. It was his kid. His responsibility.

But the instant Brooke's little body had settled in his hands, that pink fuzzy blanket all soft and warm; the instant she'd stared at him with those dark eyes—and opened her tiny mouth to scream in what he was sure was terror—he'd been hooked. He'd found that love *was* something he had a capacity for. At least that kind of love. He'd known in that instant that he'd do anything for her—even die for her—if that's what it took.

Now, standing in Tara's kitchen, he stared at the flour on her cheek, stared into her blue eyes and felt something inside him shift. Her face lit

up when he'd said she was right. Her eyes sparkled. He nearly laughed out loud. Heat blos-
somed in his chest—and he couldn't look away.
He didn't want to.

"You were right to call me on my behavior."
He slowly moved away from the wall. "I should
be the one apologizing."

"But you're not?" she whispered.

Morgan slowly shook his head. "I'd be lying
if I did."

"So you're not sorry?"

"No." He took one step and there was no space
left between them. "I'm not. Those men didn't
know you. They wanted you just because you
were a woman, alone and apparently at their
mercy. There was nothing good about their intent."

"But—"

"I know you," he whispered. "I like you. I
want—"

Tara put her finger over his lips. "Don't say
it." He watched her swallow. "Don't put it out
there. I—"

She stepped away, and he felt the cool air
where her warm finger had been.

"We can't and you know why," she finished.

"We can't what?" He grinned at her, laughing
when the color swept up her flour-dusted face.
Teasing her was the safest way to break this spell
between them. "I dare you to say it."

"You are so frustrating."

She backed away from him, just as he'd hoped, despite his disappointment. But he saw the smile playing on her lips.

"I have to get to work."

"Me, too." He headed to the back door. "See you later?"

She didn't answer, but he didn't care. The sun was out, glinting off his truck at the edge of the parking lot. She wasn't leaving and neither was he. And for the first time in months, that didn't bother him.

He climbed in the truck. His phone was on the console and it flashed to tell him he'd missed a call and had a message. As he grabbed clean clothes, he hit Play and put it on speaker.

"Hey, Morgan." Dewey's voice was loud, as if the big man were yelling into the phone. "There's a match tonight. I know I said I wasn't gonna beg. But, man, you gotta come. There ain't a one you can't beat. Come on, give a guy a break. You owe me. Tate's setting up at a barn out on County Road Eleven. 'Bout five miles out. Along the tracks. Hope you get this and decide to make us rich men. Call me."

Morgan stared at the phone. He cursed, recalling the men he'd overheard on his run. Dewey was confirming their plans. Glancing through the windshield toward the diner, he knew what choice he'd make. He had to find his daughter, and Dewey and Tate's illegal fights were the only lead he had.

He closed his eyes. He cursed and focused on getting ready for tonight. Hoping and praying he hadn't lost any of his former skills for beating the crap out of another human being. He couldn't afford to lose. He had to be able to walk away. He couldn't get caught in that world again.

Brooke's life—his future, so much—depended on it.

How DID THE man have any hearing left? Tara wondered as she approached the truck. The metal frame vibrated with the pulsing beat. Three customers had commented on the volume of the music and she'd told them she'd have a chat with him. If she knocked, he wasn't even going to hear her. But she wasn't standing out here waiting for him to notice.

He'd said *later*. Did that mean he'd come to the diner for dinner? Her place? What? It had driven her so crazy, she'd messed up two orders already. Robbie had banned her from the kitchen.

So she was out here cleaning up after that stupid raccoon again. The new Dumpsters helped, if she could get her staff to put everything in them.

Before she could change her mind, she put her foot on the running board and reached for the door handle. The door easily swung open. Letting out a blast of sound.

Tara had never really been inside one of these big semitrucks before. Climbing into the passenger seat in the dark the other night barely counted. She'd driven a delivery truck a couple times for the restaurant supply she'd worked for in Dallas during college. Yeah. It didn't compare.

She'd expected the extended cab to look like the back seat of something. She hadn't expected a miniature RV. She could only stare. Granted, the small space was dominated by a bed—she swallowed—but there was so much more.

A mini-fridge nestled behind the back of the driver's seat. Up on the wall, above the small window in one side of the cab, was a TV screen. A *large* TV screen.

Glancing at the wide mattress again, she pictured him there, remote in one hand, staring up at the screen, stretching out...

She tore her mind off her overly active imagination's wayward path. She swallowed and took a step between the two large seats. "Morgan?" There wasn't anyplace for him to be hidden. Where was he?

Cupboards lined the wall over her head, and she wished she had the nerve to open them. Curiosity teased her to look inside and learn more about the man.

A bright green, plastic folder on a small drop table over the bunk's edge caught her eye. Bold lettering on the tab of the folder said Sylvie

Thane. Staring at the proof that Sylvie really was his wife twisted something—her heart?—in her chest. She shouldn't be here. Tara turned to leave, or at least that's what her brain thought she was doing. Her body didn't budge.

The corner of a thin booklet stuck out of the file's edge. Curious, she peered at it, only able to see it was some sort of government publication.

Divorce rules for Texas. Divorce papers. She leaned closer. Dated nearly six months ago. Why were they here? She nudged the pamphlet out, reading that in the state of Texas, a divorce could be handled in sixty days. So why had he told her he was still married?

The pamphlet fell open to a well-worn page. *Notification.* The word and its explanation was highlighted in bright yellow. As she read, it all came clear. For the divorce to proceed, Sylvie had to be notified. And Morgan had to prove it. Either by her answering the documents that were still here in the folder or by written proof she'd been served.

Otherwise, no finalization.

The driver's door swung open, cool damp air washing in. Morgan climbed up, frowning at her. "Making yourself comfortable?" he yelled over the music. The sound of his voice made her jump. She nearly stumbled, grabbing the edge of the small fridge to catch herself.

She dropped the folder, and the form and

pamphlet scattered across the bed. In the normal world, it would have hit the floor, but these close quarters didn't allow for much floor space.

He stepped closer and she shrank back. There was not enough room in this vehicle for the two of them. No way. But she was held captive between the fridge and the wide expanse of the bed.

He reached past her and flipped a switch, muting the stereo.

"Yeah." She swallowed the sudden dryness in her mouth. "I, uh, need to get back to work."

"You just got here."

"Yeah. Well." Dear heaven, she nearly swung her arms like a little kid trying to distract a teacher from catching her in a lie, but feared if she moved that she'd bump into him...touch him. Touching him... *Gulp.*

That would be such a mistake.

But that didn't stop her eyes from looking, from drinking in the view. He'd changed clothes. A sleeveless T-shirt did nothing to hide the defined muscles of his chest. The camo jeans that were supposed to be loose, baggy by design—weren't.

He carefully moved closer, his gaze landing on the documents scattered on the bed. He looked at her.

"That's why you're looking for her." Not because he wanted her back. Tara swallowed. "To divorce her."

"Yeah. Except I can't find her." He tapped the page Tara had been reading. "Last option is to put an ad in the paper." His words were soft and came out slow. "Post a big ol' sign up that my marriage failed, and for what?" He picked up the pages and shoved them back into the file. "I'm not even sure Sylvie knows what a newspaper is. She sure as hell isn't going to go looking for one to see if I'm divorcing her. It's humiliating."

She saw the shame wash over his face. He looked down, as if trying to hide what she'd already seen. He focused on putting the papers away in a drawer beside the bed.

"Divorce isn't that unusual nowadays."

"She's been gone over a year. When I find her, I'm serving her those papers." He looked up then, his gaze burning through hers.

"Morgan, I—" What was she going to say? She froze, staring at him. No words came out. None even formed in her mind.

CHAPTER TEN

MORGAN MOVED CLOSER, leaning an arm against the wall beside her head. He pulled open the door to the fridge. "You, uh, want a soda—or something?" Who was he trying to distract? Cool air from inside washed over her, but it did little good with the heat of his arm, so close, so big, so…

She turned to move away, intending to slip past him, to put some space, any space, between them. Best-laid plans had her tripping over her own feet and landing exactly where she did not want to be—really, she didn't—up against that wide, muscular chest. Two strong arms wrapped around her, halting her flight.

"Where you goin'?" he whispered against her ear, his breath stirring her hair and sending a few stray strands to feather across her brow.

"I—uh, came out here to, uh—" She took a deep breath, mentally repeating her newly acquired mantra. *Focus.* He smiled. She saw him glance up and followed his gaze to the clock on the wall.

"The music. It's, uh, loud. Customers…" What was wrong with her? she asked herself, feeling like a fool. Who was she kidding? She'd just wanted to see him and hadn't been smart enough to resist. There wasn't enough room in here to kick herself, which is what she should do.

His knowing grin told her he knew what she was up to and liked it.

Whatever words she'd intended to say next melted away as she turned her head and met his stare.

"Tara," he said, soft and...pleading?

He reached for her and she couldn't—she didn't even want to—move away. His palm was rough against her cheek, but the slide of his thumb over her lips was oh-so-soft. Her eyes drifted closed as he caressed and smoothed her lips.

"Morgan," she said with a sigh, leaning into him. Her hands settled on the defined curve of his chest, feeling the even rise and fall of each breath he took. So alive. So warm and solid.

His hand moved, sliding around to palm the back of her head, his fingers burrowing into her hair. When had it fallen loose, scattering around her shoulders and sliding against her neck?

Tara waited impatiently, nearly begging him to kiss her. Needing to feel and taste him. Those papers had destroyed her resistance. He wasn't taken, at least not his heart.

Morgan took his sweet time, moving in close and settling his lips, not on hers, but on the curve of her neck. She shivered at the first touch, trembling as his arms enfolded her, aligning the full length of her with the full length of him.

Heat rolled off him, melding her to him. Her legs turned to jelly and she leaned into his strength, knowing he would catch her, probably not even noticing her weight against him.

He blazed a hot, damp trail with his tongue up the length of her neck, sighing when his mouth found her earlobe. Tugging on it with his teeth, he teased her with the implied pain and promised sweetness as he soothed the mock injury.

Along the curve of her chin, he traced her skin with a whisper touch, then, as if finally reaching home, his lips skimmed hers. Paused. Then swooped in like a hungry man who'd found the feast.

His lips took possession of hers, forcing them to part so his tongue could slip inside and taste, filling her with the promise of the pleasure he would give her.

Tara heard a sigh and belatedly knew it was hers. It shook them both. She splayed her hands on his broad back, feeling the flex of those muscles as he moved.

Morgan pulled away, and she whimpered at the distance between them. His laugh, deep, rough, scraped across her nerves in a warm, tantalizing way.

Slowly, he bent, easily scooping his hands behind her knees and lifting her against that chest.

She felt small and cherished as the blood raced through her veins. Her arms barely reached all the way around his big shoulders.

Turning ever so slightly, Morgan settled her on the mattress.

She expected him to join her, but he paused. Reaching behind his neck, he fisted the collar of his shirt and ripped the thing over his head. Taut, tanned skin stretched over muscle definition she'd never seen so up close and personal before.

The softness of the bunk closed around her as she sank into it—only to sink even deeper as his body covered hers and his lips found hers again. This time, urgent, harsh and hungry.

WHEN WAS THE last time anyone had touched him with any kind of passion or desire…or caring? Morgan's mind came up blank, empty except for the warmth and heat of Tara. God, she tasted good.

Tara bracketed his face with her slim hands. For a long minute, she looked at him, as if drinking in every detail of his face. He wanted to flinch away from her intensity, but he forced himself to hold still, bracing for her to have second thoughts.

She frowned.

Here it comes. "What?" he ventured.

She shook her head. Instead of pulling away, she put pressure on his neck, urging him closer, drawing him in. Her lips brushed his. "You're not what I expected."

"What do you mean?" He kissed her briefly, teasing them both.

"I don't know." She smiled. "You muddle my brain."

He chuckled, relief sliding over him. "Okay. Let me know when you figure it out."

"Okay." She laughed. Impatient, she captured his mouth with hers, this time not moving away, not pulling back, but deepening the kiss herself. Her sweet tongue prodded him, then dove in to match his earlier moves. She slid an arm around his neck, holding tight.

He was lost in her. No one was ever going to find him again.

She felt so small in his hands, and he liked that, liked the power rushing inside him. Not to hurt or control her but to protect her. Support her. Cherish her.

Pulling back, Morgan stared at her. She was wearing her chef garb, the jacket with a row of big clear buttons running down one side. Fascinated, he curled his fingers over the top one and pushed it through the hole. The stand-up collar parted, giving him a view of pink skin.

He had to taste it. Couldn't wait for even one more inch to be revealed with another button. He leaned in, startled by the heat of her skin.

He couldn't get enough.

Tara put her hand, tiny and hot, in the center of his chest and gently pushed. He jerked back, afraid he'd missed a signal, a word that told him she'd changed her mind. She laughed, a deep, hot, throaty sound.

Instead of sliding off the bunk, she rose on her knees, kneeling in front of him. Slowly, she reached for the next button, making it look large compared to her small fingers. She pushed it through the fabric. First one. Then another. And another.

The thick, white fabric parted, and Morgan stared hungrily as inches of warm flesh appeared. The gentle curve of her generous breast. The irritating lacy cup of a bra he briefly fantasized about pulling away…until he was distracted by the flat tanned skin of her belly.

She tossed the jacket over the edge of the bunk, not even watching where it landed. Her fingers trembled, however, as they slid lower to the catch of her pants.

"Let me." He leaned up on an elbow, unable to resist touching her. He swallowed as her soft skin reacted to just his finger trailing down the length of her—from her chin, down to the swell of her breast, where he dipped inside the lace for just a tease.

Her nipple pebbled against his fingertip, and they both groaned. Anticipation of how she'd taste made his mouth water and he caught himself licking his lips.

"Morgan," she moaned.

He pulled his finger back, rising to kneel in front of her. She was so tiny here, on her knees. He reached for the hook at her waist. The zipper slid down easily, slowly, not silently. As if announcing his arrival.

Rather than pushing the pants down, getting rid of the barrier, he instead slid his hand inside. Dear heaven, her skin was so hot. He slid lower, over the soft curls, and touched what he wanted to possess.

She was wet. So very wet. For him.

Carefully, he stroked her, watching as her eyelids drifted closed, and she leaned against his arm crossing her back, her covered breasts begging for him.

"Take it off," he croaked. "I have to taste you."

Without him moving either hand, Tara managed to reach around and unhook the dainty bra. Gravity helped pull it away, showing him the sweet curves, and the pale pink nipples, ready and waiting for him.

He quickened his finger's stroke and her breath came faster, harsher. "Please—" she cried out, nearly cresting the wave.

"Please what, babe?" he whispered, finally dipping his head to take one distended nipple deep into his mouth. At the same instant, he inched his finger deeper. Then deeper still until her cry of release dissolved into quick hot spasms. He let her fly, drinking in every sweet drop.

SHE'D JUST COME apart in his hands. She should be embarrassed. She wasn't. Not even close. Slowly lifting her eyelids, Tara looked into Morgan's smile. And smiled back.

She reached up, pulling his lips to hers, and pushed herself closer. All those glorious male muscles felt like heaven against her bare breasts.

Morgan slid his hands to her hips, against her skin, sliding the rest of her clothing off, down over her legs as he laid her back. Stretched out, she felt his gaze trail over every inch of her.

"Beautiful," he whispered.

"And you're too dressed."

"And it's going to stay that way." His smile dimmed only slightly.

"What?"

"No condoms, baby." He shrugged. "And I didn't see you bring a purse or anything with you."

"I—" Now she *was* embarrassed. She was thinking like a clueless teenager. "I didn't intend—"

"I know. It's no problem." Morgan put a finger over her lips to stop the next excuse she'd come up with. "I don't take chances. I knew before we started this. So, lie back and relax."

"But, Morgan—" She tried to sit up, tried to reach for him.

"I can take care of that, too." He leaned down and silenced her with a kiss that took her sanity along with her next words.

He stretched out beside her, his big frame taking up most of the space. It didn't matter as he pulled her to lie beside him, her head on his shoulder.

His hands slid up and down her back, over her curves, cupping her ass possessively, then up to feather over her ribs. His touch relaxed her, and she felt herself drifting nearly to sleep.

She tried to resist touching him, really she did. She didn't want to be a cruel tease, but her fingers itched to feel his skin.

Slowly, tentatively, she rubbed her fingertips in the shallow valley at his breastbone, then she trailed down to the hard ridges gracing his abdomen. Soft strands of hair tickled her fingertips, the trail leading to the waistband of the pants he'd left on. To protect her.

She played until a soft moan escaped him. Glancing up, she saw that he'd clenched his jaw and had his eyes closed tight. "Morgan. Let me…" She stumbled over the words. Instead, she slid her hand down to the fly of his jeans. The hard, hot ridge of his erection throbbed even through the thick material. "Let me touch you. Like you touched me."

She looked at his face again. His eyes were open, heat pouring out of them, scorching her. She ached where he'd touched her before.

She couldn't look away but found her way by touch. The metal closure resisted her insistent touch. When he reached down to help, she thought she might lose it then and there. The fabric parted and she had to experience all of him. She looked down.

Her hand looked so small compared to his length, but she managed to encircle him and hold on. Slowly, she explored him, feeling the solidness, the softness, the heated damp, all of him.

"Don't stop, baby," he asked so softly she almost didn't hear him. "I'm so close."

He surprised her by cupping her bare breast, tweaking her nipple and nearly distracting her from her mission. He seemed determined to stretch out their pleasure, but as her climax threatened, it only made her focus on him sharper, hotter.

She ached inside, wanting him there, but knowing he was right, damn him. When his other hand found the damp between her thighs again, she cried out, convulsing against his touch. He moved against her palm, arching hard into her touch.

This time he shattered with her, and it was his growl of pleasure that bounced off the walls.

SOMEONE WAS POUNDING. On something hard. Tara opened her eyes to darkness.

"Stay here."

That was Morgan's voice. Everything came rushing back. That she remembered, but what was going on now? She felt the mattress move and could tell he was refastening his jeans. She felt her cheeks flame.

"I'll be right back," he whispered.

He stood and suddenly a small light over the fridge blazed bright in the tiny space.

"What time is it?" Tara covered her eyes against the sudden light.

"I don't know. Late. Sorry." He didn't bother to put on a shirt. The pounding started again. "Stay here."

He turned to climb down, then stopped. "Just so you know, I'm not hiding you. I don't want you getting any crap." He smiled, then disappeared out the driver's door of the truck.

As soon as he left, she scrambled off the mattress and fished her missing clothes from beside the bed. How had they gotten there? She didn't want to know and let herself smile as she redressed.

She hadn't had very many serious relationships. And she certainly wasn't the one-night-stand type. Relationships always got her into trouble because she was so focused, and sometimes that focus got too much like tunnel vision.

She'd decided to put all her energy into her business, but now she had to figure out how to do both. She had to. She wanted both Morgan and her business in her life.

The door opened and she stepped into the shadows.

"Thanks, man. I'll be right back." Morgan shut the door and was right there again.

"Hi." She smiled up at him.

"Hi." He smiled back and reached out to finish re-buttoning her shirt, this time straight. "I wish I could stay and undo all this all over again." He kissed her, fast and deep. "But I gotta go."

He reached over her head and pulled a clean shirt and his jacket out of a cupboard.

"Where to?" She asked it casually, but his hesitation took all the casual out of everything. He didn't want to tell her. And the longer they stood, staring at each other, the more she realized he wasn't going to.

Why did that realization hurt?

"I really gotta go." He turned and opened the door again. "Give me about ten minutes, then leave. There aren't too many people out here."

Only her customers and staff. "Yeah. Sure." He closed the door with a loud wham, and she sank to sit on the edge of the bunk. He was gone, and she had no idea what he thought of anything.

Her cheeks warmed and she buried her face in her hands.

Ten minutes was a hell of a long time all of a sudden.

TARA STARED AT the nearly full parking lot. Not very many people? Right. What parking lot had Morgan been looking at? She hurried toward the diner, knowing her staff had expected her back ages ago. Maybe with the crowd, they'd been too busy to notice. Yeah, right.

Several people were actually standing around the doorway, waiting to be seated. She slipped through, a rush of excitement going through her. This was what she'd hoped for, what she needed to make a go of this place.

"Wow, we might not be able to get a seat," a woman said, making Tara turn around.

"We'll get in," the man beside her reassured her. "I don't mind waiting, if you don't." Tara had to see this guy. Even her brother Wyatt, the kindest of her siblings, wouldn't make such a syrupy sweet promise.

He was young. And the woman with him was about the same age. They gave each other what she used to think of as puppy-dog eyes. Before the urge to roll her eyes grew too strong to ignore, she headed into the kitchen to see where she should help.

"Must be nice to be a rich business owner who

doesn't have to work." A voice came from around the corner before Tara entered the prep area. She froze. She had to think a minute to figure out who it was. One of the part-time evening waitresses—Kaitlyn. She'd just started here.

Tara gulped back her disappointment.

"You don't know what's going on," Wendy said around the clatter of dishes.

Tara started to step around the corner, then froze. "She's always watching us. I hate that. She doesn't trust us." The sneer in the girl's voice hurt.

"You're paranoid," Wendy said.

"I am not."

"Then why are you so worried about what she thinks? Doing something you shouldn't?"

"No," Kaitlyn said too quickly.

"That wasn't very convincing." Wendy's voice was louder, as if she'd just turned around to face where Tara stood. "Stop being stupid and just do your job. It's a new place. She's just watching to see how things are going."

Wendy came around the corner then, a serving tray hoisted up on her shoulder. She paused, catching herself from tripping, barely. Tara met her employee's gaze, making sure not to look away.

"Where have you been? Are you okay?"

Tara didn't even know how to answer. She saw the real concern in Wendy's eyes.

"Fine." She stepped toward the swinging doors. "Just got caught up. Sorry."

The silence was heavy. Wendy nodded, though she looked closely at Tara, as if searching for something beyond her words.

Tara stepped through the doors. She didn't think Kaitlyn had known she was there. She knew she could never really be friends with her employees, but she thought she had a good relationship with them all. The reality that a lot of it was a lie hurt.

Slowly, Tara stepped around the corner, making sure Kaitlyn saw her. Did the girl wonder if she'd been there before? Did she care that Tara might have overheard their conversation?

Tara kept walking, heading for her office. She didn't owe anyone any explanations. She'd left the diner, not even thinking about how long she'd be gone. She hadn't planned to end up in Morgan's arms, or feel so comfortable there that she fell asleep.

Inside the small office, she sank into the wooden chair in the corner. Its usual comfort did little good today.

She was doing it again, wasn't she? Letting a guy distract her, letting someone else affect her ability to succeed. The last shivers of pleasure from being with Morgan slowly melted away.

MORGAN MADE DEWEY drop him off a mile from the site. "I want to scope out the place first. I'm not promising anything."

Dewey had frowned but nodded. He knew Morgan well enough to know that he'd lose if he pushed him. There was only one reason Morgan was even here, and fighting was the least of his wishes.

Something Dewey had said, about Tate calling the authorities when Mack got too rough, came to mind. He wondered if the authorities were in on this deal since this location was entirely too obvious.

He took several trips around the area before approaching the door.

He'd worked too danged hard to clean up his reputation and leave his past behind to risk a trip to jail. He might get sucked in again, but a part of him hoped he'd be able to pull back. Finally, convinced it was clear, he hit the side door, slipping inside before anyone could see him. He stayed in the shadows as best he could. He'd just go in quick, look around, then leave. If he didn't find Sylvie… He'd deal with that disappointment after.

The old days rushed back with a contact adrenaline high. His stomach turned from the intensity that hung in the air. Simultaneously, he wanted to jump into the ring to join in and head out the door to run as fast as he could in the opposite direction.

People, mostly men like those twentysomethings he'd seen earlier, filled the area between a circle of bright yellow school buses. Really, school buses? He almost rolled his eyes.

There were a few women mixed in. He wanted to find Sylvie, but not here. Not like this. Because if she was here, where was Brooke? Who was she with? Worrying about her left a weight in his gut.

Slowly, Morgan wove through the crowd, pushing gently to make progress. He didn't want to be recognized, and he didn't think he would be. He'd been out of the game long enough.

"Thane!" A voice broke through the din, and Morgan cringed. *No, please, don't know me.* He tried to keep going, knowing that if Sylvie were here, she'd be running now. He needed to get out of the crowd, get far enough away to see her leave.

"It's Thane!" Another voice broke the night. He couldn't ignore them now.

"I'm not here for a match," he told the beefy guy ahead of him.

"Yeah?" The guy crossed thick arms over his wide, muscled chest. "You sure?"

"Positive." Morgan wasn't in the mood to fight, but neither was he one to back down from a challenge. Especially not when the one doing the asking was big as a house and someone Morgan had clocked before.

"Not looking for a rematch?" Bull growled, leaning in close.

Morgan lifted his hands in surrender. "Not to-night, man." He took a step back. "I'm retired."

Just then, a woman's all-too-familiar laugh came across the crowd. Morgan spun around, at first not seeing her, then catching a glimpse of someone who looked like Sylvie. Sort of.

The same height, same body—but the blue eyes that he'd once thought were beautiful he now saw were cold as ice. Dear heaven, had there ever been any warmth in Sylvie's eyes? Did she look at their daughter with those eyes? She didn't look in his direction.

"Sylvie," he whispered and took a couple of steps toward her. She looked so different. If she hadn't laughed, he doubted he'd have recognized her with blue hair and tattoos. A shiver of fear told him he couldn't lose her now. He might never find her again. He struggled to control his desperation.

Sylvie tipped her head back and laughed again, this time at the man beside her. She actually batted her eyelashes at the fool. Drama had always been her talent, and she knew how to play the crowd. Bull was practically salivating as he stared at her. "You aren't getting near her, Morgan. She's mine. She doesn't want to see you."

That hurt, but he swallowed the injury. "I don't believe you." And he didn't, not really. But that tiny feather of doubt was difficult to completely ignore.

Then she was moving away from him through the mass of bodies, bodies that managed to step in between them, blocking him. "Sylvie," he called, the sound of his voice disappearing in the noise of the crowd. Morgan turned to follow her.

"Don't even think about followin' the lady," Bull said.

Morgan knew he could take on the mountain of a man and maybe win. Maybe. He'd been out of this too long. And while he'd kept up the workouts, he wasn't sure how well he'd really fare. Bull looked like he had other things in mind than a fair fight.

Morgan wasn't going to back down, though. He'd never been good about that. His father had taught him well. Backing down only made the beating worse. "You going to stop me?"

"Yeah, I am."

Morgan saw Bull's fist up close and personal an instant before he ducked away—an instant too slow. Pain shot through his right cheek, and the red he saw was as much from his busted face as it was the roar of rage that exploded inside him.

No backing down now. No following Sylvie, either, damn it.

He'd failed tonight. But he wasn't ready to give up. The big man in front of him stumbled back from the power behind Morgan's first punch, and he continued to retreat with each consecutive blow. None of the fist falls that Bull threw could keep Morgan back, though two shots to the ribs nearly did. Nothing slowed him down. He relished the pain.

For the first time in months, his blood rushed in his veins, and he felt alive.

When the big man finally fell on his backside in the dirt, he didn't get up. Morgan stopped, something he was fairly certain Bull wouldn't have done.

Standing there in the now dim light, inside a circle of strangers who yelled words he couldn't hear through the rushing in his ears and the sawing of the breath in his lungs, Morgan stared.

What was wrong with him? He'd left this all behind and *she'd* dragged him into it. He cursed, loud and long before turning and stalking through the crowd. She had to still be here, but it was like looking for a needle in a haystack. He headed to the exit. Maybe he'd see her leave.

The night air engulfed him, cooling his anger and the sweat on his body. He took in half a dozen gulps before his equilibrium returned.

He called himself every shade of a fool. The crowd was still inside, calling out for the next match. Fickle and foolish, those people saw the fights as nothing more than a way to make money and be entertained.

He'd been like that once upon a time. Before he'd learned the reality of icing injuries in the wee hours of the morning.

The pain grew. In his hand, radiating up his arm. In his face. Where the hell was Dewey? He cursed, waiting and watching. Just in case Sylvie showed again.

Time stretched out. Nothing. It was going to be a mighty long walk to town.

CHAPTER ELEVEN

THE WIND CUT through the night, chilling Tara. She pulled her jacket tighter, taking her time crossing the wet pavement. It felt almost cold enough for the standing water from the past few days to freeze.

While she now had plenty of staff, they were in no way ready to be on their own if she fell and got hurt. She couldn't afford to leave them in charge. Not yet, but hopefully at some point.

She'd parked on the far corner of the lot when she'd got here, leaving room closer to the door for customers. Lots of customers was a good thing. Really. Except when it was the end of the night, and she had to battle against the weather.

Now she almost regretted that decision. *Brrr.*

Morgan's truck was still parked at the edge of the lot, dark and silent. He wasn't back. Where had he gone in such a hurry? That same question had plagued her all through her shift.

Still more rain came down as she hurried through the dark. In the few minutes it took to walk to her car, she was drenched. Her fingers were cold and slippery. She had to pull the door handle twice, losing her grip the first time. Her fingertips burned from the slip. Damn it.

The dome light came on, light puddling at her feet with the raindrops. She tossed her purse, which landed on the seat with a squish. Great. She'd have to dry it out, too.

With a sigh of relief, she plopped behind the wheel and leaned back. She slammed the door closed, thankful for the relative warmth. The yard light glowed off the drops on the windshield, and in the distance, brake lights from cars at the stop-light spread red, then the green light added its glow on the glass.

Something moved. There. Up by the building. Leaning forward, she squinted, then felt stupid. Turning the key, she switched on the wipers so she could see. There. Near the back door. A shadow moved. Not low to the ground like a cat or dog or that pesky raccoon. No, this was taller.

A man. She smacked the button on the door handle, hearing the comforting thunk of the locks falling into place.

It wasn't Wade. He was inside. Even his nico-tine habit wasn't standing up to these days of rain. And it was definitely a man, not any of her girls.

The man moved. First to the back door, where he lifted a hand, and she knew he was knocking, though she couldn't hear the sound. Would any-one inside hear him?

His head bent, he leaned against the door, his

hand slipping down. Tara rummaged in her purse. Where was her phone? She tried to remember where it was. Damn. She was fairly certain it was still sitting on her desk.

Should she leave? What if he broke in? What if he tried to harm one of her employees or a customer leaving this late?

She couldn't afford to lose anything. She could drive to the police station. But what would he do by the time the cops, or she, got back here? She knew better than to confront anyone. But maybe if she drove closer, she could scare him away.

Tara pulled the car slowly across the lot. She expected the man to leave. To get away from the door. When he didn't leave, when he actually seemed to stand his ground and face her oncoming car, she got a little ticked.

What was he doing? This was her place!

"Go away," she said to the windshield, knowing he couldn't hear her. Heck, she could barely hear the car's engine over the drumming of raindrops. He just stood there.

His shadow separated from the wall as the headlight beams reached him. The light moved up his body. His big, muscular body.

"Morgan!" She slammed on the brakes before she ran into him and the building. "What are you doing here?" She shook her head, feeling like a fool again. She shoved the car into Park and stared through the pouring rain.

He stepped forward, his face appearing in the light beam. She gasped. His arm went out and his hand splayed on the hood of her car. He stumbled but caught himself, barely. She shoved open the door and jumped out.

"What happened?" He looked awful. His other arm was close to his side and the right side of his face was covered in dark purple bruises. A deep cut ran through his right eyebrow, and a trail of blood slid down the side of his face.

The eyes that stared at her were unfocused and he blinked several times as he stood—leaned—there. "Tara?"

"Come on." Before he fell on his face and she'd never get him on his feet again, she slipped beneath his arm and leaned into him. "Come with me." She used that voice she'd perfected when Wendy and Wade got into it, the one that didn't allow for any disagreement. It seemed to work on Morgan, as well, as he nodded and let her lead him to the passenger door.

This one didn't open any easier than the driver's had, but her hands weren't as cold as they'd been before. The heat coming off Morgan's body washed over her, and she made herself focus on putting one foot in front of the other to get him in the car. The rest she'd deal with later. Much later.

He fell into the car, the entire chassis shifting with the impact. "Turn around." She pushed him to get his legs in. He leaned his head back, favoring his obviously injured arm as he buckled the seat belt and settled inside the car. She slammed the door and hurried around to climb in beside him.

"What happened?" She didn't look at him, instead focusing on cranking the heat and aiming the vents toward him and toward her freezing hands.

He didn't say anything. For half an instant, she thought maybe he'd passed out, but when she finally looked at him again and found him staring at her, she froze. No, he was very much awake.

Their gazes caught and held. He wasn't going to answer her. When he leaned back again and closed his eyes, she was certain he wasn't.

"Guess we're just going to sit here." She could be stubborn, too. "Isn't like this is the first time I've spent the night here."

Was that a smile? She hoped so.

"Here's the deal." He looked at her again. "Don't ask any questions. You do not want to know the answers. Really. Just take me to an urgent care."

She'd take him to the urgent care, but she got the impression he expected her to drop him off. Yeah, that wasn't happening. She'd find out, even if he wouldn't tell her.

Setting the car in motion, she headed toward the urgent care.

He didn't talk, and neither did she.

NOT BEING RELATED to someone you took for emergency care sucked. Tara sat in the waiting area alone. Morgan was in with a doctor, and he wasn't letting her know anything. Nothing.

And the doctor was supporting that secretiveness. Privacy rights, really?

Except for the stupid fact that he looked like hell, looked like he was in a great deal of pain, she'd leave him here to walk to his truck. Or take a nearly nonexistent cab.

She drummed her fingers on the arm of the chair. Then she stood and grabbed a well-worn sports magazine.

Uninterested, she tossed the magazine onto the table.

Just when she'd decided she'd open that door— go back and demand to know what was going on—the door opened from the other side, and Morgan stepped out.

He still looked like hell, except all the broken pieces had been bandaged back together. He actually tried to smile at her, but grimaced instead. That bruise was going to take a while to fade.

Butterfly bandages on his forehead and chin told her those were deep cuts. The wrap around his left forearm looked suspiciously like a splint. He had a plastic bag in his "good" hand, which was a relative term if you didn't count the now-cleaned and dried scrapes on his knuckles. The bag's contents rattled, sounding suspiciously like prescription medication.

"I was pretty sure you'd dumped me here and left," he said.

"I thought about it."

"Thanks for sticking around." His slight grunt of pain as he fought the smile made her heart contract.

"You're welcome, I think. Can you leave now?"

"Yeah, the doc's done with me." He followed her to the doors that slid open as they approached. "I really do appreciate this, Tara."

She stopped, turning around so swiftly he had to catch himself before running into her. "I'm guessing you're not going to explain what all this is about, are you?"

Morgan shook his head. "I…" He barely stopped himself from running a hand down his face. That would probably hurt like hell and undo a great deal of the doctor's handiwork. "I will. Eventually. But not right now."

Whatever had happened, it wasn't good, and he was still suffering, both physically and emotionally.

"Okay, you're off the hook for now. But I want your promise you'll tell me."

"I promise."

He didn't cross his fingers behind his back— she leaned around to look—which made him laugh, painfully again. Without a time frame, who knew when he'd tell her anything? She was too tired to fight, and he was in too much pain. She'd let him off the hook for now, but she *would* get answers.

"WHAT THE HECK happened to you?" Wendy's voice cut across the din of the diner the next morning. Tara wasn't sure why the comment made her look up, but it did. She wished she hadn't. Morgan sat at the counter, a cup of coffee in his hands, steam wafting in front of his face.

A face that sported bruises, a black eye and several lacerations. She had to stop herself from stepping toward him. It hadn't been that long since she'd dropped him off at the truck. Was it possible he looked worse now?

"Nothing serious," he mumbled and focused on the newspaper he'd spread out. "Hey, can you get me a special?" he ordered without looking up.

Tara watched Wendy stare at him for a long minute before she answered. "Sure." The waitress headed to the kitchen, silent.

Before Wendy caught her watching, Tara scurried around the corner and focused on the dessert tray she was prepping for lunch. She did not want to discuss Morgan with Wendy, and she certainly wasn't explaining why she already knew about his injuries.

Her cheeks burned as other memories of yesterday followed. She focused on the frosting she was piping onto the cupcake. It had to be perfect…

"Hey," Wendy whispered at her elbow and she slipped, blue frosting spilling off the edge of the chocolate in a glop.

"Hey, what?"

"Did you see Morgan?"

How was she supposed to answer that? She either lied and said no or admitted she knew. Wendy saved her from answering, by speaking again. "He looks awful."

Morgan didn't know how to look awful. Tara dragged her mind from that path. "Wh-what do you mean?"

"He's hurt."

He had injuries, but Tara wasn't sure he hurt. Did the man even know how to feel? Okay, she was being uncharitable, but the ache at how he shut her out was too acute still, too painful. She wasn't ready to forgive him yet. "He's a customer, Wendy." She pulled out a knife and tried to repair the damaged frosting. "His private life is none of our business."

"Yeah, but…"

Tara hated that phrase. It always preceded something inappropriate. "No 'yeah buts.' He's not our concern. Serve him and move on. I need you to focus on your job today."

They didn't have time to get caught up in every customer's little problems. Lord knew there were plenty of them here. Which reminded her. "Have you seen that little girl in here again?"

Wendy focused on the order tray, prepping Morgan's special. "Which one, the little girl with the purple dragon?"

"Yeah."

"No, I haven't."

The swinging doors slammed open, the metal frame smacking the edge of the counter hard enough to scare them both. Tara nearly dropped the frosting bag, and Wendy did drop the plate of toast she'd been about to set on the tray.

"What the hell is with you?" Robbie yelled from the kitchen.

Morgan stood in the doorway, his eye swollen and red-rimmed, his chin a once-bloody mess. He looked like he was on the verge of killing someone or morphing into a monster who would. Tara took a step back, not sure what to think. Was he having a reaction to those meds they'd given him?

Robbie stepped out from behind the wall between the kitchen and the prep area, his scrawny frame no match for Morgan, but the knife he had in his fist would sure do damage if need be.

Morgan's eyes flashed with a fever's level of emotion, something Tara couldn't quite identify, but he tamped it down quickly, as if he'd had a lot of practice. He didn't leave, and he didn't retreat from the offensive stance, but he did relax. "You saw a girl with a purple dragon?" His gaze flew between Wendy and Tara. "Was she with Sylvie?"

"Who's Sylvie?" Wendy asked.

"His *friend*," Tara sneered the second word, figuring she was somehow a part of what had happened to him last night. Morgan glared at her but didn't disabuse her of the notion.

"It wasn't her." Tara said, feeling a twinge of sympathy for him, just a twinge as pain sparked in his eyes. "It was a young woman, a girl really. She was here with her boyfriend. The little girl said she was her babysitter."

Could a man, so big and strong, look crestfallen? If he could, Morgan did. "The little girl. What did she look like? How old was she?"

Something didn't match here. Tara put the icing down and wiped her hands on the towel. "What's going on, Morgan? Why would that matter?"

His hands were in fists at his side, and she could tell he was clenching his jaw. It had to hurt. He turned to leave. She couldn't let him go. "She was five or six years old. Blond hair, in two ponytails."

"What color were her eyes?"

"Uh—" She had to think. "Brown."

"The dragon. How…how big?"

Tara frowned and tried to remember that, as well. "This big?" She spread her hands about a foot apart. "It had plastic black eyes and a green bow around its neck."

The anguish in Morgan's eyes was too painful to watch. Yet she couldn't look away, unable to abandon him like this. "What aren't you telling us?"

Morgan didn't answer. He was pulling his phone out of his pocket and heading to the door. She didn't know who he was calling, but the intensity on his battered face told her something had changed. Drastically.

MORGAN DIDN'T LIKE SURPRISES. So, the next morning when he walked into the diner and found Jack on the stool at the end of the counter where Morgan sat nearly every day, he stopped and glared at his brother. "What are you doing here, Jack?"

Wendy and Tara stood behind the counter, pretending to be busy, but both of them shot furtive glances between the brothers.

"Looking for you."

"Why?"

Jack took his time taking a sip of his coffee. He set down the cup carefully, slowly, before looking at him again. "Someone—" he glanced over at the women, as if just noticing their interest "—told me you're fighting again." He took another deep drink of his coffee. "Looks like they were right."

Damn Dewey. He'd only talked to him this morning. He had a lot of explaining to do, but Morgan would deal with him later.

"What of it?" Morgan moved closer to his

brother and sat beside him. He gave Jack credit for having the chops not to move or flinch away.

"Morgan, are you nuts?" Jack turned on him, anger blazing in his eyes. "This isn't the answer. We'll find the money. Haul a few more—"

"This isn't about the money." He stared, incredulous, at Jack. "I'm not that stupid. Give me some credit."

"Then you'd better start explaining."

"She's there," Morgan whispered.

"Brooke?"

"No, idiot." Morgan rolled his eyes. "Sylvie."

"Where's Brooke?"

"I don't know." He nearly pounded his fist on the counter as Jack's words illustrated his frustration. But he didn't want to startle Jack or Tara's staff. He'd done enough damage yesterday when he'd lost it. "If I knew that, do you think I'd do this?"

"I didn't know." Jack shrugged. "You used to do it all the time."

"Yeah, when I had to." Morgan looked over at Tara. This was not something he wanted to discuss in front of her. She probably already thought he was nuts. This wasn't going to help.

But she surprised him then, walking over to stand on the other side of the counter. He didn't dare look at her, didn't dare face her and see the censure in her gaze. It was one of the hardest things he'd ever done.

The sweet scent of her wrapped around him, and her heat followed, tugging at him. He wasn't good at resisting her. Damn. He finally gave in as the silence grew and met her gaze.

No anger, no pity, no disgust. Just curiosity. "Who's Brooke?"

He knew everything hinged on his answer. Knew without even asking or thinking hard about it that the future was there for the taking, there for him to reach out and grab hold. He cleared his throat. "My daughter."

The look of pain on her face, as if he'd slapped her, surprised him.

"The little girl with the toy dragon?"

"Yeah."

"Why didn't you tell me?" she demanded, her hurt all too painful to him.

"She's seen Brooke?" Jack interrupted. "When?" To Tara he said, "Do you know where she is?"

"I—"

Morgan looked at Jack, at Wendy, who stood there drying the already dry plate. Finally, at Tara. The only person here whose opinion really mattered. "Not yet," he answered Jack but didn't look away from Tara. "I tend to focus on Sylvie. If I find her, I find Brooke." How did he explain that thinking about Brooke was too painful, too hard?

She gasped. "You didn't trust me enough to share that?" Her anger flashed bright.

"No." This wasn't going to go well. "I trust you. I—" Slowly, Morgan stood, then took a couple steps backward to keep from vaulting the damn counter to reach for her. "I can't take the risk."

"What the hell does that mean?"

He didn't answer, simply turned and headed out. He'd never be able to explain.

He'd lost too many people in his life. They'd left him. Death. Drinking. Hell, his wife had actually *run away* from him.

He'd been stupid to even toy with the idea that maybe he'd be different with Tara.

Brooke…might be all he had. If he had anyone.

The rain had returned—had it ever really stopped?—and the ice-cold drops fell over him. He didn't care. Not this time. He walked with purpose to the truck. He revved the diesel engine and roared out of the parking lot.

In the rearview mirror, he saw Tara come out of the diner's door. He saw Jack behind her, saw his brother reach out to grab her as she started to run after the truck.

Safety be damned, he flipped the mirror aside and focused on the road. He needed to call Dewey and get a fight lined up. It didn't matter how badly Morgan was beaten or if he lost. He'd forfeit the fight and go after her if he caught even a glimpse of Sylvie.

Once that was done—he prayed Sylvie was there—he'd get his daughter and go home.

CHAPTER TWELVE

"WHAT DO YOU MEAN, he never told you? You are Tara, right?"

Tara stared at the man she'd just learned existed a short while ago. The man who was a smaller, albeit just as feisty, version of Morgan. His brother, Jack.

"Oh, that's so...Morgan." Jack laughed. A smooth, warm sound, unlike the roughness that characterized Morgan's laugh—something she suddenly missed.

"What's that supposed to mean?" She faced him, hands on her hips.

"Have you ever tried to get my stubborn brother to admit anything he doesn't want to?"

Like where he went so suddenly yesterday? Or what happened? Or anything about what the doctor said?

Not once had Morgan shared any of the things Jack was telling her now. Things Jack seemed to think she knew.

But apparently, Jack knew about her. How many secrets did Morgan have?

Tara returned inside, focusing on clearing tables, on any task to keep herself from feeling the betrayal that was a ridiculous reaction. She'd known Morgan only a few weeks. Why did she think he owed her any explanations?

She froze when a hand landed on her arm. Why was she disappointed it was Jack?

"Look." He glanced around. "Morgan would kick my ass if he knew I told you this, but cut him some slack."

"I don't know what you mean." She didn't like the fact that this stranger had read her so easily. Were the Thane brothers psychic or something?

"Yes, you do. You're thinking he's a liar. He's not. He's the best man I know." There was strain in his voice as if him convincing her was vital. "After Mom died and Dad, well, Dad fell off the face of the earth, Morgan took over."

Jack's eyes grew distant. "He drove truck to put me through school. He fought dozens of fights." His gaze came back to hers. "One of those fights? Someone nearly killed him with a choke hold. The damage to his voice is a reminder of that."

She froze, staring at Jack, whose face was so similar to Morgan's. She'd noticed the rasp in Morgan's voice but never really thought about it. It was who he was. But now that she heard Jack talk, it was more obvious. "Who would do that?"

Jack laughed, harsh and dark. "You're so sheltered," he whispered. "No wonder he's drawn to you." Jack took a couple steps away. "If you have any influence, talk him out of this. Please?" He shook his head sadly before leaving the restaurant.

Wendy stepped out of the kitchen just then, Jack's change in her hand. "Where'd he go?"

Tara refocused on the dishes. She heard Wendy go into the kitchen, mumbling to herself. Tara mentally cursed and sank onto the chair at the empty table.

Now what?

THREE DAYS HAD passed since she'd last seen Morgan. Tara kept looking for him. Whenever the door opened, she'd look up. It was never him.

When she walked to her car each night, she fought the urge to look over at the empty spot where his truck had sat.

Every night, when she finally went to sleep—exhausted—her dreams filled with him. Of the hours with him in the truck. Of him sitting there at the counter.

Was he ever coming back?

After her third nearly sleepless night, she stood staring at her closet. During culinary school, Tara had spent a chunk of her hard-earned income on chef jackets, matching pants and various head pieces that fit all the images she carried of what a great chef should look like.

Now, she stared at several hundred dollars'

worth of waste. Not ruined—wasted because she never wore any of it, aside from a chef's jacket.

Here, in the small-town diner, these staid, almost formal clothes seemed out of place. In the heat of a real kitchen, the fabric didn't hold up any better than the comfortable clothes she'd always worn to cook. The steam, the heat, the spills—there wasn't much difference.

Except she'd spent a whole lot more money and worried more about the money she'd lose when they were ruined.

It really wasn't about utility. It had been about image. Should she get rid of them? Donate or sell them to someone wrapped up in that dream of what a chef was supposed to be?

Or should she get back into who she'd always planned? Was this a way to get her focus back?

Shaking her head, Tara tried to laugh at herself. Slowly, she took each item out and looked at it, realizing that she'd bought an awful lot of white clothing. Which was stupid. With her pale coloring and light hair, white made her look like death warmed over. Grimacing, she tossed all the white items onto the bed. She'd donate those.

What was left were the few colorful things she'd barely worn, not wanting to stand out in school. Now? Now she was in charge and could wear whatever she danged well pleased.

She stared at a bright maroon shirt for a long time. Big, silver buttons ran down the left side from a mandarin collar. It was similar to the one Morgan had—

No! *Do not go down that path.* She focused on the shirt, on the here and now.

She'd never even worn this shirt except when she'd tried it on in the shop. She'd kept telling herself—someday.

Was today someday? That's what the sign over her diner said.

Holding the hanger up in front of her, she turned to the mirror. The bright-colored shirt still appealed to her, just as it had on that day in the store. She twisted and turned to see the varied angles. The darker color was a good contrast to her hair, and the reddish tone cast a faint pink tint to her skin. She liked it.

Okay, today, she was going to take that step and leave all the boring white behind. She was going to do what she'd always wanted to do. She pulled the shirt off the hanger, tugged it over her head. She looked into the mirror again and smiled.

Yes. This was the right thing. This was her taking control and focusing on what was important. *Her* business.

She finished dressing and headed to the door, feeling better than she had in a while. Today, she was going to cook. She was going to make food the way she'd always wanted. And that's all she was going to do.

She didn't even think about Morgan. Much.

WHEN TARA WALKED in the front door of her diner, the sun was barely up, and she froze. He was back. *Figures*.

Morgan sat in his usual spot, a newspaper in front of him, a coffee in hand.

"He came in about an hour ago," Wendy said as she passed, carrying a tray of dirty dishes.

She was not going to get sucked in again, Tara told herself as she walked across the dining room. She had a business to run, and Morgan Thane had no place in that plan.

She headed toward the kitchen, letting the swinging doors swish behind her, hard. Normally, she caught them, but she just wanted to get away. Maybe hide.

After dropping her things in the office, Tara stomped over to the baker's table. Pulling the eggs out of the fridge, she smacked them against the side of the big bowl that perpetually sat there, ready to use. *Crack, sploosh.* The eggs fell into the growing puddle of yolks and whites.

She didn't have to look at the recipe. This was one of Mom's, one Tara had made since she was a kid. She yanked a wire whisk from the rack above and proceeded to beat the eggs into a frothy mix.

"I'm sorry." Morgan's voice startled Tara. She dropped the whisk, and the metal handle flipped over the bowl's rim to skitter down the front of her pretty shirt.

She turned and stared—or was she glaring?—

at him. He took a step back. Glare, she'd bet. Looking away, she tried to control her features.

"Sorry," he repeated. "Again." He stepped toward her, close, warm and smelling of the coffee he'd been sipping, the faint scent of the damp morning and something else. Something she didn't even try to identify. It was the smell of Morgan—a man who drove her crazy.

"It's fine." She grabbed a dish towel and mopped at the glop of egg on her shirt. At least it would wash out. The shirt wasn't ruined.

"No, it's not." He didn't go away. "I shouldn't have startled you. Among other things."

She fought the chagrined smile as she turned back to the eggs. *Focus*, she reminded herself, *focus*.

"Can I help?"

"Uh…no." She wasn't used to having anyone offer to help in the kitchen. Her staff, yes, but no one else. Not her brothers and certainly not customers. "Grab a chair from the office." She pointed to the open door, since the industrial kitchen wasn't normally a place people sat and there wasn't much other choice. "I don't mind the company."

Maybe he'd offer up that explanation he'd promised her. She refused to ask. He had to take the first steps here.

Morgan came back with her mother's chair, and she almost said something. It looked so small next to him. He spun it around, sat and stacked his big arms across the back. She should take a picture, except her phone was in her purse in the office.

The silence while she worked was uncomfortable. Did he notice it, too?

"I owe you an explanation," he said.

"Ya think?" She looked pointedly at him and he laughed.

"Yeah, I do. About more than just the trip to the urgent care." He paused as if thinking over what to say. "I left the other day and didn't even say goodbye, and I'm sorry for that."

"I appreciate that." She waited for him to continue. This was all on him.

"I went home." He paused. "Jack seems to have taken a liking to you."

"Really? He seems nice enough."

"Don't let him fool you. He's tough."

"That doesn't make him bad." Who were they really talking about here? Neither of them spoke for a long time.

"I did some things I should have done long before now." He paused, waiting until she looked over at him. "I saw my attorney." He waited for that to soak in. "He's going to file the divorce as contested. The authorities will be looking for Sylvie now. I won't much longer."

She frowned. "What do you mean, much longer?" This didn't sound good and the look on his face didn't help.

"My dad was an abusive asshole," he said without preamble. "He treated Jack and me like punching bags. As soon as I graduated, I got out and on the road. I knew I needed money and fast, so I drove dangerous loads for extra money and started bulking up." He took a deep breath before continuing. "I wanted to make sure he'd never hurt Jack or me again."

She wanted to stop him but knew this was what he needed to say, and she needed to hear it.

"I met people—" His eyes grew distant and pain-filled. "People who noticed, and I started fighting in back-alley matches. It was more money than I'd ever thought I'd make. It allowed me to get my brother out of Dad's house and put him through college."

Then she realized what he was telling her. She carefully set the bowl aside and stepped over to him. "That's what you did the other night? How you got hurt?" The bruises had faded, but they were far from gone.

"Not exactly. I went there, yes." He shot to his feet as if he couldn't sit any longer. He paced the length of the pastry table, then turned to face her. "That's how Sylvie and I originally met. At those fights. I heard of one here and I went to see if I could find her."

"And did you?"

"Yeah?" His answer was more question than affirmation. He paced again. "I found her, but a guy called Bull got between her and me." He flinched and rubbed his jaw with his hand as if it still hurt. "He's a mean one. I've beat him before, but that was a long time ago."

"You can't go back there," she said, moving closer to him, knowing full well that's what he intended. "I—" How could she tell him she wouldn't let him? She didn't control him. They barely had a friendship.

"I am going back, Tara." He stopped just inches away from her and put his hands on her shoulders. "That's part of why I'm telling you this. I'm scheduled to fight tomorrow night."

"No!"

"I'm committed. And before you get all upset, I'm not just going in there to find her. Another person I saw at home was a high school buddy of mine who's a cop." He laughed like that was a big joke.

"What did he say? He told you not to do it, right?"

"Not exactly. We talked, that's all. I know I can't continue fighting. Besides not wanting to, it's only a matter of time before the cops find out. I can't afford a record. But for now—" He shrugged. "It's my only choice."

Jack's words echoed in her mind. *Talk him out of it.* Morgan would think she was crazy if she laughed aloud instead of just inside her head. Yeah, it sounded so easy. Not. She put the finished batter into the cake pan, then wiped her hands on the towel at her waist.

Morgan headed toward the door. She reached out, grabbing the loose fabric of his shirtsleeve, then moved her hand to curl around his arm. The splint was gone, and she couldn't help but wonder if it was really healed. Remembering how he'd looked after that last fight made her shiver.

"Don't go," she whispered, then cleared her throat and reiterated, "Stay here."

He looked at her hand, then into her eyes. "I'm not going to change my mind." But he didn't pull away.

She stared at his throat, where there was no visual evidence of that long-ago injury. The rasp in his voice that Jack had mentioned stood out now. Why hadn't she noticed it before? She'd never admit it to Jack, or even to Morgan himself, but that growl was part of what made him so appealing, part of what sent shivers up and down her spine.

What else was damaged inside him?

"I—I know." She took a tiny step closer to him. "I mean now. Tonight. Stay here. With me."

Maybe she'd come up with something to convince him it was too dangerous or show him that the fight wasn't worth the risk.

"Don't try to distract me." He smiled despite the warning in his voice. "You're not going to change my mind."

"Doesn't mean I can't enjoy trying."

He laughed and swept her into a loose embrace. "Oh, baby...I thought you'd never ask."

She considered that progress. For now.

WHAT WAS THAT god-awful buzzing sound? It took what seemed like forever for Tara's brain to click into place and figure out that it was her alarm clock.

It took even longer for her brain to realize the alarm was on the other side of the bed. And a very large, very sound-asleep body was between her and it. Of course, she didn't grasp those implications fully until she was reaching across Morgan, and while the clock had been silenced, the heat racing through her had not.

She wasn't wearing anything more than she had been when she'd fallen into sated sleep. Rough, warm hands engulfed her hips, holding her gently in place. There was no mistaking the hard, hot length beneath the covers, nor the answering thrum of her heartbeat.

"Do you usually get up in the middle of the night?" His hand slid up the curve of her bare back.

"Y-yes." He was distracting her. Delicious memories of how he'd kept her awake well past her bedtime flooded into her mind and washed over her body.

"Ah the joys of all-night diners." Morgan's lips

found the sensitive spot beneath her ear. "And all-night pharmacies." He reached toward the nightstand—again.

"How much time before you have to leave?" His lips found the side of her neck and she shivered as he tasted her.

"Probably not enough."

He flipped her onto her back and settled the heaviness of his erection at the juncture of her thighs. "There's always time enough." His lips came down on hers, hard and insistent. She responded in kind, curling her fingers into his shoulders and holding on tight as he thrust quick and hard inside her.

He felt so good, and she didn't remember ever coming awake so fast. But she was wide awake now, her body wanting more, wanting all of his.

And he wasn't holding anything back. The strength she admired in him nearly overwhelmed her. His shoulders, wide and strong, made her feel small and yet protected. The muscles of his arms, so large and solid, made her feel weak and yet not, more like he acknowledged he could and should share his strength with her.

"Come with me," he growled in her ear and the pleading command was enough to push her over the edge.

"Morgan!" His name tore from her lips and shattered in the air around them as she shattered around him. He trembled in her arms, collapsing on top of her as he struggled to catch his breath.

"Morgan," she whispered his name, tasting it just an instant before he kissed her long and sweet.

He didn't let her go, instead turning over and pulling her with him and into his arms, snuggling her head in the crook of his shoulder.

Time ticked by, but she stayed there waiting for the snooze to go off. She didn't want to leave him.

She needed to get up, but questions spun around in her head. Was he expecting to stay here? Why hadn't they figured this out? She blushed. Like any of this was planned?

Then she remembered tonight. All the heat left the room and she shivered.

"You're thinking again."

"No, I'm—" She was lying.

"I can fix that." Morgan rolled her over again, and he was right. She stopped thinking.

JACK SAT IN the back booth of Tara's diner. The whole crew rushed around, refilling coffee cups, carrying out big trays full of meals, laughing, smiling and collecting payment. It was a beautiful insanity that intrigued him.

He normally spent his day in an office staring at a computer screen. He had very little interaction that wasn't through the computer or briefly with one of the drivers who dropped in. This place intrigued him like nothing else ever had.

Wendy came over, her order pad ready. "Oh," she said and smiled. "It's you. How's it goin'? Jack, right?"

"Yeah."

"I have your change from the other day." She fished in her apron pocket.

"Oh, no, keep it." He waved her actions away. "You earned it."

Silence stretched out as he racked his brain for something else to say, something intelligent or witty. Something that would make sense, that would impress her. He drew a blank.

"So, uh, can I get you something?" She finally broke the silence.

"Uh, yeah. Coffee. And uh—" He fumbled with the big laminated menu. "A sandwich. Corned beef on rye. Yeah. That sounds good." It was the first one he saw. He'd looked at this menu dozens of times, but he couldn't even read the danged thing right now.

"Sure." She frowned but wrote his order down anyway. "Fries with that?"

"Yeah."

"That'll be right up." She turned and started to walk away.

"Wait." He leaned over, hoping something brilliant would come to mind. "You, uh, forgot the menu." He mentally rolled his eyes.

"Oh, we leave them back here." She took the menu and leaned all the way over the table and tucked it behind the metal napkin dispenser. Pausing, she turned her head toward him, meeting his gaze, the upper part of her body stretched out across the entire length of the table. "Like that," she whispered.

Jack's mouth went totally dry. Words, thoughts, sanity failed him. He could only stare.

Wendy straightened and brushed against his arm in the same instant. Jack snatched his hand back as if she were a flame. Which she was. And he was the flippin' moth.

Wendy sauntered away, her hips swaying slowly, gently, teasing. He could only stare after her.

WENDY HUSTLED THROUGH the diner's double doors to the kitchen, making sure the blasted thing didn't smack her in the backside like it did about half the time. Tara was always telling her to slow down going through them. She had to keep reminding herself.

"Who's your friend?" Kaitlyn leaned against the counter, texting with someone, probably her dork of a boyfriend.

"No one."

Wendy busied herself setting up the tray for Jack's meal. She was not in the mood to talk to anyone, least of all Kaitlyn, who was proving to be a real pain to work with.

What was wrong with her? Wendy was a good girl, but he'd looked at her so befuddled and tongue-tied, she'd had to shake him out of it. When his gaze had met hers, as she'd stretched out there on the table…

She hadn't wanted to look away. She hadn't wanted to move away. She'd wanted him to move closer.

Suddenly, the ketchup bottle slipped from her fingers, smacking the edge of the tray and popping open when it hit the tile floor. The pool of red goo spread at her feet, splotches landing on her neat, nearly-white shoes. "Dang it!"

Kaitlyn giggled and moved farther down the counter, focusing on her phone as if the giggle hadn't told Wendy she'd seen. The girl wouldn't help clean up anything—why would she help with this?

Hastily, Wendy grabbed the mop and cleaned the spill. She'd just finished scrubbing the last of the splotches from her shoes when Wade called, "Order up," through the pass-through.

Kaitlyn hadn't moved. Which meant there would probably be diners out in the dining room waiting for refills and services. With a sigh, Wendy hefted the tray with Jack's order up on her shoulder and headed through the door.

Why was she disappointed that she might have

to wait on other customers? Why was she even surprised that the lazy girl was leaving her with all the work? She headed to Jack's table.

He was staring at his phone but hastily put it down when she approached. She smiled warmly, hoping to hide her mortification at her earlier behavior. "Here you go," she said too brightly.

"Oh, great." He pushed his phone across the table toward the napkin holder.

Wendy's cheeks warmed with the blush at the reminder of how she'd slid across that table as easily as the phone. She settled the plate in front of him, filling his water glass and setting the carafe down where he could reach it. "Can I get you anything else?" She leaned back, crossing her arms over the empty tray.

"Uh, no. This is great." He looked at her then, and she couldn't look away. "You, uh, have…" Jack reached out and ran a finger down the length of her arm. "Ketchup," he said on a soft growl.

Heat ran up her arm, sizzling into her brain. *Breathe*, she reminded herself as she took a step back. *Breathe.* "I had a little accident." She lifted her arm and saw the trail his fingertip had left in the smear. A white napkin appeared in her peripheral vision as he handed her one.

When she stood there, frozen, he wiped off her arm for her. She couldn't stop watching him, watching his big hand move over her skin. Her mind went blank and she stepped back another

step. "Thanks," she whispered, then turned
around before she made an even bigger fool of
herself, not to mention shocking all the other diners.

She glanced over her shoulder as she turned
tail and ran. He was watching her and the heat
in his eyes made the big kitchen seem practically arctic.

What was wrong with her?

With him?

She looked down at her ketchup-stained shoes,
at the rumpled uniform, knowing her hair was
limp and hanging loose. Looking up, she saw her
distorted reflection in the metal door's surface. It
only made her look worse. Made her feel worse.

The door swung open, that loud whumping
sound startling her, making her jump. She tried
to pull herself together. She looked up and found
Jack standing there.

"Did you—uh, need something?" She tried to
keep her voice from wobbling.

He looked as uncomfortable as she felt. "Uh,
yeah." He swallowed and tried again. "Maybe
some ketchup?" He pointedly looked at her arm
and smiled.

Their eyes met and she couldn't look away.
He moved closer. Slowly. Suddenly, he was just
inches away, so close she could see the tiny lines
around his eyes and the thick lashes that framed
the dark blue.

"I'll bring it out."

"That's okay. There's some here." He leaned in and she knew there wasn't a single drop on her face. "Right. Here."

His kiss was short and sweet. Then he left her there, speechless and staring after him when he returned to the dining room.

Oh. My. She didn't move. She couldn't. *Oh. My,* she repeated to herself another half dozen times before she could think straight again. What the—

She stalked through the doors, hearing them swing back and forth a dozen times. She didn't stop until she reached the table again. "What was that for?"

CHAPTER THIRTEEN

Not wanting to lose the glow of the time she'd spent with him, Tara drove to the diner in silence. Morgan sat in the passenger seat, looking rested, gorgeous and entirely too big to fit in her Jeep's close space. She parked near Morgan's truck, as images of what lay ahead flashed in her mind. Jack had called earlier with a load for him, and Morgan planned to take it.

"I know what he's doing," Morgan had told her at her apartment. "I can get the load and make it back in plenty of time for the match."

Her heart sank, wishing Jack had found him a load that took him to someplace like Alabama or something. Of course, he wouldn't have taken it, but still, she wished.

"He doesn't realize how late the fight is." He grinned. "I'm not educating him."

Her grip tightened on the steering wheel. "Don't do this," she whispered. The idea that he'd be hurt as bad as or worse than before suddenly felt like a weight in her chest. It scared her.

"Don't what?" He leaned in close. "Leave?"

He was teasing, still caught up in the now, not the future.

His lips were so close. She almost leaned in to kiss him, to distract herself from her thoughts. "No." She swallowed. "Fight." She faced him. "There has to be another way. Please."

Morgan pulled back as if she'd slapped him. "Don't ask me that." His hand curled around the door handle. "I've spent a year looking for her. Taking the safe route won't get Brooke back. I've tried that." He shoved open the door. "Go to work, Tara. Don't worry about me."

"How do I not worry?" She glared at him. "What if you're hurt so bad you can't take care of your daughter?" Breathing was a challenge as her anger grew. "What if—"

"Stop it, Tara. I may get banged up, but have faith in me. I've won plenty of these fights."

"Winning doesn't mean you don't get hurt."

He took a deep breath and she held hers, hoping he was at least considering it. The hard glare he turned on her deflated all that hope. "Go to work, Tara. I'll be fine."

The passenger door closed with a wham, and Tara climbed out, as well. She pulled open the back door of the diner as the big engine roared to life. Her heart sank.

Would she find him at the back door again tonight? Would they take another trip to the urgent care, or worse yet, the ER? She couldn't think about it. Couldn't let herself worry for an entire day.

Maybe she should just call the police herself. And tell them what? She had no clue where the fights were going to be. She didn't know anything except rumor, really. All she'd accomplish would be to, most likely, get Morgan arrested and ruin any chances he had at finding Sylvie and Brooke.

And Tara would probably lose him.

But maybe it would be worth it if it kept him alive and in one, uninjured piece.

The diner was nearly full, and her staff hustled to and from the kitchen. She had to focus on that, had to remind herself once again that *this* was her life, her livelihood, her dream.

She was surprised, however, to walk into the dining room and find her sisters sitting in a booth. Little Lucas was nestled in his carrier on one of the toddler seats. Seeing their smiling faces brightened up the otherwise gloomy day.

"What are you guys doing here?"

Addie looked at Mandy. "Why wouldn't we be here?" She winked. "This is the best restaurant in town."

"Thanks." Tara smirked. "But I think you're a bit biased."

"She's telling the truth." Mandy waved at the plate in front of her. "This is like visiting Mom."

"You were able to use the recipe cards." Addie grinned. "I'm pleased."

"Some of them. Others don't transfer as well, but I'm still working on them." Tara hadn't had much time lately to work on any new items for the menu.

Mandy took a bite of the French toast. "Keep working. Need any help with taste testing?" She laughed. They all did.

It felt good to be with her family where she understood them, and on the whole, they tried to understand her.

"There's one recipe I'd like to add to the collection," Tara hinted, settling on the edge of the booth next to Addie.

"That's not open for discussion, Tara." Addie's smile faded and Tara regretted taking it away, but having Addie's amazing cookies here would be good for business. It would pay homage not only to Mom but their entire family.

"I know. And I understand. Really. I just love those cookies, and I know my customers would love them as much."

"Maybe Addie could make the cookies for you. Then you don't have to give up your recipe." Mandy suggested.

"Oh, Addie, would you?" Tara's heart leaped. For the first time in days, something besides Morgan and the frustrations of him took the forefront in her mind.

"I'll think about it." Addie actually looked like she was considering the idea.

Tara threw her arms around her. "I'd love you forever if you did." She pulled a line from when she'd been the baby of the house and wanted something badly. It had worked then, and she hoped it worked now.

And just like when she'd been a kid, Addie slipped an arm around her. It felt so good. She wanted so badly to confide in them, wanted to talk to her sisters like she had over the years. They'd always been there for her, and she knew they'd be there for her now, but she didn't know what to say or even how to explain.

She didn't understand what was happening in her world.

"What's the matter?" Addie hugged her, running a hand over Tara's hair much like Mom used to do.

With a deep sigh, Tara pulled slowly away. "Maybe I'm just tired. It's a good tired. Business is good."

"You sure that's all?" Addie knew her too well. Tara had never successfully lied to her.

"I—" She shrugged, then nodded. The look on Addie's face said she wasn't buying it.

"You know we're here for you," Addie said.

"Yeah, I was kidding about the taste testing, but I'm not kidding about helping. I'm happy to pitch in like I did when we had the fires," Mandy offered.

She loved her sisters. "Thanks. The staff is

awesome. It's—well—" Looking around, hoping for some type of distraction, she was surprised to see Jack Thane finishing his lunch. She'd thought he'd called Morgan from Dallas.

He saw her and came over. "Hey, Tara." He glanced around, probably looking for Morgan.

"Hi, Jack. What are you doing here?" She stood, wanting to move away from the too-interested glances of her sisters.

"Did you talk to him?" Jack asked after introductions were complete.

Tara blushed. She'd more than talked with Morgan. Both her sisters stared at her, Addie's eyebrows lifting in curiosity. Tara took Jack's arm and thought about dragging him away, but her sisters would just grill her when he left. "Yeah."

"Did you convince him to give up on the fight?"

"I tried." She took a deep breath. "He knew what I was trying to do. He's not going to back out."

"Damn it."

"Did he tell you that he talked to someone named Mitch?"

"The cop?"

"Yeah."

"No, he didn't say anything. What's Mitch going to do?"

"I don't know." She hoped her despair didn't show. "What can he do?"

"I'll call him to see what I can find out."

"Will you let me know?"

"If I find out anything, yeah." Jack fell silent for a moment. "Thanks for at least trying, Tara. If he survives, he'll be lucky to have you."

"Thanks. I don't think he'd agree with you."

Jack laughed but didn't argue with her. "Nice to meet you all." He spoke to her sisters, then headed to the door.

Tara turned to find three sets of eyes staring at her. Wendy's were the only ones with any comprehension in them.

"What?"

"I think you need to explain what's going on." Addie spoke in that adult-talking-to-a-kid voice she'd used growing up—the same one she probably used with her students.

"Yeah." Mandy nodded. "Who's Jack?"

Wendy's mouth opened as if she intended to explain.

"Don't say a word," Tara told her. "This isn't any of their business. It's not even ours." She didn't want her sisters involved with this mess any more than she liked her staff being a part of it.

"Oh, now you definitely better start explaining." Addie's voice grew stern.

"I have work to do." Tara stood. "And so do you." She looked pointedly at Wendy.

"Yeah. Nice seeing you ladies again." Wendy

forced a smile and walked away, gathering up dirty dishes at a nearby table before heading to the kitchen.

The diner was filled with noise, but the silence at the table was thick. Tara knew she'd not only upset Addie, but Mandy's look of disappointment said she'd hurt her feelings, as well.

"It's not that I don't want to tell you," she began, only to be interrupted—saved—when Wendy came to their table. She had the diner's phone in her hand.

"It's for you," she said before stomping away.

Great. "Someday Café. This is Tara, how can I help you?"

"Ah, babe, the list is long." Morgan's deep, rough voice slid over her every nerve. Belatedly she realized she was blushing—again—and her sisters were staring. "Oh, uh, hello."

"I'm guessing you're not alone. Who's there with you?"

"My sisters."

"Ouch. Still mad at me?"

"Yes." She turned away, from her sisters' intent stares. "Unless you've changed your mind." His silence only made it worse. "Do you need something?"

"No. Just wanted to see if you're okay."

"No, I'm not okay." But she couldn't let the harsh words linger between them. "Be careful," she said softly. Her worry didn't take away her feelings for him. All her fears that her sisters had distracted her from came back in full force. "Please."

He was silent a long time. "I always am. Trust me, Tara. I do."

She didn't let herself think about that reference too much. He'd taken precautions with her that she'd have tossed to the wind. He'd stepped in to help her without thinking twice. He'd taken care of Jack for so long, and he was driving himself into exhaustion to save his daughter from a horrible situation.

He was exactly what Jack had called him. A very good man.

And she'd fallen in love with him. Head over heels, no-holds-barred in love with him.

Wide-eyed, Tara looked over at her big sister Addie, and after Morgan hung up, she sank to the bench beside her. Addie enveloped her in a warm reassuring hug and didn't even ask why.

A STEADY STREAM of diners kept Tara's worry at bay and her just busy enough to fill her mind with orders and inane conversation for the rest of the shift. She put together the list for next week's groceries and even had time to work the line, putting together some plates. She didn't often get that opportunity anymore.

Work filled her mind so that she wasn't thinking about Morgan. At least that's what she kept telling herself. Still, *where was he now? What was he doing?* looped when she wasn't focused.

She grabbed two plates of pie for the party at table eleven. Coffee. They'd both ordered coffee. She'd just reached for the creamer when the door opened. She automatically looked, reprimanding herself. It wouldn't be Morgan.

When her brother DJ came in, she smiled. "I'll be right back." She delivered the plates, then hustled to where he sat. "Tammie still having problems? Pie or a burger?" She knew she was rushing to talk, wanting something to distract herself.

"Tammie's not the problem." He wasn't smiling.

"Then why are you here?" He crossed his arms over his chest. *Uh-oh.* "What happened?"

"Oh, nothing's happened—yet."

"What do you mean?"

"Damn it, Tara." He leaned forward. "Imagine my surprise when I go to my older sister's house to help her move some furniture, and she tells me you're seeing some guy named Morgan."

Tara's smile faded. She should have known there were no secrets in this family. "And?" She leaned against the counter, waiting for the usual lecture.

When he didn't immediately start in on her, she was surprised. "I'm waiting, DJ. Go ahead, give me hell." With a huff, she gathered dishes and prepared to ignore him.

"Morgan Thane?"

That made her stop. She turned around, hands full of plates. "How did you know?"

He cursed again, this time getting a dirty look from the older couple at table four.

"He is not someone you should be involved with."

"And you know this how?"

DJ ran a hand through his hair. "He's involved in things you don't know about."

Tara rolled her eyes. "If you mean the fighting, I know." She walked to the counter. "The question I have is, how do you know about it?"

"Well…"

She set the plates down before she either dropped them or threw them at him. "You better tell me, brother dear."

This time, DJ was the one who rolled his eyes. "It's not that big a secret." He threw up his hands. "There's been talk around town about an underground fight. It's not that odd. The hands go to 'em sometimes." He was referring to the men who worked on Wyatt's ranch. "I've been to a couple over the years. They're pretty rough."

"You know about them? How come I've never heard about it before?"

DJ shrugged. "We always knew about them,

even when we were kids. Maybe because you were a girl?"

"Does Addie know?"

"You'll have to ask her."

Then a thought crossed her mind. "Do you know where they are?" She came around the counter, grabbing his arm. "Do you know where this one is?"

"Oh, no." DJ shook his head. "I see those wheels turning in your head. No. That's no place for you."

"That's not your choice."

He cursed again.

She'd seen the results of those fights on Morgan's face. "DJ, I'm not a kid. I know you and the others all think of me as your little sister. But look at this place." She lifted her hands. "A kid can't do this. A kid doesn't work this damned hard."

"Come on, Tara."

"No. You don't get to walk in here and try to play big brother and not…and not do something for me."

Morgan had refused to discuss the fights or anything to do with them. Last night, all her brilliant plans to distract him had backfired, and he'd spent the night distracting her. It had been glorious and wonderful, and she hadn't wanted it to end.

Today's realization only made it worse and increased her urgency. "I've tried to talk him out of it," she said. Then she considered and did something she didn't think Morgan would be very pleased about.

She told DJ everything—well, everything except the private parts. That would *not* convince DJ to help her.

"What makes you think he's going to listen to you?" DJ finally asked.

He wasn't. That was the problem. She and Jack had already tried all that. "He won't. But if we can find Sylvie, then he won't have to fight."

"I don't know if that's true. Those crowds get rowdy. They won't like it if he backs out."

"We have to try."

DJ cursed again. Table four was probably never coming back. She couldn't care right now.

"On one condition…"

"Oh, thank you!" Tara threw her arms around DJ's neck. "Thank you."

"You haven't heard this condition."

"I don't care. Anything."

"I'm calling Wyatt."

"Okay, that's not what I wanted to hear." She didn't like the idea of Wyatt's disapproval. Even now, she saw that look he and Addie had shared in the kitchen when she'd told them about buying this place. "Do we have to?"

"Yeah. He'll make sure some of the boys are there. I am not letting you go by yourself, and I'm not stupid enough to even consider going there without them."

"All right." She reluctantly gave in, just as she knew he expected. "Here." She handed him the handset of the diner's phone. She had no idea where her cell phone was—again.

"Uh—" He held up his cell phone. "I got my own." He hit Speed Dial, and they both waited for Wyatt to answer.

THE NIGHT SKY shone with stars, and the remnants of a fading moon lit the landscape. It was the first clear night Tara could remember in weeks. The shadowed outline of the steel-frame building stood dark against the fading light.

Wyatt's voice came out of the darkness behind them. "If Pal Haymaker weren't already dead, I'd think this was his doing."

Tara shivered at the memory of the old rancher who'd always been a thorn in her family's side. He'd nearly destroyed the entire county, and had managed to ruin his own family with his greed, last year. People were still trying to recover from that devestating fire.

DJ was ahead and Tara knew her brothers and the other hands from the ranch had surrounded her. They'd watched too many old Westerns.

"I think we are actually on Haymaker property," DJ said.

"Great." Wyatt was not happy about that. She could hear it in his voice.

She'd been to dozens of events around the county, and this felt like most of them. Cowboys and their pickups filled the field around the building. She could see the lit end of cigarettes, but otherwise, moonlight was all they had to guide them.

The ground beneath their feet was damp and squishy, but the thick grasses made it not quite a total mess.

There weren't any windows in the building—she had no idea where they were going. But DJ and Wyatt seemed to know.

As they walked, the thick grasses scraped against her jeans, and the men mumbled quietly to each other. If she didn't know better, this would be like going to any of the country dances or rodeos that happened here each summer.

She had an awful lot of questions for both Wyatt and DJ once this was all over with. But that would have to wait.

Then she saw him. She hadn't expected Morgan to be out here. She wasn't sure what she'd expected, but there he was.

Morgan stood staring at the building. Tara couldn't help but stare at him. The shadows accentuated the breadth of his shoulders. He didn't move, and she wondered what was going through his mind. Did she really want to know?

Unable to speak, she took a couple steps toward him. Gravel crackled beneath her feet. His head whipped around, and she felt rather than saw the glare that shot through her.

"What are you doing here, Tara?"

"Following you." She was in for it. No holding back now.

"Go home, Tara." He walked away from her, a purpose in his step. "You don't belong here."

"And you do?" She crossed her arms, as much to keep from reaching out for him as to look stronger.

"That's what we keep trying to tell her." DJ stepped forward.

"And you are?" Morgan glared at him.

That was not going to help, and she hurried to explain. "These are my brothers. DJ and Wyatt. And some of Wyatt's employees."

No one shook hands, no one even moved, except maybe to breathe but she wasn't totally sure about that.

"I'm sure there's room inside." Morgan lifted an arm toward the door. "If that's why you're here. Otherwise, if you'll excuse me, I have a match." He started walking.

She should have known he wouldn't stop for her. He just kept walking, his steps loud against the gravel. She hurried to get into step beside him and heard the others close behind.

As they drew closer to the metal barn, she

heard the sounds of loud voices. Cheers and whistles broke through the night.

"Go. Home. Tara." Morgan stopped at a metal fire door, his hand on the knob. "Do me a favor, gentlemen. Take her home."

Tara crossed her arms. "Nope. Not going without you."

"Oh, we've tried," DJ said.

Morgan glared at her. She glared back. "Why are you doing this?" she asked.

"You know why."

"No, I don't. Not this time. Is she here?"

"I don't know—yet."

Suddenly, the door flew open and two men stumbled out. Tara squealed as they nearly landed on her and she jumped back.

"Fine." Morgan's hand clamped around her wrist, and with little effort, he pulled her to his side. "Stay with me. Don't even think about going anywhere, you got it?"

She nodded.

Morgan turned to the crowd of men behind her. "At least try to blend in."

Inside, the door slammed with a vibration she doubted anyone heard. The noise level inside was deafening, with voices bouncing off all four metal walls.

Down a flight of stairs, where a group of big rigs were parked, a crowd of people gathered around a circle of dirt. Mostly men, though she did see a few women scattered around. Morgan ignored her except to drag her with him as he made his way down the steps.

A voice came out of the dark. "Hey, Dewey. You sure about this?" A big hulk of a man separated himself from the crowd. He looked the way she expected a brawler to look. Big, rough, with shoulders that made Morgan's seem small. She felt miniature.

"I'm sure." A scraggly looking man grinned. He had his hands full of money, the bills nestled in between his fingers as if he were trying to keep each pile separate. "You just wait and see, Will. Just you wait and see. Welcome back, Thane."

Morgan grunted. "Let's just get this done." He barely moved his mouth, his jaw was clenched tight. "Or you just gonna stand there and yammer?"

"No, man." The man with the money grinned. "Let's get down to business." He led the way through the crowd, which parted as Morgan followed.

What was she supposed to do? The crowd closed in on her, and the scent of dust and other undefinable odors, not so pleasant, engulfed her. Where were her brothers? She looked back. They were close, but the crowd swarmed around them.

The vise of Morgan's hand was all that kept her from being swept away, as well. She hurried to keep up.

The open path behind them vanished. Engulfing her. Pushing her toward the wide-open dirt ring.

When Morgan stopped, she nearly plowed into his back, catching her breath as she caught herself, her hand against his broad, muscular spine. Heat seeped into her palm, and she yanked her hand back. He didn't even notice.

The thin man whose fists were full of money stepped into the circle. Morgan stayed put. He let go of her hand and a shiver of fear slid through her. Without his anchor, she'd be swept away. As if sensing her fear, Morgan turned to face her. "Stay with them. You hear me?"

She turned to find Wyatt and DJ standing just inches behind her. She nodded, realizing what they'd all meant trying to warn her away from this.

Morgan stepped away, but the crowd didn't follow him like before. He stood there, flexing, clenching his hands at his sides. The muscles of his arms bunched beneath his suntanned skin.

"You're in for a treat tonight, folks," the man in the center of the circle cried above the crowd. "He's back. Morgan Thane. And he's aching to bring on the pain."

Morgan's jaw twitched, but that was all the reaction Tara saw to the man's words. She gulped. Was this for real?

Across the circle, another man stepped out of

the crowd. "Yeah?" His fists at his sides. "You think you can beat me?"

"He sure as shootin' can, Kenny," Dewey cried with a hoot of laughter. "Care to put your money where your mouth is?"

"This ain't no toothpaste commercial, Dewey." The man leaned in close, breathing into the smaller man's face. "Let's get down to business."

Morgan turned his gaze to the money man, and, with a knowing glare, jerked his chin toward Tara. Dewey turned and met her wide-eyed stare. He nodded and moved to stand right in front of her. She had to shift to the side to see.

Where a normal boxing ring had a bell, this place had an air horn. Tara slammed her hands over her ears as the sound cut through her brain. She dropped her hands as the two men shifted toward each other.

Morgan was moving around slowly, prowling the clearing, never taking his intense gaze from the big man before him. Her heartbeat pounded hard. She realized she wasn't breathing and forced her lungs to expand. She couldn't afford to do anything stupid like pass out. She'd be trampled under the crowd's stomping feet.

The big bruiser of a man took the first swing, his fist hitting nothing but air.

CHAPTER FOURTEEN

MORGAN KNEW HE was going to win. Not that the fight was rigged—something common in the illegal rings—but because he'd done his homework. He'd pumped Dewey for information and learned Kenny's weaknesses. Kenny had gotten old and too comfortable in his prowess. He banked on new guys being too afraid of him. And it often worked.

Morgan knew better.

He also knew that he had to focus on the fight or get the shit beat out of him again, which meant he couldn't scan the crowd to search for Sylvie. Instead, he cut a deal with Dewey.

Dewey didn't care how he got his money, as long as he got it. Morgan had sweetened the pot for the greedy bastard. If Dewey found Sylvie before Morgan did, there was a big fat reward in it.

Dewey knew where Sylvie was, Morgan was sure of it. He'd hinted that he'd tell Morgan for the cost of a fight. Morgan had agreed. He'd have agreed to just about anything for that information.

Morgan should have thought of that idea months ago.

Still, when Kenny's fist connected for the first time, Morgan cursed. It still hurt like hell, but the pain gave his anger focus. Yeah, he was gonna win.

And he was going to find Sylvie. He'd known her too long. While she'd changed, she hadn't changed that much. She couldn't stand not having his full attention. He just had to wait for her to show herself. And act like he wasn't looking for her, pretend he was ignoring her. That'd trip her up.

So with Dewey on the lookout for Sylvie, Morgan focused on putting Kenny on his ass in the dirt.

Blood stained Morgan's knuckles. His? Or from Kenny's nose? It looked a bit more crooked than before.

The mountain of a man was going to have a nasty shiner in the morning. Still, Morgan wasn't off the hook, either. His hand needed a bucket of ice. It stung. As did his jaw.

"That all you got, Thane?" Kenny growled, prowling around Morgan with his fists raised. Morgan's focus honed in on the guy's shoulders, looking for him to telegraph his next move.

"Not even." Morgan laughed, though not in humor. "Your age is showing, old man."

Kenny swung and Morgan managed to duck. But Kenny's efforts weren't a total waste. His other fist plowed into Morgan's ribs, shoving the air out of his lungs. Morgan jerked back, sucking in air, trying to save his equilibrium. And stave off the pain. He moved slowly away. Shaking his head, he kept his eyes on Kenny. Looking away would be the end of it all.

So MUCH FOR good intentions. Tara tried to watch the fight, but after Morgan's first swing, she was behind DJ, hiding her face in her brother's shoulder. She consoled herself that at least she hadn't buried her face in her hands like a total wimp. DJ's broad shoulders served as a block just fine.

She'd seen her brothers get into it as kids, and a few fights in bars, but she'd never seen anything like this.

It didn't help that DJ's muscles bunched and moved as if he was out there, swinging punches himself. The men from the ranch cried out encouragement and punched the air around them.

She couldn't. She just couldn't.

This was harsh and just plain cruel. How could Morgan hit someone with his bare fists, intending to hurt them? How could anyone tolerate that much pain, knowing it was coming?

"You want to leave?" DJ asked over his shoulder.

"No." She might not be able to watch, but she was here for a reason and she wasn't backing down from that. She didn't have to *watch* the fight.

But listening became almost worse. The crowd

was really into it, but even over their yelling, she heard the footfalls of Morgan and his opponent, heard the sickening sound of knuckles against skin. She shivered despite the heat of all the packed-in bodies.

Tentatively, she looked up. Morgan's back was to her, so she couldn't see how badly he was hurt. He stood straight and tall and moved easily, so seemingly not bad. The other guy hulked around the ring and seemed to avoid Morgan rather than come at him.

Finally, time must have run out and the air horn sounded once again. Had he won? Was it over? Tara took a step away from DJ, hoping to get out of here and know Morgan wasn't at risk anymore.

But the men simply stepped back, opposite each other, taking deep breaths. It was only a break. Tara took her own deep breaths as she looked at Morgan.

There was a nasty cut above his eye from where blood dripped down the side of his face. Another dribble of red pooled at the corner of his lip. Just then, he reached up and wiped it with the back of his big, red-knuckled hand. She tore her gaze away.

"There's three rounds," DJ explained. Tara's heart sank and she swallowed hard to release the pressure in her chest. Only a third of the way through?

Morgan didn't look at her. He didn't look

around at all, simply stared at the man across from him—intense and watchful.

"What's happening? Why aren't they taking a break?"

"They're both making sure the other one doesn't pull anything," DJ explained.

"Like what?"

"Like cheating."

Just then, a pair of hands hit the center of Tara's back, right between her shoulder blades, hard. She stumbled forward with a loud cry of surprise. She hit DJ's solid shoulder before nearly falling on her face in the dirt. She barely caught herself at the last second.

"What the—" She turned to stare at the spot where she'd been standing, where Wyatt had hold of a woman's arm. The woman was struggling hard to get away, but Wyatt was stronger than her.

Tara stared. *Sylvie.*

Morgan wasn't far away. He hadn't moved, but his focus was definitely still on the fight. Then, as if shaking out of the trance, he glanced over at the commotion just outside the ring.

"Sylvie!" He turned toward them. The big man he'd been fighting took that as a cue to move, and Tara barely scampered out of the way as he swung at Morgan.

Morgan easily shoved the man aside. But instead of coming over to her, Morgan headed toward Sylvie. The crowd followed, and Tara was soon engulfed by onlookers. She didn't have any choice but to move. It was that or be trampled.

Somewhere in the distance, buried in all the noise, she heard Dewey trying to get people's attention. He even tried blasting the air horn a couple times, but they weren't interested.

DJ appeared out of the crowd, with Wyatt and several of the other ranch hands. DJ took Tara's arm, guiding her toward the door.

"Where are we going?" Where was Morgan? What was going on?

"We're getting out of here. Now." Wyatt led the way.

"Not until I find out what's going on."

DJ didn't let go of her arm, but he stopped. "He's in that mess—with her." He pointed back the way they'd come with his free hand. "He's not thinking about you and certainly not headed this way."

That hurt. But she had to find out what was happening. She pulled loose of DJ's grip and moved only a few steps before she saw them. Morgan was easily a head taller than the rest of the crowd. DJ was right. He was headed in the other direction. She took a few steps toward him, planning to follow and talk with him.

Then she saw what else he was doing. His arm was around Sylvie. He was holding on to her, guiding her through the crowd to a completely different exit.

Blue lights suddenly flashed through the open door across the building and the cracks between the boards.

"Come on," DJ yelled, grabbing her arm again. Morgan didn't look around, didn't even look back to see where Tara might be. All too soon, she was out the door and Morgan had vanished into the night.

With Sylvie.

"LET GO." Tara pulled her arm loose from DJ's grip again. It wasn't that he was hurting her. She just needed space between herself and anyone else.

"Hey, no problem." DJ stepped back, lifting his hands away.

They reached Wyatt's truck, which they'd parked on the other side of the field from the barn. Wyatt hadn't wanted Haymaker's crew to see his truck on their land. Now they didn't have to fight crowds to get out, and the whole appearance of the police wasn't a problem.

The flash of the blue lights faded as they disappeared behind the ridge, leaving only faint moonlight to light the way. She looked up, seeing clouds moving in again.

Perfect. The rain fit her mood right now.

Wyatt climbed in and started the pickup's engine. The ranch hands climbed into the truck bed as easily as they would a car. Tara sat between her brothers as they headed toward town. No one spoke.

Finally, Wyatt pulled up in front of her apartment. "We'll talk tomorrow." He looked pointedly at her.

"No, we won't," she said defiantly. "I'm not talking about this to you. Not to any of you."

"Tara—" DJ said.

"I'm not kidding." She stepped away from the vehicle. "Thanks for taking me. Now go home to your wives. Get some sleep and forget tonight happened." That's what she would do her best to do.

Right after she let herself dissolve into a bucket of tears. Maybe a gallon or two of ice cream would help, too. She was halfway up the walk when her phone rang. She struggled to fish it out of her pocket. It was nearly 2:00 a.m. Who would call her this time of night? Morgan?

Cursing her own stupidity for getting her hopes up, she stared at the number on the screen. The diner? What the—

"Hello?"

"Tara!" Wade's voice was edgy. "We got a problem."

"What's the matter?" She turned around, seeing that her brothers and the crew were still at the curb.

"The creek's overflowing. We got water coming in the back door."

Glancing up, she saw the storm clouds dancing overhead. They led her gaze to the horizon where the cloud bank was dark and thick to the north. She cursed. That rain was coming from upstream and headed this way. "I'm on my way."

DJ rolled the window down. "What's the matter?"

"The diner. Wade says there's water from the creek coming in the back door."

"Hop in," Wyatt yelled. "We'll take care of you, Tara."

For the first time in a while, she wanted to hug her brothers. They'd done so much for her and were still doing more. "Thank you." She climbed into the truck.

But she still wasn't discussing Morgan with them.

MORGAN WASN'T LETTING Sylvie out of his sight. If he had to hold on to her like this for a week, he'd do it.

"Let me go," she screeched at him, trying to pull her arm away from his grasp.

"Oh, I don't think so." He had to clench his jaw to keep from saying all the things he wanted to say to her. "I'm not letting you go anywhere until we've settled this."

"There's nothing to settle."

"Oh, yes, there is." He dragged her across the

parking lot to Dewey's pickup. The man was nowhere to be seen, damn it.

And neither was Tara, for which he was thankful. Her brothers would get her out of here, keep her safe. The ranchers were good, solid men. The kind of men he could count on.

Not that he'd ever get that chance. He'd known instantly that they didn't think too highly of him.

Blue lights strobed through the night. He didn't have the time he'd hoped to deal with Sylvie. And he certainly wasn't letting the cops get her—he'd never see her again.

"Look," he pulled his soon-to-be-ex around to face him. "If you want to avoid the cops, then you'd better cooperate with me."

This close, even in the dim light, he saw the differences in her. Taking her chin in his abused hand, he tilted her face up to him. She wouldn't look into his eyes. "What are you on?"

"Nothin'." She pulled her chin from his grasp, briefly glancing angrily at him.

That glance was enough to show him the overbright sparkle in her eyes. She was high. Even high, it took her only an instant to decide he was the lesser of the evils. "Okay," she begrudgingly agreed.

He peered back at her, looking for some sign, some sliver of the girl he'd been attracted to not that long ago. Was she gone? Or just buried too deep to see? Had she ever really been there, or had his wishful thinking made it all up?

They'd had some good times. They'd brought Brooke into this world. Where was that girl?

She tried to pull away. "Come on." Morgan wove through the rows of cars, keeping his head down and heading toward the road. He wasn't going to walk on it, that would be too obvious, but he recalled a trail on the other side of those trees. Thank goodness he'd taken the time to learn the area on his runs.

The trail followed the creek that ran behind Tara's diner. He'd used it the last time he'd fought, coming to her door much more quickly than following the road.

He wasn't going to stop at Tara's diner, though. No, he intended to keep her out of this mess completely. He dragged Sylvie along with him, kept his hand tight, but not bruising tight, around her wrist.

"Morgan, stop. You're hurting me," she whined.

"No, I'm not. And no, we're not stopping until I'm sure those cops aren't coming after us." He kept going, and she managed to keep up.

The sound of rushing water was loud in the night, and the ground beneath their feet was soggy. It slowed their progress, but Morgan didn't think anyone was coming after them. Finally, the trail widened to a spot that was almost big enough to be a beach of sorts. He turned to face Sylvie.

"What the hell were you thinking?" He almost didn't yell the words.

"Whatcha talking about? Your new girlfriend don't like the circle?" Sylvie's voice sounded slurred, almost like a four-year-old's taunting him.

"She's not my girlfriend." He couldn't give her that piece of information to use against him.

"You walked in holding her hand."

"Was that what that little stunt was about?" He didn't hear footsteps or anything behind them. "Start explaining. And start with where the hell Brooke is."

Sylvie was struggling to catch her breath, but that didn't stop her from leaning against him. "Ah, come on, Morgan. When did you get to be so not fun?"

"Life isn't all about fun." She was trying to work her hand free from his grasp. "It's not going to work." He tightened his fingers ever so slightly. "Where is Brooke?"

"Oh, um…with the babysitter. Somewhere. I told her I'd be back around two, so she took her for the night."

Relief almost made him relax. "Where does she live? We'll go get her, and then I'll let you go."

Sylvie stared at him for a long time. "Well, I—" She stopped midthought, frowning. "I don't exactly know for sure."

"What?"

"She always comes to the store and picks Brooke up there. I don't ever drop her off." She shrugged as if giving his daughter to an unknown stranger to take god-knows-where was normal.

He was about to lose it. "Then we'll go to the store and wait."

"Jimmy won't like that."

"Who's Jimmy?" He pulled her close, putting his face right in hers.

"My boss. He don't like kids much. We rent a room from him."

"A room? A single room?"

"Hey, it's all I can afford."

"Doing what exactly?"

"Hey, I'm good at sales." She lifted her chin defiantly, nearly stumbling despite the fact she was standing still. "We make really nice T-shirts."

The pictures in Morgan's head kept getting worse and worse. The mysterious T-shirt vendor came to mind. Was that Jimmy? Was the woman who'd said she didn't know Brooke the babysitter?

He started walking again, dragging Sylvie with him. He needed to clear his head before he talked to her anymore. The flashlight app on his phone helped get them there more quickly.

It also showed him the rush of the water beside them. Clouds were moving overhead, gobbling up the stars. It'd be raining again soon.

Finally, he saw the lights of town, saw the familiar outline of Tara's diner and the hulking frame of his truck on the other side of the water. They'd have to go to the bridge farther down to cross.

"Hey. Is that your truck over there?" Sylvie asked.

"Yeah."

Finally, they reached the familiar wooden bridge, and Morgan was surprised to see water lapping at the bottom boards, occasionally spilling over the top. It had rained for days, soaking the ground. Maybe too much now. He thought about that tree he'd seen the other day. How dangerous was it now?

Morgan stepped onto the wet bridge.

"I'm not going over that," Sylvie screeched. "We'll drown."

"We aren't going to drown." He faced her. "You can either walk over that bridge with me, or I'll carry you." He leaned closer to her again. "I don't much care, but one way or another, you're crossing it and I'm getting Brooke back. Tonight."

She huffed but stopped pulling against his grip. As if to accentuate his plan, those clouds that had been coming in settled close and started to dump even more water on them.

"Come on," he said. "Unless you want to get drenched."

Tentatively, Sylvie stepped onto the wood slats.

He didn't rush her. While he was beyond angry with her, he wasn't trying to be cruel.

Finally, they reached the other side, and Morgan had to admit that it felt good to be on solid ground. That bridge wasn't as steady as it had been a few days ago. If the water kept rising, it probably wouldn't hold.

Morgan headed to the truck, still dragging Sylvie behind him. He glanced at the rear of the diner, then yanked his gaze and his mind back. Tara didn't need to be part of any of this.

He prayed her brothers took her home, took her away from all this insanity.

Sylvie didn't say anything, and the more the rain fell, the less she resisted. As he opened the cab door, he felt her shiver and knew that, if nothing else, her need to be warm and dry would keep her from trying to get away.

It was a temporary solution, but whatever worked. He lifted Sylvie inside ahead of him. He knew he was taking a chance that she'd try to run when he let go of her, but in here, in these close quarters, he knew he'd catch her.

He yanked towels out of a cabinet and tossed her one. "I don't have any dry clothes to offer you."

"I can borrow something of yours." She leaned in to put her hand in the middle of his chest. Her fingers were cold as ice.

"I don't think so." He removed her hand and

spread a towel on the edge of the bunk. "Go ahead. Have a seat." He wanted away from her as soon as possible.

"Oh, you're no fun." She pouted.

"I'm no fun?" He rolled his eyes. "I didn't know we were playing games, Sylvie." Slowly, he reached into the drawer by the bunk and pulled out the folder. He might not have Brooke yet, but he would, and he wasn't wasting this chance. He handed it to her. "Read it. And sign."

"What is it?"

He shook the folder until she took it. He took a step back since that was all the room there was and crossed his arms. Waiting.

She scowled but took it, pulling out the pages. "You're really divorcing me?" She actually looked indignant.

"Yeah." He hurt, not because she was upset or his heart was broken, but because he saw this as a failure. But that was all. Even before he'd come to the realization they weren't going to make it, neither of them had been happy. "You knew that when you took off with Brooke. We never should have gotten married, Sylvie." There, he'd put the truth out there.

Morgan glanced out the windshield at the diner. So much possibility sat over there.

"You're just mean." Sylvie interrupted his thoughts.

"I'm mean?" The urge to hit something returned, almost too strong to resist. "You took my daughter a year ago. One entire year I haven't seen her. And *I'm* mean?"

Sylvie didn't say or do anything. She didn't look at the papers, simply sat there staring angrily at him.

"Do you need some help?" He yanked open another drawer and handed her a pen. "This should work."

"Then what?"

"Then in sixty days, it's final. We're divorced and can get on with our lives." How wonderful those words sounded, even accompanied by his sense of failure.

"What about Brooke?" Sylvie whispered.

"She's coming with me." He no longer even tried to look calm. "I won't let you have her until I know you won't take off again."

"That's not fair."

"Fair? Fair?" Morgan flexed his hands, noticing for the first time the ache in his knuckles. Damn, he should ice his hands. Not an option. He leaned in, so she had to look at him and know he was serious.

"Here's the deal. I won't turn you over to the cops as long as you cooperate. I won't tell them how you took Brooke—I won't tell them anything. But you cross me, and I won't promise anything."

"Fine," she spat. "I don't want to be married to a jerk like you anymore, anyway."

Jerk. She'd called him worse. How much had she said to Brooke? he wondered, wishing he had his daughter now so he'd know. He was close. So close.

He watched, his eyes hungry until she'd dotted every *I* and crossed that final *T.* Before she could do anything else, he took the paperwork from her and shoved it into the lockbox over their heads. He wasn't taking any chances with it until he could turn it in to the courts.

He looked out the windshield toward the diner again. He wanted to walk across that asphalt and tell Tara, wanted to share this accomplishment, this first step to actually having a chance with her, but he couldn't.

Sylvie was the first step. Now he had to find Brooke. Then, and only then, would he be free.

It ONLY TOOK a few minutes to reach the diner. Sure enough, water was pouring over the banks of the creek. What had been a quaint meandering creek was now a raging rush of water.

Wyatt turned to one of the men and tossed him the keys. "Go wake up Gordon Currington. Have him open the hardware store so we can get some sandbags."

The man nodded, then tore out of the lot as fast as the pickup would go.

"Come on." Wyatt led the way into the diner.

Tara looked around. There weren't any customers, but Wade and Wendy were in the kitchen trying to block the flow of water from under the door. Every towel and linen she owned was stuffed in the doorframe. It was helping, but there was still a rivulet of water meandering across the tile floor.

"I disconnected and turned off the gas," Wade told DJ as he looked at the big stove. DJ nodded. Wendy sloshed through the water, carting dry goods from out of the storeroom. The water hadn't reached it yet, but it was headed that way.

Tara's heart sank. She blinked away the burning in her eyes. Was there anything left to lose? No! She'd worked too hard for this. She would not lose.

"Where do you want this?" A voice came out of the storeroom and Jack appeared in the doorway with his arms full of sacks of flour.

"What are you doing here?" she asked.

He glanced over at Wendy, who blushed furiously. Tara looked closer. The waitress's hair was mussed, her lips swollen as if they been well-kissed.

"Offering a hand," Jack said, waiting for direction.

"Put that on the counter out front." DJ stepped in, his own arms full of supplies. "Come on."

When the man with Wyatt's pickup returned

a short time later, the bed was full of bags filled with sand. The rest of the men, along with Tara and Wendy, worked to build a wall of sandbags around the back of the diner.

Almost as if the creek knew it was beat, which Tara knew was nothing more than her exhausted brain being wishful, the creek started to recede. The water meekly slipped back into its banks.

DJ was mopping up the mess that had reached several feet into the kitchen.

"I can do that," Tara said.

"So can I." DJ smiled at her. "Mom taught us all how to mop, Tara." He laughed. "It's okay to let someone help you, ya know."

She smiled. "I know."

Wade had made a big urn of coffee and she poured them each a cup. "Here."

DJ took it and set it on the steel baker's table. Putting the mop bucket away, he came back and took a deep drink. "Heaven. Come on, hon. You need some sleep."

"So do you." She sipped her own coffee, as if it would ward off the impending exhaustion.

They went into the dining room to find the morning crew just arriving with the sun. Kaitlyn frowned. "Are we open?"

Wade shrugged. "Disaster averted. Looks good to me." He'd reconnected the gas and turned on the stove. "Robbie here yet?"

"Yeah," the day cook called as he walked in. "What can I do to help?"

Nearly everyone was here. Her brothers, their crew who'd helped her throughout the night, her staff. All these people were here to help her keep going, to help her business succeed.

Everyone but Morgan.

"Thanks, all of you." Tara cleared her throat. "You're awesome. I love you all," she whispered, her emotions running high.

The roar of a truck engine broke the silence of the quiet morning. Everyone turned to watch Morgan's semi-tractor pull out of the parking lot. Morgan was behind the wheel.

"What the heck?" Jack ran to the door, staring out through the wet glass. "Was that Sylvie with him? He found her?"

You could have heard a pin drop.

CHAPTER FIFTEEN

TARA WATCHED MORGAN'S TRUCK, minus the long trailer, move through the nearly empty parking lot.

The sunrise was sneaking between the fading storm's cloud line and the horizon, outlining the frame of the truck with a pretty, red-gold glow.

Then Jack's words sunk in. Sylvie was in the truck with him. Tara had seen them leave the fight together, seen Morgan's arm around Sylvie, holding her tight. He'd been searching for her for a year. Was Brooke with them? Had he finally gotten everything he'd been searching for? Since the trailer was still here, she knew he'd be back.

Tara looked around. At her staff, who looked as exhausted as she felt, at the men from her brother's ranch and her brothers who'd gone with her to the fight. They'd stayed up all night stacking sandbags to keep the water out of her diner. At everyone who wasn't Morgan.

Tara shivered, as much from the cold and damp as her own doubts. If he had everything he'd been searching for, where did she fit in?

"Damn him," she whispered, her breath fogging the glass of the door that she hadn't even realized she'd walked to. Damn him for making her forget her priorities and want something else—want more. Wasn't this exactly what she'd warned herself about?

Turning, she faced the crowd. Every one of them stared back, some in trepidation—her brothers mostly—others openly curious. "Don't worry," she assured DJ and Wyatt. "I'm not going to lose it."

Instead, she walked through the empty dining room, through the prep area and the kitchen, to her office. She grabbed her purse and her jacket, then marched out. "Everyone go home. You were awesome last night. You saved us." She hugged Wendy and Wade. "Robbie, you and Kaitlyn can handle today?" At the man's nod, she walked outside and climbed into Wyatt's truck.

The men piled into the truck bed, much as they had last night, only more subdued. They were exhausted. So was she. She closed her eyes, leaning her head back on the seat.

"You want to come out to the ranch?" Wyatt spoke in nearly a whisper.

She shook her head. That was the one thing she wanted to do more than anything, go back home where it was safe and Juanita and Addie—and maybe even Emily—would take care of her.

"I need to come back in a few hours." The diner was firmly set as her focus. "But thank you." She tilted her head sideways and rested it on her big brother's strong shoulder. That would have to be enough. For now.

MORGAN HAD GONE past this kitschy T-shirt shop a couple dozen times. Always on an early-morning or late-night run. Never when it was open. He felt like a fool. He should have been more thorough… and more what?

He shrugged. Hindsight was twenty-twenty. He didn't have time to second-guess himself.

Sylvie dozed, sleeping off whatever crap she'd put into her system, while he sat in the driver's seat and stared out the window at the still-closed store. Maybe he could mentally make the doors open sooner, make the owner, her boss, what was his name—Jimmy?—open the damned doors.

Time stretched out. Despite the long, punishing night, adrenaline wouldn't let him sleep.

Twice, he thumbed his phone to life and considered calling Tara. Twice, he cleared the screen before he finished dialing. She'd been so out of her element last night and had looked completely lost. He'd liked that, liked the contrast that she was to this awful world he couldn't seem to escape.

What would Brooke think of Tara? Actually, they'd already met. What *did* Brooke think of her? She'd already taken a liking to Tara's cookies, apparently. No big surprise there. Brooke had always loved sweets, and Tara made amazing desserts.

Something in his chest ached at the image of Brooke sitting at Tara's counter. His hand itched to touch her, to hold his little girl. He wasn't so sure he'd ever be able to let her out of his sight again. But he'd have to. She needed to go to school, to live a normal life. A healthy life.

Sylvie snorted in her sleep, and Morgan rolled his eyes.

Yeah, Tara was from a different world. One he had no business wanting, but one he ached to be a part of anyway.

He glanced at Sylvie. He'd never felt with her what he felt for Tara and part of him felt the guilt—just a part. He'd been telling the truth when he'd told Sylvie they never should have gotten married. They shouldn't have.

But he'd been lonely, looking for a home, a family to come off the road to. At one point, Sylvie had offered that illusion, but it had been short-lived. Too soon, she'd gotten tired of playing house and he was itching to get on the road and away.

The few good memories he'd held on to took a beating whenever she did something like this.

It was different with Tara. With her, there was no itch to leave, no longing to get away. Just the opposite. He never wanted to leave. He'd learned that lesson the hard way.

"You got any aspirin?" Sylvie stuck her head through the space between the seats and brought reality roaring back. Her hair was a mess, her makeup was smeared and he didn't even let himself notice anything else—too depressing.

"Cupboard above the fridge."

He heard her rummaging around. She didn't say thanks. Didn't speak anymore, for which he was glad. He wasn't yet beyond the point of wanting to give her a piece of his mind.

"Let's go." She yanked a brush—his hairbrush—through the tangled mess of her hair as she slipped into the front of the cab. He cringed. Luckily, he knew where to buy a new one.

"Give me a minute." Morgan climbed out of the truck and came around to open the door for her. Not that he was being a gentleman—he didn't trust her.

"Don't you go pissing Jimmy off," Sylvie said as they finally entered the cluttered little shop a few minutes after it opened.

Too late. Jimmy was the same asshole from the street fair. There was no sign of anyone else.

"You're late," the man said as Sylvie walked in.

"It's not my fault," she whined.

"That'd be mine," Morgan said, waiting for Jimmy to look at him.

Jimmy jumped, then narrowed his eyes and decided somewhere in his pea brain to stand his ground. "What do you want?"

"Oh, nothing much." Morgan strolled through the center aisle. "Just my daughter back."

"Who?" Jimmy stared at Morgan for an instant, frowning. Then he turned to Sylvie. "This is your old man?" He took several steps toward her. "This is the washed-up fighter?"

Morgan ignored that comment, knowing Sylvie frequently manipulated the truth. She moved toward the cash register at the back of the store, as if putting a barrier between herself and Jimmy—and Morgan. Morgan followed her.

"Don't go acting surprised," she said, a lot braver behind the counter. "I told you all about him." She reached beneath the register and pulled out a neon orange purse.

"Where you going?" Jimmy asked.

"Away from here." She looked at both men, slinging the long strap of her purse over her shoulder. "I got things to do, and I certainly can do better than either of you." She stomped away from them along the length of a counter that ran along the back wall, toward a curtain that obviously covered a doorway.

Her body language spoke volumes and Morgan, used to looking for tells in his opponents, read her intent. *Damn.* She was going to run. He vaulted the long counter, landing hard against the doorframe on the other side just as she slipped past the curtain. Beyond the fabric barrier was a storeroom filled with boxes set every which way.

By the time he reached it, the back door stood wide open. And Sylvie was nowhere to be seen.

He ran out the door, jumping down the broken steps into the alley. He couldn't hear footsteps, didn't hear her retreat. Had she really gone? Or was she hiding somewhere in that mess inside? He turned, intent on going back to look, but froze.

Jimmy stood in the open doorway, a shotgun aimed straight at Morgan. "You get out of here, or I'll call the cops and tell 'em you were breaking in."

"No, you won't."

Sylvie had said she didn't know where the babysitter lived. Was that the truth? Did Jimmy know? "Tell me where Brooke is and I'll leave you alone." Morgan leaned closer to the man, glaring at him. "Maybe I should be the one to call the cops."

"I don't know or care where she is." Jimmy gave the gun a shake, as if using it to emphasize his words. It looked old enough that being rough with it might make it go off. "So, get out of here."

Still, Morgan couldn't give up. Not yet. The ache in his gut at losing Sylvie now, at the idea of not getting Brooke after all this, ate holes through him.

Morgan backed up and lifted his hands. "Look, I'm going. See?" Getting shot right now wouldn't solve anything.

"Yeah, you keep going. And tell that bimbo

you brought in here that she's fired." He looked up and down the alley. "You hear that, Sylvie? You're fired."

Then Jimmy turned and slammed the door. Morgan heard the lock click in place.

Morgan wasn't stupid. He had a pretty good idea that Sylvie was in that shop, hiding behind some of those boxes. He wanted to scream, and he took back all those earlier thoughts that he should protect her from Jimmy's wrath.

Hell. She deserved his wrath—if it was even remotely real.

Morgan had to go half a block before there was enough space between the buildings for him to walk through. It was a narrow gap, littered with trash and weeds. He moved through as quickly as he could and found himself on Main Street.

He stood there for a long minute, trying to figure out what to do. Chasing after Sylvie would be a waste because he really didn't think she'd gone anywhere. Would walking through the front door be stupid, knowing that Jimmy had a gun? If he waited long enough, would she come out?

He was heartily sick of waiting. A year was too damned long?

"Whatcha doing?"

Startled, Morgan turned to see a young girl beside the hardware store where he stood. She had bright gold hair, pulled precisely to the sides of her head into two ponytails. Pink ribbons held the bands in place. For an instant, his heart skipped a beat.

If only it were Brooke. Sylvie used to try to tame their daughter's wild curls, but after an hour, her hair was usually falling down. It had driven Sylvie a bit crazy, but he'd always thought it was rather adorable.

"I'm, uh, looking for a friend." The last thing he needed was the girl around an idiot with a gun. "What are you doing?"

"Walking. My mom said I could go to the candy store by myself." She looked back the way she'd obviously come and waved at a woman standing in the doorway of a small shop on the corner.

He tried to smile and lifted a hand in greeting to the woman. The candy store was another two doors down. He'd bet everything he had that until this child returned to her side, with whatever candy she was going to get, that mom would be glued to that doorway.

An ache grew in his chest. While the girl reminded him of Brooke, the woman was nothing like Sylvie. He wished… No, he was just being stupid.

"You have a safe trip," he said to the girl, then continued on his trek, not wanting to give that mother any more apprehension than already showed on her face.

"Bye-bye." The girl waved and marched on to

the store as he continued down the street. Morgan waited until the girl was safely inside the candy store before shoving the front door of the T-shirt shop open again.

He felt minimally better walking inside. There was at least one witness out there. And now a couple customers were here, as well. He hoped he didn't need their presence, but it helped.

Jimmy was nowhere to be seen, but the jingling of the bell overhead made him appear in the curtained doorway again. Sylvie didn't appear.

"Prove she's not in there." Morgan took a step inside.

"You...you stay back." Jimmy still held the gun, shaking it again, as he narrowed his eyes.

Morgan saw Jimmy glance around at the customers, heard the shuffle of footsteps heading to the door.

Morgan had faced plenty of dangers in his life, mostly in the form of fists, but weapons weren't uncommon. "Come on, man. Help me out." He inched closer. "Just let me look to make sure she's not there."

"I said stay back." He aimed the gun and gave it another one of those weird shakes.

Why was the fool so jittery? And while Morgan was glad, why hadn't the fool shot him already? Was Jimmy high? What were he and Sylvie involved in? God, where was Brooke? What had they exposed her to?

"Just tell me where Brooke or Sylvie is and I'll gladly leave you alone."

Jimmy rolled his eyes. "They ain't here."

"Then tell me where they are."

"What's in it for me?"

The speculative gleam in Jimmy's eyes made Morgan's stomach turn. "What are you saying?"

"What's the information worth to you?"

"You'd take money to tell me?"

"I might consider it. For the right price."

"What price?"

Jimmy named an exorbitant amount, then nearly doubled over with his cackling laugh. "You'd pay it, wouldn't you? You sucker. They ain't worth that much, but I'll take it if you got it."

Anger and something akin to panic took over. Morgan lunged for the idiot with the gun, half expecting to hear the roar of the shotgun's blast. When he didn't hear anything, he only briefly thanked the heavens above. He didn't have any more time than that as something harder than any fist he'd ever met, slammed into the side of his face.

Morgan stumbled, pain shooting through his skull as the darkness slid over him. "Brooke," he whispered as he hit the floor, then cursed, thinking briefly how Tara was going to be pissed if she had to take him to urgent care again.

"WHAT THE HELL do you think you're doing?" Jack rounded the front bumper of Morgan's truck, then stopped dead in his tracks. "You look like hell."

"Thanks, little brother. You're looking particularly lovely yourself." Morgan pulled the ice pack away from his right eye, stared at it for an instant as if that could make it work better, then put it back over his eye. He was seated on the edge of the truck's running board.

"I lost her," Morgan whispered. He shot to his feet, palming the ice bag as if strangling it would relieve the desire to do something similar to someone else.

"What exactly do you mean, you lost her?"

"I had her. Sylvie." Morgan turned on him, and Jack barely resisted the urge to back away. The man was one scary dude when he was riled. "She was at the fight last night, and I grabbed her. I brought her here. I had her."

"Yeah, we saw her."

"We?"

"Tara and her staff were all here this morning when you drove off." Jack relaxed, realizing that the pain—both physical and internal—Morgan felt right now wasn't going to stop anytime soon.

Morgan cursed and sank onto the running board. He put the ice pack back on his eye again and cursed with a wince.

"What happened?" Jack spoke softly. Morgan

needed to talk, but he'd fight against it. Dad had hit him too hard, too many times, for him to easily let go.

"She left Brooke with a sitter and doesn't even know where the hell the woman lives." A long silence. "I made her go to her job where she said the woman would bring Brooke back."

"And did she?"

"I don't know."

Jack waited. Dad had beat that silence into him, as well.

"Her boyfriend gave me this," Morgan pulled the ice pack away from his eye. Looking closer, Jack realized it wasn't a fist print on his brother's face.

"With what?"

"The butt end of his shotgun."

"What?"

"Idiot apparently doesn't keep it loaded," Morgan mumbled. "Thank God, or Brooke wouldn't have any parents left."

"Damn, Morgan." Jack sat next to his brother. "This has gone too far. You need to call in the authorities."

"I know." The defeat was thick in Morgan's voice. The pain just as strong. "I called Mitch again." Their old friend, now a detective on the Dallas police force, had already offered to help Morgan. Guess stubborn had finally been beat out of Morgan, and Jack mourned the loss. It was one of Morgan's most irritating, yet admirable, traits.

As if just noticing where they were and that Jack was here, Morgan asked, "What the hell are you doing here?"

"Spent the night helping Tara. That creek's rising so we sandbagged the alley."

Morgan cursed again. He stood and walked around the front of the truck. He stared at the building. Jack ignored the hurt in his brother's eyes. "How ticked is she?"

"I don't know. Her brothers took her home to get some sleep."

"This is her dream. She's worked too damned hard for it. It's not fair she might lose it."

"Who keeps telling me life isn't fair?"

"Shut up, Jack." There wasn't much venom in Morgan's voice. Jack laughed and clapped Morgan on the shoulder.

"Get some sleep. You're going to need to be clearheaded pretty damn soon." Jack walked away, heading to the diner.

"Where you going?" Morgan asked. Wendy stepped away from the shadows and waved. "Forget I asked."

Jack climbed into the passenger seat of a car, Wendy behind the wheel. Morgan watched them disappear into the sun's glare.

His eye ached, but the real pain was deep in his chest as he stood there. Alone.

CHAPTER SIXTEEN

Two DAYS LATER—a day and a half of which it rained—the sandbags were still in place. And holding. Tara breathed a sigh of relief. The rain hadn't let up, but the creek stayed in its banks. Barely. Upstream, according to the weatherman, was getting a break from the downpour, and as a result, so were they.

Tara sat at the old-fashioned counter, where scattered papers and her laptop covered the surface. Customers were few and far between this late in the evening, and with the flood alerts that kept going out, people were staying closer to home.

Tara was trying to multitask—help in the dining room and get the taxes done. Apparently, Uncle Sam didn't care much about flood warnings.

With a heavy sigh, she sat back and took several meant-to-be-relaxing stretches. She'd been at this too long, and looking at all of it, she wasn't sure she'd accomplished a blessed thing.

She needed to take a break. Standing, she walked to the French doors. Outside, the world was soggy. Fat raindrops fell on the flagstones. A small river slipped over those same stones and tumbled over the edge, down into the shadowed bed of the creek.

She could see the top of the water. Normally, the creek was little more than a trickle at the bottom of the pathway. Tonight the water reached nearly to the top. How deep was the creek bed? She couldn't remember. Would it overflow again? Would the sandbags hold?

Was it supposed to stop raining anytime soon? She'd been so busy, she hadn't had time to watch the news or do more than listen to the sound bites on the radio. Now she wished she'd taken more time. Deciding to get online and check, she half turned when a movement outside caught her eye. Was someone out there in this awful rain?

She leaned closer to the glass, trying to see out. She could see movement but couldn't make out the person or even if it was man or a woman. Just a figure moving slowly down the hill toward the parking lot.

Hastily, she moved to the other door, following the person's movement down the incline. They leaped over the puddled water, a splash shooting into the air around them as they landed. Then they disappeared into the shadows beneath the trees. She couldn't see them anymore.

In the relative quiet of the near-empty restaurant, Tara heard her phone blare. Not her ringtone, not a call coming in. She pulled the phone out of her pocket and looked at the glowing screen. A weather alert.

Like a wave across the room, phones in various diners' purses or pockets made a similar noise.

"Hey, what's that?" Wade stuck his face in the opening of the pass-through.

"Weather alert." Tara walked into the prep area and thumbed the screen. Her face reflected his frown. "Flood warning actually."

"Where?" Wendy came into the kitchen, her hands full of dirty dishes, her phone in her pocket glowing through the thin fabric. Most likely the same warning.

"Let me see." Tara read the message, trying to concentrate at the same time she tried to hit the right key to stop the obnoxious noise of the warning. "East of town."

Wade cursed and scooted into the kitchen.

"Don't you live out that way, Wade?" Wendy asked. There was no answer from the kitchen.

Tara walked around to the door. The cook was at the grill, but she could tell he was worried. His shoulders were tight as he worked.

"Do you need to go?" She could handle the grill.

"Nope." He flipped half a dozen burgers onto the grill. "My place is up on the hillside. It's safe."

North, south, east, west, didn't matter. What did was up and downstream at this point. East of here was the hill country. Uphill country. She stood watching him work, her mind focusing on something else. The town had been built in the valley. They sat frighteningly close to the creek.

Tara went out the back door and looked across the alley. Rain still fell in sheets, the wind strong, raking through the thick cottonwood branches, bending the big trees nearly in half. She stared at the creek.

The tiny meandering creek reached the top of its meager banks. The grasses that normally grew tall, that Ricky Raccoon and Tabby Cat—as they'd been dubbed by her staff—usually hid in, slipping through the tall blades to sneak up on each other, were flattened to the ground. Battered by the rain that hadn't stopped for long.

Where had the animals gone? She hadn't seen Ricky in days, hadn't had any critters getting into the trash since Wyatt's crew had put up the sandbags.

What happened to raccoons when it rained? Where did stray cats hide? She looked around, wondering, hoping that she might see them lurking somewhere where she could get them. Save them if she needed to.

Maybe they were smarter than she was. Should she close up? Should she—

"Everyone's leaving," Wendy announced, coming through the door. "It's gonna be dead now."

Tara turned and went inside. She had other

things to worry about right now. Still, she looked over her shoulder one last time, wishing she knew if the animals were safe and sound.

"Here's what we're going to do," she announced to Wade and Wendy once she'd closed the door. Time to make the right, adult decision.

"We're closing. This is crazy. Wendy, hustle everyone else along and don't seat anyone else. Wade, finish up those meals and start shutting down." She headed toward where she'd left her paperwork. She'd take it with her and do it at her place. Was there anything else in the office she couldn't afford to get wet?

"Great." Wade stared at the fresh burgers he'd thrown on the grill with a scowl. "What am I supposed to do with these?"

Tara turned around, letting herself smile. "Put them out back just in case Tabby and Ricky show up."

"Should I put them on a plate?" He was being sarcastic, but she saw him and Wendy exchange a smile. They cared about the little guys, too.

In less than half an hour, they had what they could pack up. Wendy had already left, and Wade was finishing putting supplies from the storeroom in his truck. Tara had all the paperwork in her car, ready to go.

A sound at the front door made her turn around. "I'm sorry, we're—"

Tara stared at the little girl standing in the

doorway, almost afraid to move, afraid Brooke would vanish. "Hello."

"Hi." The girl stepped inside, and Tara saw Brooke shiver. She pulled the wet, purple dragon close, almost as if the fluffy thing could keep her warm. The yellow T-shirt and soaked blue jeans weren't doing much good in that department.

Tara wasn't sure what to do. She didn't want to scare Brooke and didn't want to chase her away. It was too wet and dangerous outside, and Tara didn't want the girl going back to where she'd come from. The adults in her world certainly weren't paying attention.

"What can I do for you?" Tara cautiously asked.

"Um." The girl stepped closer. "Lanara—" she held up the toy "—is hungry."

Tara followed the girl's lead. "She is? Well, that's not good." Tara pretended to ponder the problem. "I don't know much about dragons. Can you help me figure out what to feed her?"

Brooke nodded, a smile beginning on the corner of her lips.

"What do dragons like?" Tara moved carefully behind the counter. "Do you two want to sit at the counter?"

Again, Brooke nodded, struggling to climb up on the stool where her father so frequently sat. Tara wanted to call Morgan but needed to get the girl settled first. "Is Lanara cold?" Tara asked. "I have a couple sweaters that you guys could borrow."

Brooke frowned as if thinking about it. "I don't know." She shivered. "I guess that'd be okay."

Tara didn't want to leave the girl, afraid she'd disappear before she got back. She needed the sweaters, though, or the girl would catch pneumonia. As she hustled past the phone, she grabbed the handset. Trying to hurry and focus on the numbers flashing on the screen as she reviewed the previous calls list, she nearly stumbled. Which one was Morgan's?

Forcing herself to focus, she put the phone in her pocket and grabbed the sweaters she and Wendy kept by the back door. She hustled back, breathing a huge sigh of relief to find the girl and her trusty dragon still seated at the counter.

"Here you go. Lanara and Brooke, right?"

"Yep. I'm Brooke." She smiled and let Tara wrap the too-big, blue sweater around her—after she tucked the other around the stuffed toy.

"What a pretty name." Tara moved behind the counter and pulled out two bowls. "Do dragons like stew?" There was still plenty in the pot.

Brooke wrinkled her nose. "No. They like samiches."

"Ah." Tara put the bowls back. At this point, she'd do anything for this kid, to keep her here and safe. She might still be upset with Morgan, but this girl needed to be taken care of by someone. "What kind of sandwiches?"

"All kinds."

"Peanut butter ones?"

"Those are okay." She wasn't very enthusiastic.

"What about grilled cheese?"

"Yes. Those are Lanara's favorite. With extra cheese."

"I see she has very good taste." Tara hated to move away to make the food for the girl but didn't know what else to do. "You know…" She frowned as if she were thinking hard. "It's a lot warmer in the kitchen, where I'll make Lanara's sandwiches. Would you two like to come back there with me?"

"Yes, please." Brooke shivered and glanced at the door as the wind suddenly howled and rattled the glass.

"Okay, then come with me." Tara held the big swinging door open for Brooke. The girl hopped down from the stool and grabbed Lanara as she passed.

The kitchen *was* much warmer, but Brooke still shivered every few minutes. "Let me get you a special chair." Tara pulled her mom's wooden chair from the office and set it at the pastry table. "This is one of my favorite chairs. And Lanara can sit here, what do you think?" Tara dragged the stepladder that Wade used in the storeroom over beside the chair. Brooke nodded and smiled.

Tara pulled out all the ingredients for the sandwiches and warmed up the griddle.

"Can you make Lanara two samiches? If she can't eat them both, I'll help her," Brooke offered.

"That's a great idea." Tara quickly prepared the sandwiches. Finally, the sandwiches ready, she put them on separate plates.

"Do you…or does Lanara like chips?"

"Yes. Lots."

"What kind?" She lifted up several of the small bags she served with her sandwiches.

"Reglar." Brooke mispronounced the word, not seeming to notice.

Tara put down the plates, one in front of the stuffed animal and the other on the side toward Brooke. "So you can help her."

"I don't think she can eat both of them," Brooke very solemnly said. "I'll help her."

"Okay." Tara leaned on the pastry table, resting her chin on her fists as she watched the girl gobble up the food.

"You make good stuff," Brooke said around a bite of food.

"Don't talk with your mouth full," Tara said. "And thank you." She smiled.

When the sandwich was half-done, and Brooke showed no signs of slowing down, Tara ventured to ask her a couple questions. "So, Brooke. Where's your mom?" The last thing she needed was Sylvie coming in here accusing her of something, especially if she couldn't get in touch with Morgan.

The girl shrugged and focused more on her sandwich, slowing only slightly in her chewing. "I think she's out with Jimmy."

"Who's Jimmy?"

"Her boss. We stay at his house."

"Oh." That didn't sound good. "Where were you before you came here tonight?"

"Can I have more chips?"

"Of course."

"Lanara wants them." Brooke had already eaten hers and was halfway through the portion Tara had put on the plate for the dragon. She put more on Brooke's plate.

"Lanara is awfully hungry," Tara observed.

"She didn't get anything to eat all day, 'cept an icky granola bar that Mandy—that's the babysitter—had in her purse this morning."

Tara managed not to yell or groan. She had to call Morgan. She might be mad at him, and she might not be happy about some of the recent events between them, but this little girl couldn't go without any more. She was already too thin and soaked through from the rain. Rain she had no business being out in alone.

Tara tried hard not to start asking a million questions about Sylvie and what life was like with her. Right now, that wasn't her responsibility. Keeping this girl safe was.

She pulled out the phone and the girl hastily looked up. "Are...are you calling my mom?" Why didn't that sound like something the girl wanted?

"I wasn't going to. Do you want me to?"

Brooke's tiny baby teeth bit into her lip as if she were thinking. "Can I stay here with you?"

Tara swallowed the hurt that came with the sound of the girl's voice growing softer. "Of course, but don't you think she's missing you?"

Brooke shook her head slowly, staring down at the rest of her uneaten sandwich. "I—me and Lanara—we got a secret."

Tara shivered, and she wasn't cold in the big warm kitchen. "You do?"

Slowly, Brooke climbed off the wooden chair and reached for the stuffed dragon. She pulled it close. "My daddy gave Lanara to me for my birthday," Brooke whispered.

Tara remembered Brooke telling her that before. Tara watched as the little girl turned the dragon around.

There were three safety pins on the dragon's back, as if she'd been torn and someone had tried to fix the tear. What if one of those pins popped? Brooke could be poked or hurt. But her little fingers easily opened the pins, as if she'd done it dozens of times before.

Carefully, the girl reached into the torn toy, shoving through the white cotton batting that filled it. She pulled something out from inside the toy. "Don't tell I got this. Mama would get mad."

"I swear." Tara made the zipper sign over her mouth, hoping she wouldn't regret her promise.

Brooke came around the big metal table and stood beside Tara. She extended a piece of paper to Tara. "This is my daddy."

Tara's heart ached as she looked at the old, computer-printed picture of Morgan. Someone had torn the picture into several pieces, then taped it together. He was laughing and posing with the purple dragon that didn't look nearly as bedraggled as it did now.

"I'm gonna go find him."

"Oh. You are? Why?"

Brooke looked at Tara then, and the sadness in the little girl's eyes was too much. She felt her own eyes well with tears. "I wanna go home," Brooke whispered. "I don't like Jimmy. At home, Mama played with me and tucked me into bed."

"She doesn't do that now?"

Brooke simply shook her head, her ponytails bouncing now that they were beginning to dry. "I was at Lisa Hanson's house for a sleepover the other day." Brooke walked to the dragon and focused very hard on putting the picture inside the stuffing and re-pinning it. "Her daddy tucked her into bed." Brooke rubbed her eyes with a fist. "I miss Daddy," she whispered.

"Oh, sweetie." Tara wanted to sweep the little

girl into her arms and never let her go. "Would you like me to help you?" The question hung heavy in the air.

"I saw a big truck here the other day. My daddy used to have a big truck like that."

"He did?"

"Uh-huh. And he'd let me ride in it. Do you think the truck man would know my daddy?"

Tara swallowed the lump in her throat. "I'll bet he would. You know, I have his phone number. Would you like me to call him?"

Brooke seemed to think about it a long time, then slowly nodded. "Yes, please."

Tara couldn't ask for a better opening. She took the diner's phone and scrolled for Morgan's number. It wouldn't have his name, but she knew around what time he'd called. Surely, there weren't that many numbers.

Amazing how many people called in a day. Finally, she found the one she was pretty sure was his. *Please, let it be his. Let him answer even if he knows it's me.*

MORGAN ALMOST DIDN'T answer the phone. The rain was coming down hard, and while he knew this road well, he was never comfortable driving the rig with a phone in one hand. He slowed, which was surprising since he was already creeping along. Water splashed up, loud on both sides of the cab as he pushed the truck through yet another pool of standing water in the middle of the road. He hit the speaker button and propped the phone on the console.

"Hello?" He didn't take his eye off the road to see who it might be.

"Morgan?" Something akin to relief and joy washed over him. He hadn't thought Tara was speaking to him. If he were her, he wasn't sure he would. He hadn't seen her since he'd left with Sylvie.

"Yeah? Tara? What's up?" He tried not to get his hopes up that she was calling because she actually wanted to talk to him.

"I'm at the diner." He heard her say, then a long silence where the phone seemed to blip out. "We're…dinner…"

"I only got part of that. You're breaking up." His heart sank. He wanted to talk with her, wanted to clear the air between them. She was talking, but he couldn't understand the odd syllables. Then he heard a full word. "Brooke…" Another long pause. "Here." Then the phone cut out completely. The silence was too heavy not to be absolute.

"Tara?" He waited, hoping the call was still connected. "Tara?" No answer this time, either. He cursed and had to force himself to not slam his foot on the brake pedal. He took several deep breaths as he kept driving. Trying to see through each swipe of the wiper blades and the path in the beam of the headlights through the thick dark.

THE CALL CUT OUT, and Tara didn't even try to call Morgan back. She knew he was out on the road, and with the rain coming down, it couldn't be safe to be on the phone. She'd said all the things to him he needed to hear. She just hoped he'd heard.

The diner was empty except for her and Brooke. Wade had made a few trips in and out. He wouldn't leave until she did.

Her phone blared again, and she looked over at the screen, hoping that maybe Morgan was calling back. Instead, it was another weather alert. The loud, piercing tones echoed around the room.

"What's that?" Brooke looked up from her third grilled cheese sandwich.

"A weather alert."

"Oh." The girl fell silent, looking at the dragon. "Do Lanara and I gotta go?"

Tara sat on the stool next to Brooke. "That depends. Where are you going?"

Tara watched Brooke slowly, deliberately put the remainder of her sandwich on the plate. She looked out the windows, her eyes wide. "To Jimmy's?"

Why would the girl ask that as a question? "Do you want to go to Jimmy's? I can take you."

The girl stared at the crust on the plate. Slowly, she shook her head, her now-dry ponytails bouncing against her shoulders.

The weather alert went off again. Could it possibly be more insistent? The phone's screen filled with a map of the county and the words *flood warning* scrolled across it.

Wade came out of the kitchen then, and even his usually calm, weathered face looked alarmed. "We need to get going, Tara. I'm disconnecting the gas and turning off the stove."

"I'm not going until you do." She met his eyes.

"I'm right behind you," he assured her. "That creek is at the top of the banks. It's going over, and soon."

"Will the sandbags hold?" All the work Wyatt's men had put in had to hold. It had to keep her dream safe.

"I don't know." Wade disappeared into the kitchen and returned carrying her jacket and her purse. The man was serious. He'd never touch her purse otherwise. He'd pulled on his own jacket. "Let's go. You, too, little one." He roughly grabbed the stuffed dragon and lifted Brooke off the stool.

He didn't really give Tara much choice, and the next shrill of the phone made her hustle ahead of him. She unlocked the passenger door of her car and they got Brooke strapped into the seat, Lanara settled safely on her lap.

"I'm scared." Brooke's eyes shone in the darkness.

"You'll be fine, kiddo," Wade assured her, snapping the seat belt tight. "Miss Tara'll get you to a safe place. Now be strong for that dragon. Don't worry her."

"You're a good man, Wade." Tara hugged her cook. "Now, get out of here." His pickup was a few feet away from her little car.

"Not until I get that gas line off. Then, I'm out of here. Get going." He almost buckled her in, as well, closing the driver's door behind her. He didn't wait for her to turn out of the parking lot before he was sprinting into the diner. She trusted him and knew he'd take care of everything. She just prayed he'd also take care of himself.

As she drove past the alley, she saw the water slipping over the creek's bank, heading toward the back door of the diner. Her dream. Was she seeing the beginning of the end?

"Where are we going?" Brooke whispered, hugging Lanara tight, her face against the worn fabric of the dragon.

Tara thought about taking Brooke to her apartment, but in the most recent warning, the big red field had covered the entire town. All of it would be at risk.

"Would you like to come with me to my brother's ranch?" Tara asked carefully. That would be one of the safest places in the county. The old ranch house sat up on the hill that overlooked most of the valley. Outside the warning zone.

"Can I go with you, please?" Brooke asked so softly, so politely.

"Of course." The whisper of uncertainty was so strong in her voice. Tara wished she could reach over and hug the little girl tight. She wanted to strangle Sylvie. How dare she leave Brooke on her own, leave her to the mercy of the elements like this? Tara tried not to think uncharitable thoughts, like maybe she deserved to be worried out of her mind about the girl not being where she could find her.

What if something happened to Sylvie? How would Brooke react? What would Sylvie have done if Brooke hadn't found her way to the diner, to the company of someone who actually took care of her? Tara's mind filled with all the horrors that could happen to a little girl wandering the streets of any town.

Suddenly, she understood all too clearly why Morgan did what he did, trying to find her.

"Do you know how to dial a cell phone?" she asked Brooke. The girl came out of her fear long enough to give her one of those stupid-adult looks. "Okay, yeah, I know. My phone is in that side pocket of my purse. Can you get it out?"

The girl nodded and reached for the phone. It looked so big in her tiny hands. "Who are we calling? My mom?"

"Well, actually I want you to call your dad."

"My dad?" The girl stared at her, wide-eyed. Tara hadn't told her she knew Morgan. She hadn't been sure what her or Sylvie's reaction would be.

"Yeah. His number is in my list." Thank God she'd thought to put it in her phone after calling him. "See that button on the bottom? Push it twice." The girl was six, and Tara didn't know how much she could read. Brooke turned the screen toward Tara, who was afraid to look away from the road.

The rain was coming down so thick she could barely see beyond the bumper. It was going to take forever for them to drive the miles to the ranch at this rate. She didn't care if it took all night. They needed to get there safe.

She hastily glanced away. "See that one that starts with the letter *M*?"

"Uh-huh."

"Push that button."

She could see out of the corner of her eye that the line was ringing. Hopefully, they were calling Morgan.

"Hello," his familiar voice filled the interior of the car.

"Daddy?"

"Brooke?" Even here, through the sound of the pounding rain, Tara heard the joy and pain in his voice.

"I'm with the diner lady."

Dear heaven, Tara wondered if she'd told the kid her name. She'd gotten in the car with her.

Who else would she have gone with? Damn, Sylvie.

"What? I can't hear you. Where are you?" There was controlled desperation in his voice. The connection wasn't any better than before. She had to tell him where they were going, hope he got something.

"It's Tara. We're going to Wyatt's ranch. Brooke's with me. Wyatt's ranch."

"Where?" he yelled.

"The ranch. Wyatt's ranch."

He didn't say anything more. Dear God, she hoped he was okay. Hoped she hadn't scared him more than she'd explained. But she would keep Brooke safe until she could get them together. Brooke deserved it.

Begrudgingly, she realized so did he. He'd spent a year looking for this little girl.

"Daddy?" Brooke held the phone close to her mouth. "Daddy?"

"The storm probably messed up the call." Tara tried to sound upbeat. "He'll meet us at my brother's house."

"You sure?"

"I'm positive." Oh, he'd be there. She was sure of it. She just wasn't sure when. "We'll be safe there until he comes to find us," she said to the windshield, leaning forward, hoping to see more clearly. They crept along the two-lane highway, away from town, away from the winding path of the creeks and rivers that meandered through town. Up the Texas hills to the ranch house that she'd always considered safe. Home.

CHAPTER SEVENTEEN

WIND BUFFETED THE RIG, howling around the cab and making Morgan tighten his hands on the wheel. Gusts had to be hurricane strength, which wasn't unheard of in this part of Texas but not something he wanted to be out in.

The windshield wipers could barely keep up with the rain. He struggled to keep his gaze trained on the lines he had to remain between. Thankfully, few vehicles were coming this way since the headlights were blinding on the water-covered glass.

Morgan wanted to get to Haskins Corners tonight, but that was looking more and more like stupidity at this point. His frustration grew.

Brooke was with Tara. Would she stay there? He couldn't lose her again. Hurrying would be dangerous, and in reality, he should pull over under the next overpass. Soon, he wouldn't have a choice. It was all the cover he'd find out here.

He turned off his stereo and flipped on the radio. It might be static, but he'd find a weather report somehow. He'd tried his phone a while ago, and the storm must have knocked out at least one cell tower. He had battery power, but not much else.

Old, twangy country music crackled through the speakers. Yep, he'd get reports on this channel—he just had to listen to this stuff in between. Finally, the noise came to a halt and a man's voice came on. "It's a stormin' out there tonight, folks. Hope you're home safe and not out on the roads. The state patrol has just issued a high-profile vehicle restriction until 10:00 p.m. tonight. That means you boys out in them eighteen-wheelers need to pull over.

"Take cover if you can. It's gonna be a long wait. Could be a while before this one blows through."

The disc jockey somewhere in musicland pushed a switch and another lovesick fool started crooning through the speakers. Morgan switched it off, not bothering to turn his stereo back on.

Morgan knew this road, and it was too flat and open. He'd be better off stopped, without the momentum of the truck to add to the storm's strength, but the next overpass was several miles ahead. Maybe he could find a hill.

He inched along, not seeing much beyond the headlight's beam. A gust caught the back end of the truck, and Morgan felt it slip. He struggled to balance the weight of the truck against the slide.

Stopped out here in the open was better than sliding off the road. Slowly, he applied the brakes, hoping to bring it to a halt quickly, but not too quickly.

He felt another gust yank at the back end. He hard-corrected, knowing he was doing the right thing, knowing that he could pull the truck into control if he timed everything right. He cursed, feeling the pull of inertia and doing everything he could to fight it.

The headlight beams found the edge of the road, found the soft shoulder that was just as soaked as the pavement, maybe worse as the rivers of water ran off the asphalt. Thick grass grew at the edge of the narrow strip of road, and he hoped there weren't any fences or steep drop-offs he couldn't see in the darkness.

His heart pounded against his ribs. His arms strained, but he hadn't tipped and he wasn't spinning. Not yet. A crack of lightning cut across the sky, blinding him for an instant, time he didn't have to spare.

Thunder rumbled in tune with the big tires hitting gravel, and just as he felt the truck respond to his commands, his vision returned. A stretch of barbed wire appeared ahead.

He had to hope he'd planned enough time to stop as he hit the brakes harder and hung on. If he hadn't, this was going to be a bumpy ride.

THE BIG RANCH house was lit up, with nearly every light in the place on. Who all was here?

Brooke had fallen asleep on the drive, her small head resting on top of the dragon's. She looked adorable, and if the girl hadn't been holding so tight to her phone in case Morgan called back, Tara would have snapped a picture for him.

Tara hated to wake her, so she quietly opened the car door. The rain wasn't much more than a light mist here, but it was still cold. She grabbed what she'd need and hurried around the hood of the car.

Carefully, she opened the passenger door, gently disengaging the seat belt and scooping the girl and her dragon up in her arms. Brooke barely stirred, laying her head trustingly on Tara's shoulder.

She hurried up the walk and wasn't even surprised when she reached the veranda and Wyatt was holding the screen door open for her.

He didn't say anything, just looked at her with curiosity and a raised eyebrow.

The house was full, and Tara was surprised Brooke didn't wake up. Was she okay? She thought about putting her in one of the half dozen spare rooms to sleep, but knew her waking up in a strange place would not be good.

Instead, she went to the couch and sat, Brooke still snuggled close. "Hey, Brooke," she said softly, pulling away from the girl.

Brooke clung tight, and Tara realized she wasn't asleep, not really. "It's okay," Tara said. "This is a safe place."

Brooke still didn't let go, but she turned her head to look at Tara. "Where are we?" she whispered.

"Remember, I told you we were coming to my brother's house? We're here."

"Oh." Still, Brooke didn't move.

"This is Wyatt." She turned so Brooke could see him without moving.

Wyatt, being the man he was who was always good with kids, leaned closer. "Hi. Nice to meet you. What's your name?"

"Brooke."

"Hello, Brooke. Welcome to my house."

Brooke still clung tight to the dragon and her arm squeezed Tara's neck. "He's tall," she whispered. "My daddy's tall, too."

Tara figured almost everyone was tall from the little girl's perspective, but she didn't tell her that. "Wyatt knows your daddy." Maybe that would help ease Brooke's discomfort.

"He does?"

"Uh-huh." Tara nodded. "Wyatt, you met Morgan the other night, remember?"

"Oh, yeah." Wyatt eased onto the couch beside them. "You're right, he is tall. I hear he has a big truck, too."

That did the trick. Brooke sat up, still holding on to Tara and the dragon, but not leaning so tightly against her. "It's really big. Makes a lotta noise, too."

"We can do that here, too." Wyatt smiled. "Did you two have dinner?"

"We did," Tara told him. "But maybe there're some stray cookies around?"

"I think we've got some, if Tyler hasn't eaten them all."

"Who's Tyler?" Brooke asked.

"He's our nephew. He likes cookies almost as much as I do," Wyatt explained.

"Not as much as me." Brooke smiled.

Wyatt smiled back. "Come on." He stood and led the way to the kitchen.

Tara let Brooke slide down and didn't say anything when the girl reached for her hand. "You're coming with me?"

"Of course." Tara stood. "I like cookies, too, you know."

When they reached the wide doorway that led into the kitchen, however, Brooke stopped. Family and ranch hands sat around the big table. Nearly a dozen people in all. Juanita, the cook, stood at the sink, finishing the evening's dishes.

Tyler slid off his chair. "Hi!" He came over to them. He put his hand out, like all the men on the ranch did when meeting someone. The fact that he was nine years old only made the gesture more adorable. "I'm Tyler."

"Hi." Brooke hugged Tara's leg. "I'm Brooke."

She probably didn't know how to shake hands. Tyler didn't seem to notice, shrugging and waving her to follow him. "You can sit by me. There's lots of room over here." He walked over to his seat and pulled it out.

Brooke looked at Tara, questioning.

"It's okay," Tara said. "I'm not going anywhere."

Slowly, Brooke let go of her hand and crawled onto the chair. Her chin barely reached the table's top, but she didn't seem to mind. Tyler carefully pushed the chair in a couple inches. "Here." He slid a small plate with a cookie on it toward her. "You want some milk?"

Brooke shook her head, her ponytails sliding back and forth. She took the cookie and nibbled on the edge. Her eyes were wide as she looked around at the room full of people.

The cowboys slid along the bench seat that ran the table's length, giving Tara space next to the girl. She smiled her thanks.

"Brooke and I came here when we heard the flood warnings. The whole town's included."

"You're safer here," Wyatt said. "I was going to go get you if you didn't head this way."

The kitchen door came open just then and Brooke jumped. Tara laid her hand gently on Brooke's shoulder when she saw who'd come in. "That's my other brother," she explained with a smile. "That's DJ."

DJ looked over, consciously clearing his frown. He asked Tara, "Is that...?"

"Yeah." Tara had explained everything to him at the diner before he'd agreed to take her to the fight. How much had he shared with Wyatt? Some, she guessed, as Wyatt had accepted Brooke's presence without any questions.

At least for now.

TARA'S GRANDFATHER HAD built this house, making it the heart of one of Texas's largest and most successful ranches. Growing up, Wyatt had spent most of his spare time out here with Granddad, what time he'd had when he wasn't helping Mom after Dad's death and when he wasn't in school. It hadn't been a surprise to any of them that he'd taken over when Granddad had gotten too ill to run the place.

They'd all come here as kids, feeling the love and acceptance that Granddad had showered on them. But Wyatt had always seemed a part of this place.

Now Tara felt that family love reach out and wrap around her and Brooke. Brooke must have felt it, too, as she soon relaxed and started to nod off again.

"Are you sleepy, hon?" Juanita came over to kneel beside Brooke's chair. "We got lots of big beds upstairs you and your dragon friend can snuggle down in."

Brooke shook her head, leaning toward Tara. Juanita looked at Tara, a frown in her eyes.

"I have an idea." Tara smiled at the older woman. "When I was little, I used to love to build a fort in the den, remember? Maybe we could do that tonight."

Juanita's warm grin grew. "I remember. That way Tara could stay with you. Would you like that?"

"A fort?"

"It's really cool." Tyler grinned and nodded. "The den is a big old room with a fireplace and bunches of pillows on the couches."

"Okay," Brooke softly agreed. "You'll be there?" She turned pleading eyes to Tara.

"I will." She stood and extended her hand for Brooke to take it. "I'll even get it set up for you." She looked at Wyatt, not really asking his permission but wanting some type of reassurance that she was doing the right thing. He nodded.

"Emily should be home soon." He glanced at the door. "She called a bit ago and was almost home."

Tara nodded and led Brooke to the den. It was on the other side of the family room, past the staircase. The wooden double doors were open and the room was dark. Tara hit the switch, and the lights came on the same instant the gas fireplace came to life.

"Oh." Brooke stared in awe at the flames,

and Tara wondered if she'd ever seen a gas fireplace before.

Juanita came in with an armload of blankets, and by the time she had the blanket tent with a half dozen throw pillows set up, Brooke was giggling at the woman's antics.

She still held Lanara tight, though, never letting go of the toy. Even when Juanita helped her change into an old T-shirt of Wyatt's that she'd brought as a makeshift nightgown. It nearly reached the ground.

"My, don't you look lovely." Juanita smiled at Brooke, who lay down on the same big pillow Tara had loved to snuggle on. Tara settled on the couch nearby, staring into the flames as Juanita left them alone.

"Tara?" Brooke whispered. "When I wake up, will Daddy be here?"

"I hope so, but I guess that depends on how long you sleep."

"Okay." Brooke smiled and closed her eyes, holding the stuffed dragon against her chest. It wasn't very long before her even breathing told Tara she was asleep. Even asleep, she didn't let go of the dragon.

Tara's heart hurt as she watched the sweet little girl. Looking now, she could see where she resembled Morgan. Her eyes were pure Sylvie, but with them closed, her pouty lips and nose were all Morgan's.

"She's exhausted." DJ's voice was a soft whisper as he walked into the room. Wyatt followed and closed the double doors.

"Yeah." Tara didn't move as the men sat on the couch facing the one she sat on. The only light was from the dancing flames, but she could see her brothers clearly. "I think she's had a rough time." Tears stung her throat.

"How'd you find her?" DJ knew about Morgan's yearlong search.

"I didn't. She found me." Tara shifted on the couch. "She's been in the diner a few times with her babysitter, which is why Morgan's been hanging out there. He kept hoping he'd be there when she came in."

"Hell, if that'd been my kid, I'd have moved in," DJ said.

"He about did," she agreed with a smile, remembering all the times Morgan had inhabited that end stool. "Tonight, I almost missed her. Wade and I were closing when she came in. I think she was starving. She ate three grilled cheese sandwiches."

Wyatt cursed. "She's a good kid."

"Yeah." Morgan would be proud of her. "She's scared of her mom's boyfriend. I'm not sure her mom even realizes she's gone." Surely by now Sylvie, or at least the babysitter, had noticed her missing.

"Does Morgan know you have her?" DJ leaned

forward, resting his elbows on his knees. If anyone understood how Morgan felt, it would be her brother who'd almost not known about his son.

"I don't know. We tried calling him. The connection kept breaking up. I've tried to leave him a message." She lifted her phone. "But his phone is either dead or off."

"What about her mother?" Wyatt asked.

"I have no idea where she is or how to contact her." Tara's voice rose in anger, and Brooke shifted in her sleep. They all seemed to hold their breath until she settled again. "What kind of mother lets a six-year-old run around in weather like this?" Her anger grew the longer she thought about Sylvie.

"She was the woman who pushed you the other night at the fight?" Wyatt asked through clenched teeth. Tara nodded.

Wyatt used some choice language for the woman and Tara smiled. "Yeah. That."

They all sat staring at Brooke for a long time. "What are you planning to do?" DJ finally asked.

"I'm not sure." Tara met her brother's intense stare, then looked at Wyatt. "I need to talk to Emily, but Morgan deserves to get her back."

"It may not be that simple."

"I know. But Sylvie doesn't deserve to have her."

"I agree. Still, we're not making the decisions."

"Morgan said he'd contacted a lawyer about a divorce, asking for full custody."

"They're still married?" DJ's voice rose, a hint of outrage in the words.

"Just hold on." Tara lifted a hand. "Don't go getting all judgmental. I saw the paperwork. They'd be divorced by now if he could have found her. He's telling the truth. His brother confirmed it."

"His brother?" Wyatt asked.

"Oh! I can call Jack." She didn't have his number, but she was pretty sure she knew who might. She thumbed her phone and dialed Wendy's number. Relief washed over her.

"Hello?" Wendy answered, sounding like she'd been asleep.

"Wendy? It's Tara. Sorry to bother you, but do you have Jack's phone number?"

"Hmm…uh, yeah. Just a minute. It's in my phone, but I'm talking to you on it."

That made sense. "I really need to get ahold of him. It's urgent."

"Is Morgan okay?"

"I—" She swallowed. "I think so."

"Oh, good. When I saw the news, I thought maybe it was him."

"What news?" Tara's heart beat hard in her chest, and she looked at her brothers. "Wendy?"

"You didn't hear?" Wendy's voice was soft.

"I'm sorry. There's a jackknifed rig on I-35. The news reports sounded bad."

"Oh, God." Tara looked at the little girl asleep on the big pillow. Brooke had fallen asleep expecting to see her Daddy when she woke up. What if it was Morgan, what if...? Tara couldn't even think, couldn't imagine...

"What is it?" Wyatt stood, looming over her.

"There's been an accident," Tara whispered. "A jackknifed rig."

She completely forgot about Wendy, until Wyatt took the phone and started talking to her. Tara couldn't listen, couldn't even think. She could only stare at Brooke.

So close. He'd been so close.

WATER POURED ACROSS the diner's parking lot. A single vehicle, a battered red pickup, sat in the rain. The water lapped halfway up its tires.

Morgan turned in the narrow drive, pulling up to the door, not even bothering to do more than stop. He jumped down, pounding on the glass doors. There was a light on, clear in the back. Dear God, was Brooke back there? With Tara? Alone?

He pounded harder. "Hey, anyone in there?"

Wade stuck his head out the swinging doors and ran across the dining room. He hastily unlocked the door. "I was yellin' at you that we're closed. Sorry, man." Wade let him in and struggled against the wind to close the door again. "They ain't here," he told Morgan and headed into the kitchen.

"Where are they?"

"Headed out to Wyatt's ranch. It's upriver and on a hill."

Relief so thick it threatened to knock him to his knees washed over Morgan. Brooke was safe. She was with Tara. She was with all those cowboys who'd taken such good care of Tara. He let it all sink in.

"What are you still doing here?" he asked Wade.

"Trying to get this stove disconnected. We don't need a gas leak on top o' all this water." He waved toward a stream of water coming in under the back door. "DJ put it back last time, and that man's got some serious torque power."

"Let me help."

They headed to the big stove and together pulled the coupling loose.

"Whew. That's a relief." Wade stood back and wiped his brow. "I just wish I could do somethin' about the rest." He looked sadly toward the dining room.

"What do you mean?"

Morgan stepped away from the stove and took in the area around them. On the big pastry table where he'd watched Tara make bread and so many other things, two small plates still sat side by side. The chair from Tara's office and a step stool were next to it, as if someone had sat there.

Wade saw him staring. "That little girl with Tara ate pert' near three sandwiches. Not sure where she put it. She's a skinny little thing."

Morgan couldn't move. The crust of bread had little girl teeth marks in it. Brooke's. His heart stopped, then pounded. After all this time, all this pain and anguish and work, he'd finally found Brooke? What was that stinging in his eyes?

"Hey, man, we need to get goin'. That water's a comin'." Wade was staring at the screen on his phone. Another weather alert blared through.

"She's going to lose this place," Morgan whispered.

"Maybe." Wade nodded. "Those boys did a bang-up sandbag job, but even a little water's gonna ruin that wood furniture. Took her months to find it all."

"Not if I can help it." Morgan sprinted through the dining room and flung open the glass doors. The Closed sign on the door whipped in the wind. He unlocked the back doors of the empty trailer, barely hearing the slam of the metal against the frame as they opened.

"You need some help?" Wade yelled.

"If you can spare the time. We gotta hustle."

Neither of them spoke as they set to work. Chairs. Tables. Putting the buffet, with all the linens that weren't stuffed under the back door, inside.

"Sure wish I could save that stove." Wade stood staring at it.

"There's no way, man."

"I know." Wade smiled faintly. "Just a thought."

"Anything else?"

They looked around. The patter of the rain on the French doors echoed in the nearly empty room.

"Just that chair in the kitchen. She'd be awful upset to lose that one."

So would he, he realized, as he pictured Brooke sitting on it eating the sandwiches. He hustled through the door, and snagged the little wooden chair.

"Guess that's it," Wade finally said, heading to the front door.

"Then let's get out of here." Morgan put the little chair inside and, with Wade's help, managed to get the metal doors closed and locked down. It wasn't a watertight solution, but it was a sheltered one. Better than what was heading toward the diner.

Wade locked the diner's glass doors behind them and jogged over to his pickup. The water was nearly to his knees, but he managed to get the truck to start and pulled out of the lot the same instant Morgan heard a loud crack.

The tree. Morgan watched as the big pine he'd noticed last week, on the other side of the creek, swayed in the rough wind. Back and forth.

He cursed, but before he could move, he saw it tilt, saw the big ball of roots that normally held it in the bank lift into the air.

Morgan stared as the thick green boughs come down and bounced off the hood of his steel truck. The metal over the cab buckled, and the tree slid just enough to wedge between the building and the seat where seconds later he'd have been sitting.

Water rushed over the broken bank. And headed straight toward Morgan.

CHAPTER EIGHTEEN

SITTING STILL WAS IMPOSSIBLE. Finally, Tara gave up, moving to warm her suddenly chilled hands before the flames.

"You don't know it's him," Wyatt said.

"I don't know it isn't, either." She closed her eyes, seeing Morgan in her mind's eye. She had so much to tell him, so much they hadn't resolved or discussed...or done.

Just then, the double doors opened and Wyatt's wife, Emily, stepped inside.

"Dang, it's nasty out there." She moved over to Wyatt, who pulled her into his arms and gave her a resounding kiss.

Tara looked away. Wishing...

"Hey, none of that in front of the kid," DJ teased.

"Oh, who do we have here?" Emily looked at the still-sleeping Brooke, then up at Tara. "Is this your guy's little one?"

Tara looked at DJ. "Is there anyone who doesn't know?" Though this time she was glad she wouldn't have to explain everything. As a judge in family court, Emily had more experience with this type of situation than Tara ever hoped to have. It didn't take her long to catch up.

"Except now, Tara's worried about Morgan. There's news of an accident involving a rig on I-35," Wyatt explained.

"Oh." Emily frowned. "I came that way. Traffic was bad, but I did see them moving a black truck from the ditch."

"Black," Tara whispered and sank onto the couch. Not blue. Not Morgan. Just then, her phone dinged and she grabbed it. She was only slightly disappointed that it was Wendy texting her Jack's number instead of Morgan. She quickly dialed, but only got Jack's voice mail.

"Jack. It's Tara. I'm trying to reach Morgan. Brooke's with me at my brother's ranch." She stumbled over the words. She took a deep breath and left her number for Jack, or Morgan, to call her back. Then she hung up.

All that was left to do was wait. The only sound in the room was the echo of the rain pelting the windows. The gas flames behind the glass were weirdly silent. She wished for the pop and crackle of logs, if for no other reason than to break up the night.

"I'm calling Dutch," Emily said softly, breaking the thick quiet.

"Dutch?" Tara asked.

"Sheriff Ferguson," Wyatt explained.

"No!" Brooke shot up off the pillow where

they'd all thought she was sound asleep. She scrambled into Tara's lap, curling her tiny hands tight in Tara's shirt. "Don't let her send me away, please." She hiccuped on a sob.

Tara closed her arms tight around Brooke. "I won't let anyone take you away." She frowned at Emily over Brooke's head.

Emily's eyes shone in the dim firelight. "I'm not sending you away, sweetie." Emily stood and moved to sit beside Tara. Brooke clung tighter, snuggling against Tara's shoulder. "I want to call the sheriff and let him know where you are."

"He'll take me to Mama. And Jimmy."

"He won't be able to get here," Wyatt said from the other couch. Emily glared at him, then looked at Tara and Brooke.

"If your mom has called the authorities, we have to let them know. If she hasn't..." She paused. "Well, that works in our favor."

Tara understood, and rubbing her hand up and down Brooke's back, she tried to calm the girl. "Do what you need to do to make everything legal, Emily." Tara tilted her head so she could see Brooke's face more clearly. "But the only person I'll let you go with is your dad, okay?"

That seemed to calm Brooke some. Tara felt her shirt dampen with the little girl's tears and part of her ached, wishing she could take them all away.

"I'll call from here so you'll know everything

I say, okay?" Emily didn't wait for anyone to answer as she pulled out her phone. She also lifted her briefcase off the floor and pulled out a laptop.

"Bernice? Hi, it's Judge Hawkins." The indistinct sound of a woman's voice came from the other end of the call. "Yes, we're all safe out here. Thanks." More talking. "We have an issue I'd like to report. Tara found a little girl wandering in the rain."

Tara breathed a sigh of relief and leaned her head against Brooke's. Every so often, she shuddered with a half-asleep sob.

"Yes, in town," Emily continued. "But Tara brought her out here. She didn't know where else to take her that would be safe." Emily listened. "Yes, we know you guys have your hands full. But we want to let you know in case someone's looking for her. She's safe and sound here."

More undistinguishable chatter, and Brooke seemed to calm. Her breathing was rough, but her eyes were closed.

"She asleep?" Tara mouthed to Wyatt. He leaned forward and nodded. The frown on his face was deep.

"I'm taking temporary custody of this girl, Bernie. I know it's unusual, but she's about six years old, and I'm concerned that there's something wrong or something has happened to her parents. I can't accept this or let it pass. Let Dutch know that I'm taking over the case."

Emily listened for a long minute. "Yes, yes, that's fine. We'll keep her here tonight and give you a call in the morning. Hopefully, the rain will stop soon, yes. Good night, Bernie."

The entire room breathed a sigh of relief when Emily hung up. She looked accusingly around the room. "See? I made it legal, and she's staying here with us."

She started typing on the laptop nestled in her lap. "I'm opening a case file. Let's get the facts down now. That'll help Morgan in the long run, as well."

"Thank you," Tara whispered and leaned her head on the soft cushion of the couch. Her eyes burned. For an instant, she wished she was six again and could cry herself to sleep with Brooke.

"Here." Someone nudged her shoulder, and Tara opened her eyes. DJ had a glass in each hand. "It'll help you sleep."

Tara almost laughed. "I'm a big kid now? I get a drink from Granddad's bar?" The carved wooden bar dominated one end of the room. Granddad had commissioned it from a local artisan when he'd built the house, believing it was better for his employees to party close to home and under his watchful eye. As kids, they'd all been in awe of its grandeur.

"You've earned it." DJ smiled and took a swig of his own drink—whiskey, from the scent. His was straight on the rocks, not "watered down" as he called the mixed drink he'd given her. "We all have."

Wyatt handed Emily a drink and they savored the silence.

"I'm thirsty, too," Brooke said softly.

That elicited a laugh from them all.

"We can fix that. How about one of these?" Wyatt fixed her a drink that smelled suspiciously like a Shirley Temple, complete with a maraschino cherry. The highball glass looked huge in the little girl's hands.

"That's pretty special treatment," Tara told her. "I don't remember him ever making one of those for me."

"I'll gladly make you one," Wyatt offered with a wink.

"I'll take a rain check, thanks." She lifted her drink, much stronger than Brooke's, in a mock salute and prayed it would do as DJ promised. Sleep seemed incredibly elusive right now.

WADE'S OLD FORD had seen better days, but the truck was high enough that they could make it safely through the rising water. Morgan had been convinced he'd made a colossal mistake when he'd seen that tree fall.

His truck was destroyed, but it looked like the trailer was intact. The big pine was wedged between the cab and the building, actually providing a level of protection to the back of the diner. He hoped.

"You think that trailer'll hold?" Wade asked, leaning forward over the steering wheel as if getting closer to the windshield would make seeing easier. The rain was coming down so thick, Morgan could barely see more than a few inches beyond the hood. How was the old man even driving in this?

"I hope so." Morgan glanced in the side mirror. They weren't making quick progress through the water, but his truck—what was left of it—was growing smaller in the reflection. He didn't speak, not wanting to distract Wade.

"Tara's brother's place is a ways out of town." Wade stared straight ahead. "Might take us a while to get there."

"I can't ask you to do that."

"You didn't. I'm offerin'."

"Thought your place was out east. Isn't that where the worst of the storm is?"

"Can't be much worse than this. If it is, I don't think I could get there anyway. Might not have a choice but to go out to the Hawkins place."

Morgan nodded, returning his gaze to the windshield and the view he couldn't really see. Then suddenly, they pulled out of the thick water, the engine making only a few protests as they were obviously heading uphill. The rain seemed to thin, as well, and Morgan could see the road, and the line of red taillights ahead. "Maybe you can get some information on the radio," Morgan suggested.

"Might." Wade grinned. "If it worked. Yer phone work?"

Morgan stared at the blank screen. "Nope." He didn't know if he'd run out of battery or if the thing had gotten wet.

"Mine's in the glove box. See if it's charged. I ain't looked at it for a while."

Morgan rummaged around in the very full glove box. Receipts, odd gum wrappers and small tools were all he found inside. Then he saw a curled cord and grabbed it. A phone sat next to it. Morgan flipped the ancient screen open. It lit up, faintly. One bar. A smidge of battery. Not enough to justify the phone call he ached to make. Not enough to do that *and* have anything left for an emergency.

He told Wade as much.

"Yeah, we might need to call someone if we get stuck...oh, wait." He pointed at the traffic jam they were firmly embedded in. The one surrounded by streams of water and muck.

Morgan chuckled, liking the man's outlook on life. "Yeah, there's that." He stuffed the rest of the junk into the glove box but set the nearly dead phone on the seat beside him. He'd wait.

Brooke was with Tara—she'd told him that and Wade had confirmed it. She was safe. For now.

The knot in his chest wasn't getting any smaller. He wanted his little girl back. Ached for it. *Now.*

Patience was a virtue, he told himself, pretending he had some.

TARA AWOKE. WEAK dawn sunlight filtered between the storm clouds and the horizon. There weren't any curtains on the picture window behind Wyatt's desk, and she could see the soaking-wet world outside. Levering up on her elbow, she looked at Brooke. She was curled up on the big pillow, one of Grandma's afghans snuggled over her tiny shoulders, her arms around the purple dragon that she hadn't let go of since they'd left the diner.

The diner. Was it still intact? Had the water destroyed her dreams? Tara shook her head, hoping to dislodge the images of destruction that had to have come out of last night's dreams.

She hadn't been asleep long. They'd gotten here late and she'd stayed up even later talking to Emily and her brothers.

Slowly, Tara inched off the couch and left the room on tiptoe. She left the double doors ajar, in case the girl did wake up. She hoped she didn't. Brooke was expecting her dad to be here when she woke up. And while Tara hoped for the same thing, she knew the chances were slim. And getting slimmer by the minute.

Voices came from the kitchen, and Tara followed them. Her brothers were there. Half a dozen ranch hands gathered around the table while Juanita was at the stove, flipping pancakes like a pro.

There was a new face at the table. Dutch Ferguson. The badge on his chest caught and held her gaze. What was he doing here? Was there news of the floods? About Morgan? Sylvie? She froze in the doorway, her heart pounding against her ribs.

"H-hi, Dutch," she whispered, clearing her throat before she headed to the coffeemaker. "What, uh, brings you out here so early?" Did she really want to know the answer to that question?

"Emily's call last night," Dutch explained. "I was out this way and thought I'd stop in and check." He took a minute to savor the coffee from his cup. "We did get a call about that girl."

Tara's heart sank. She couldn't let Brooke go back to her mother. Morgan might never find her again.

"You did?" That wasn't her hand shaking as she poured the coffee into a mug, really it wasn't. She didn't fill it too full, a precaution against spilling it. She liberally added cream and sugar, the clink of her spoon loud in the too-quiet room as she stirred the mixture. Finally, a sip of fortification under her belt, she slowly turned to look at the older man again.

"We got a call, yeah," Dutch repeated softly.

"Some guy named Jimmy said the little girl had been kidnapped."

Tara gasped. "I—"

The sheriff lifted his hand. "We know better. But—" he looked at Wyatt "—the call is on record."

"And time-stamped." Emily came into the kitchen then, wearing a fluffy, blue robe that Tara remembered her opening last Christmas. "What time did he call, Dutch?" Emily didn't look nearly as ruffled as Tara felt. She envied her sister-in-law.

"Bernice took the call, just like she took yours. 'Cept yours was two and a half hours before his."

"Two and a half hours?" Tara screeched. "We didn't call Bernice until Brooke was with me a couple hours."

"That's a hell of a long time for a little one to be gone and no one noticing." The anger was clear in Wyatt's voice.

"I'm not disagreeing with you, Wyatt." Dutch finished his coffee and pushed away from the table. He carried his cup to the sink. "Emily, I know when you called. Phil has the case file you started. We're in good shape there." He walked toward the door. "But right now, I got a little girl who's not with either of her parents, and I don't see either of those parents here."

Emily bypassed the coffee and fixed herself a cup of tea. She took in a deep breath of the steam that rose from the cup. "She's in my custody now. As an officer of the court, that trumps either parent until we've done an investigation."

"Never knew you to be one to argue jurisdiction, Emily." Dutch faced the room, and Tara watched the grin grow on his weathered face. "You know I'm not one to argue about that sort of thing, either."

"I do, Dutch." She smiled back. "How much time do you think we've got?"

Tara didn't understand what was going on. She was tired and stressed, and her head hurt from either the drink DJ had made her last night or lack of sleep or a dozen other stresses she'd internalized.

"I'll stall them with the investigation as long as I can." Dutch pushed the screen door open. "Let me know when—if—the father shows up. His lawyer has already filed a motion. I'm thinking you're going to grant it?" He looked at Emily, an eyebrow lifted.

"Why, Dutch, I believe we've worked together entirely too long." Emily deepened her drawl, and the men in the room laughed.

The sheriff looked at Tara and she swallowed hard, surprised at the deep emotion in his worn eyes. "Did you need something, Sheriff?" She tried to keep her voice even.

"You took a mighty big risk last night. I've been all over this county in the past twenty-four hours. I've seen the destruction. Most of the time, I'd give you a lecture about setting out like that in the dark. But you did a good thing, getting that girl to someplace safe." The old man cleared his throat, not saying another word as he headed to his car.

Tara frowned, wondering what had caused the sadness in the older man's eyes. She frowned and looked at Emily. Wyatt stared into his coffee, and the men around the table were silent.

"What am I missing?" Tara asked.

Emily was the one who answered, her voice soft. "Dutch lost his son several years ago. He was just eighteen." Emily paused to take a slow sip of her tea before she finished. "He drowned."

"If you hadn't been there for Brooke, she'd have probably been caught in the flooding last night." Wyatt finally looked up. "You probably saved her life."

"How bad is it?" She hadn't asked Dutch about the damage in town, more concerned about him taking Brooke. Silence stretched out. Obviously, it wasn't good.

"The creek banks broke," Wyatt explained. "The east side of town got at least three feet of water."

The Someday Café, her work, her dream, sat on the east side of town, right on the banks of that creek. Her eyes burned and she blinked hard, fast, refusing to fall apart—yet. No one said it, no one had to. It was gone. Everything had to be destroyed.

Closing her eyes, she visualized every inch of the place she'd worked so hard to build. The blue paint she'd spent days putting on the walls. The eclectic collection of furniture from every garage sale she could find. The industrial stove that she, Wade and Robbie used to make all those amazing meals. Their pride and joy. The counter stool where Morgan had sat, watching and waiting to find Brooke.

Brooke. The idea of her, of anyone out in that raging water all alone, made her shiver.

Where was Morgan?

TIME PASSED SLOWLY. The men went about their chores but stayed close in the yard, not riding out on the range. Wyatt was with them, as was DJ. Emily stayed in the house with Tara and Brooke.

News came slowly from town, and Juanita was in the kitchen watching the early morning news, giving them updates every few minutes. When she came rushing into the den, both women looked up. "Hurry, come see." She waved them toward the television.

A helicopter was flying over Haskins Corners, the town hardest hit by the flooding, according to the news anchor. "The small town has been cut off since yesterday, though rescue workers have been working through the night to help people out of their homes. Let's show you some of that footage now."

"Is that our town?" Brooke asked and crawled up on Tara's lap, the purple dragon still in tow.

"Yes, it is. Oh, look." Juanita pointed at the screen. "There's your diner."

They all watched as the helicopter dipped toward the creek bank where it had broken. Where the worst of the water had come out of the creek. A giant pine was on its side—Tara hastily stood and moved closer, sitting Brooke on the chair.

"That's Morgan's truck." Tara lowered her trembling voice, glancing at Brooke. "Under—" her heart beat in her ears "—the tree."

"Are you sure?" Emily asked.

"Positive." How many times had she looked at that truck? When had he gotten there? The truck's cab was badly damaged—the broad branches of the tree covered over half the trailer and blocked the view of the whole back of the building. Water still rushed across the entire property.

There weren't any other vehicles in the parking lot, and Tara let herself believe that Wade had kept his word and gotten out of there as soon as she left.

The helicopter moved over the rest of town. Main Street looked like a river, and cars sat in the middle of the wide, flowing water, abandoned, ruined.

"Tara?" Brooke squirmed on the chair, her purple dragon clasped in a tight hug. The photo of Morgan was still snuggled inside, and Tara wondered if it would survive all this.

"Yeah, hon?"

"What if…what if Daddy doesn't come?" She was staring at the television with wide, frightened eyes.

"He'll come."

Emily looked over at her, one eyebrow lifted.

"What?" Tara asked.

"Don't make promises you can't keep," Emily whispered, even though they both knew Brooke could hear them.

"He'll be here," she repeated, convinced she was telling the truth.

But as the next hours slipped by and the sun rose higher in the sky, Tara's certainty wobbled. She paced, going to the picture window that overlooked the entire property. From here, she could see most of the valley, the herd in the distance, the charred earth that was beginning to return to life with new growth.

The recent rains had done some good, nourishing the abused soil and seeds. Behind her, Juanita kept the TV on, but there was no new footage. No new information, just the same reports, over and over.

Tara had gotten ahold of nearly everyone on her staff. Only Wade wasn't answering his phone. He didn't have a cell phone that she knew of, and his home was east, where the damage was the worst. She tried not to worry about that, about the additional fact that her calls to Morgan and Jack hadn't been returned, either.

Could they even get to town? Should they try? "Maybe we should—" Her words were cut off by the loud rumble of an engine.

Brooke hastily scrambled off the couch. "Daddy!" she cried and ran to the door. She struggled to open it, the heavy wood sticking from all the recent damp. The slam of the screen door was loud as Brooke lunged out of it.

Tara was right behind her. "Brooke, wait!" There was no guarantee it was Morgan. The girl would be so disappointed.

A battered pickup came up the drive, stopping in the middle of the muddy lane. The men streamed out of the barns. And Tara heard footsteps behind her.

Relief nearly tripped her up when Wade climbed out from behind the wheel. He looked tired but in one piece.

The passenger door opened then, and the whole world melted away.

Morgan. He was here. He was safe.

Both he and Wade looked worse for the wear, their clothes rumpled, their eyes tired. But they were both smiling.

"Daddy!" Brooke cried from halfway down the sidewalk, her ponytails streaming behind her as she ran. Morgan was down on his knees in an instant as she flew into his arms. He looked so big, and she so tiny. He seemed to engulf her.

"Oh, Brooke," he whispered, though the pent-up pain in his voice carried across the entire yard. He kissed her head and ran his big hand over her hair as if making sure she was real.

Tara slowed her step, stopping several feet away. They needed this time, needed space, she was sure, though she ached to touch him, to make sure he was okay. Make sure she wasn't dreaming.

The purple dragon lay on the worn walk, forgotten, no longer a needed comfort. Tara bent to pick it up, her vision blurred. When she was upright again, she looked at Morgan and Brooke.

With his daughter in his arms, Morgan was staring at her. The intensity of his gaze stole Tara's breath. Tears filled his eyes, spilling onto his rough cheeks. He rose to his feet then, swinging Brooke up onto his hip, her head on his shoulder and arm around his neck.

His stride was long and sure as he came right up to Tara.

"Thank you," he said, then pulled her with his free arm to his side. "Thank you," he repeated as his lips found hers.

CHAPTER NINETEEN

MORGAN FOLLOWED TARA into the comfortable kitchen of the Hawkins ranch with a fair amount of trepidation. Kissing the girl for saving the day had been one of his better ideas. At least in his mind. The dozen sets of eyes staring at him when he'd pulled away from Tara hadn't been quite as…enthusiastic.

Before he could recover, though, an older woman had come out of the house and called everyone inside. Lunch was ready, and even his unexpected arrival wasn't about to stop this crew from eating. She bustled around the kitchen, putting huge platters of food on the big wooden table.

"Have a seat." The woman smiled and waved them toward the table.

Morgan would have liked Tara to sit with them, but she was bustling around, too, not meeting his eye.

"Daddy?" Brooke's tiny voice broke through the din the same way it broke his heart. He'd never heard a more beautiful sound. He had to fight to swallow the lump in his throat.

"Yeah, baby?" He sat beside Brooke and barely

resisted the urge to scoop her up in his arms again. She felt so small against him.

"Don't go away."

"No, honey. I'm not going anywhere."

Brooke snuggled close and held on tight. He could keep her here like this forever. Slowly, she pulled back just a little, so she could look up at him. "Mama said you didn't want us no more."

He didn't say, "Mama lied," though the words were on the tip of his tongue. "Maybe she misunderstood. I'll *always* want you." Right now wasn't the time to bash Sylvie or let the reality of what they still had to deal with—custody—into the situation. Now was the time for him to just hold and love his little girl.

"Are we gonna go home?" she asked.

"Yeah, soon." He smiled at her, feeling the warmth of her grin wash over him.

"Welcome to our home." A slim, young woman moved along the table, filling water glasses from a pitcher. "I'm Emily Hawkins." She extended her hand to him, and he took it, surprised at the strength in her handshake. "It's been nice having Brooke visit us."

Her eyes were astute and never wavered as she looked at him. Moving away, she sidled up next to Wyatt and got a brief kiss for her efforts. The cowboy was a lucky man, if the love shining in her eyes was any indication. Morgan glanced at Tara, not sure what to think.

"Thanks for having us," Morgan said to the entire room, his voice quickly drowned by the chaos of the crowd. The mounds of food soon disappeared, leaving empty plates behind. This had to be where Tara had learned to cook.

Finally, Wyatt and his men prepared to get back to work, gathering at the door. A young cowboy stuck his head around the corner. "Hey, Boss. Dutch is back." A puzzled look passed between the ranch owner and his wife. Morgan glanced at Tara, who'd kept her distance through the meal and was now sitting quietly beside her brother on the other side of the table. Her face paled and she clasped her hands together.

"Who's Dutch?" Morgan asked Tara, not sure if he was butting into family business.

"The sheriff," Wade volunteered from the counter where he was helping the cook—whose name Morgan had learned was Juanita, and who was married to the ranch's foreman. "Maybe he's got news about the diner."

Morgan had nearly forgotten about the diner, his truck, the flooding—all of it had vanished as soon as he'd seen Brooke. The sadness in Tara's eyes brought it all slamming back.

"Afternoon, ma'am," an older, burly man with a badge on his chest said from the doorway.

Morgan barely had time to register that before Sylvie burst into the room.

"There you are," Sylvie said, strutting to where

Brooke stood hugging Morgan's side. "Come on, Brooke, it's time to go."

Brooke only pushed closer to Morgan, hiding her face against his leg. "Don't wanna."

That's when Sylvie did what Morgan had feared she'd do earlier. Her temper flashed in her eyes as she rounded on him. "What did you say to her?" She turned to the sheriff. "Arrest him, Sheriff."

"Uh, ma'am, why exactly would I do that?"

"He took my daughter and put her at risk." Sylvie reached for Brooke's arm. "Come on, Brooke."

"No!" the little girl cried and tried to pull away from Sylvie's hold.

"That's enough, Sylvie." Morgan's hands were fisted at his side, but he relaxed enough to put his arm around Brooke's shoulders. "You've traumatized her enough."

"Traumatized? See?" Again, she turned to the sheriff. "This is why you need to arrest him. I realize this is the boonies, but surely you know how to arrest someone."

Brooke's sob broke the quiet of the room, and Morgan bent to lift her into his arms. She snuggled against his shoulder, reminding him of when she'd been a baby and he'd walked the floor to soothe her to sleep. The idea of Sylvie being able to take her again was like a knife in his gut. He couldn't let her go.

"Now, ma'am, let's calm down here." Dutch stepped forward, nearly in between them. "Wyatt, you got someplace private we can all go for a chat?"

Wyatt nodded. "You can use the den. Follow me." Wyatt led the way into a room with a fireplace and a bar that covered an entire wall. On the opposite end of the room, a large, wooden desk sat in front of a picture window that overlooked half the county. It was beautiful.

Was this where Tara had grown up? Morgan couldn't help but feel the inadequacy of his own past in comparison. She entered after everyone else had gotten settled, hanging back by the door.

"This is ridiculous," Sylvie started to say as soon as everyone stepped inside. "Brooke and I are leaving. Now."

"You're welcome to leave, Sylvie," Morgan said through clenched teeth. "Brooke isn't going anywhere with you."

"Wanna bet?" Again, Sylvie reached for their daughter.

"That's enough." Emily might be small, but her voice carried across the room. She'd come in at the head of this group and was seated behind the massive desk.

"And who the hell are you?" Sylvie stood with her hands on her hips. Morgan thought he actually saw the woman's lips twitch with a smile.

Brooke clung to Morgan's neck, her arms nearly too tight.

"It's okay, baby," he whispered, wishing this weren't happening in front of Brooke. She didn't need to see this.

Needing to feel grounded, he looked at Tara, who was leaning against the wall just inside the doors. She wasn't looking at him, but seeing her there eased some of the tension in his chest. She glared at Sylvie with more venom than he'd thought possible.

"I'm Emily Hawkins." She looked directly at Sylvie. "*Judge* Emily Hawkins, senior magistrate in family court." She didn't even blink. "I took temporary custody of your daughter last evening, when it was apparent neither of her parents were around to look after her well-being."

"Excuse me?" Sylvie glared. "I left her with a babysitter. She—" Sylvie pointed at Tara. "She took her and...and kidnapped her."

"You sure that's the story you want to go with?" Emily looked at Tara, then at Sylvie.

"It's true."

"No, it's not." Brooke said, lifting her head but not loosening her grip. Her bottom lip trembled, but it didn't stop her from speaking. "I went there all by myself. She made me grilled cheeses."

Morgan wanted to hug his daughter tighter. For once, that independent streak of hers was a blessing.

Sylvie turned and frowned at Brooke. "What have I told you about talking when you're not supposed to?" Sylvie snapped. "We'll discuss your disobedience later. We're leaving. Now."

"Not so fast." Emily stood then. "Dutch. I'm pretty sure my courtroom is unavailable due to the flooding."

"Yeah. The entire courthouse is closed off today."

"Can you give me a hand? I'm calling an emergency hearing here. Now."

"What are you talking about?" Sylvie looked around the room as if they were all crazy.

Morgan almost felt sorry for her. Almost. "Sylvie, quit while you're ahead. Judge Hawkins said she works for family court." He walked over to her, still not letting go of Brooke. "Right now, neither of us has custody. Sorry, baby." He patted Brooke's back, wishing he could protect her from what was going on.

"You can't do that," Sylvie told Emily.

"Actually, she can." The sheriff stepped forward. "And she is."

"Brooke is my daughter. Mine."

"She's *our* daughter," Morgan corrected her. "But we could both lose her if you don't cut it out."

"You're the one screwing this up, Morgan. Just like you've screwed up everything else."

"Stop it!" Brooke squirmed and let go of Morgan's neck. "Let me go."

Morgan instantly put his daughter on the ground, his heart hurting as he waited for her to go over to Sylvie. Everyone in the room watched as she yanked the purple dragon from its spot on the couch, then ran over to Tara. Thankfully, Tara knelt beside the girl and gave her a hug.

"Daddy?" Brooke's voice wobbled, shaking his heart just a bit. Her eyes were wide and frightened.

"It's okay, sweetie," he lied. He hadn't a clue how any of this was going to work out.

Sylvie stared at Tara, like angry darts flying through the air. "What do you think you're doing?" Sylvie took a step toward Brooke and Morgan went to follow.

Emily stepped in instead. "I'd suggest you think about what you say and do next." Her glare was hard, but it all vanished when she knelt beside Brooke. "Remember how last night we talked about following the rules and making everything right?"

Brooke nodded, still leaning against Tara's side.

"This is part of that. Now I need to talk to your parents. Is that okay with you?" Emily waited patiently, giving Brooke a sense of control, something he doubted she'd had much of in the last year.

Brooke looked at Morgan, then at Sylvie, then finally, surprisingly, at Tara. Tara nodded, and Brooke pushed away from her side. "Okay."

"Maybe Juanita can take you to the barns to see the horses while we talk," Emily suggested. "Would you like that?"

Juanita stepped forward then, crouching beside Emily. Brooke looked at Morgan and the indecision in her eyes was almost too painful to see, but he couldn't look away. He had to be strong for his daughter.

Brooke was hesitant to go with Juanita—afraid Morgan would leave her. "I'm not going anywhere," he reassured her. "Not without you."

How long would it take for her trust to return? Would it ever?

"You got real horses?" Brooke turned to Juanita.

"We do." Juanita smiled. "And Tyler even has pigs, Pork Chop and Hamlet, down the hill."

Brooke actually laughed and his heart squeezed. "Those are funny names."

The tension in the room eased, and Morgan unclenched his fists. "Go with Juanita. I'll be right here when you come back. I swear." Letting her go was the hardest thing he'd ever done.

"I'll be waiting, too." Sylvie tried to sound sincere. He was being uncharitable, but a year of worry and anger was more than his charity could overcome. Sylvie did a bad job of hiding her need to win Brooke back. She'd never been good at sharing what she believed was hers. Morgan just wished she cared more about what Brooke wanted.

Slowly, Brooke nodded. After she took Juanita's hand, Tara leaned down. "Why don't you leave Lanara here? The horses might be scared of a dragon."

"Oh…okay." She extended the stuffed animal to Tara. "But only you get her. She likes you." Tara softly gasped, then slowly nodded. His heart squeezed.

"We'll be right back," Juanita said. Brooke looked over her shoulder all the way to the door. The room fell silent after they left.

"Let's get started," Emily said, her voice easily filling the room as she resettled behind the desk.

It hurt that his daughter had wanted away from him, that she was having to go through this mess that he and Sylvie had made of their lives.

TARA WATCHED BROOKE LEAVE, realizing what an amazing daughter Morgan had. She knew how scared Brooke was of her father leaving her, of going back with her mother, but it humbled Tara that Brooke trusted her. She couldn't let the girl down.

She knew everyone expected Emily to speak, but Tara surprised them by stepping forward, holding up the stuffed dragon. "You all need to see this."

"I told her to throw that ratty thing away," Sylvie said. "I didn't know she still had it."

"Morgan, turn it over," Tara whispered, ignoring Sylvie's outburst.

He did as she asked and she saw the pain flash in his eyes. The pinned-together back of the stuffed animal made it look even more disreputable. The safety pins looked so out of place against the matted fur.

"Why didn't you fix it for her?" Morgan softly asked Sylvie.

"Duh. You know I can't sew."

Poor Brooke had put up with a torn toy because of it. Tara reached past Morgan when he didn't move. His heat washed over her, and she wanted to put her arms around him and hold on tight. This was going to hurt him. But Emily needed to see this, and he had to know.

"Brooke didn't want it fixed," Tara whispered. She opened the pins and pulled the fabric apart.

"What the—?" Morgan looked at Tara, then at what she was doing. She reached inside and pulled out the crumpled photo.

"She's been carrying this around." Tara put the photo in the center of the desk. "She had to hide it here from you," she said to Sylvie, barely controlling the accusation in her voice. "This says a whole lot about what that little girl has wanted for the last year." She faced Emily.

Watching the hurt and realization dawn in Morgan's eyes cut through Tara. He'd been trying so hard to find Brooke, and the confirmation that she'd wanted him to find her was overwhelming to them all. Even Sylvie stared silently at the picture.

"I—I didn't know," she whispered.

Angry words flew through Tara's mind, but she pressed her lips together. It wasn't her place to voice an opinion about how Sylvie had ignored her daughter. It wasn't her place to hurt Morgan more.

Emily, however, had no such qualms. "My guess is that you were too busy to pay attention to your daughter." The anger in Emily's voice was stronger than Tara had ever heard. "Just like you ignored her last night, when she could have drowned in those floodwaters."

"I paid for a babysitter." Sylvie tried to defend herself, but even she looked defeated.

Emily leaned back in Wyatt's big desk chair. "I'm not going to make any final rulings today. There will need to be another full hearing." Emily paused for a long time, thinking. Tara wished she could read her sister-in-law's mind.

Finally, she spoke again. "But we are going to settle a few things. Morgan, I know your attorney has filed a motion for full custody. I've read it." She looked up from the computer screen. "Is that still what you want?"

Morgan didn't hesitate. "It's not about what I want." He took a deep breath. "It's about what's best for Brooke."

"Give me a break," Sylvie said under her breath.

Emily looked at Sylvie. "Do you have something to say at this point?"

Emily gave Sylvie every chance to explain her comment. Tara held her breath, hoping for Brooke's sake that for once Sylvie could put her daughter before herself.

"She's *my* daughter." Sylvia said and Tara's hopes faded. "*I* know what's best for her."

"Taking her away from her home, from a father she obviously loves and who loves her in return is in her best interest how?" Emily asked.

"You saw how she reacts when we talk to each other." Sylvie threw her arms wide. "I had to get away."

"For a year?" Emily asked.

"Yes. I had things to do. Being a truck driver's wife sucks."

"Hmm." Emily paused before she asked, "If Brooke hadn't gone to Tara's diner, if we weren't here today, would you have any plans to take your daughter to her father?"

Morgan's sharp intake of breath was loud in the room.

"Why would I do that?"

Tara closed her eyes, afraid of what Morgan was feeling and thinking. When she opened her eyes again, he hadn't moved, but his gaze dark. His anger and anguish filled the room.

"Morgan?" Emily's voice broke in, and he slowly returned his gaze to Emily.

"Yes, ma'am?"

"I'm granting your motion for full custody. It's temporary, until a formal hearing can be held."

Tara figured this was the part where Emily would probably bang a gavel or something if they were in an actual courtroom. She'd never been in Emily's courtroom, but she had a feeling it was a fair and just place.

"But—" Sylvie tried to protest.

"Don't push your luck." Emily faced Sylvie. "I get the impression you took that little girl away from her father a year ago for no other reason than spite. You're the one who's put her at risk. You've barely taken care of her." Emily's anger was rising.

"I did my best."

"Maybe," Emily conceded. "But it's time for someone besides you to judge that. Dutch?"

"Yes?" The older man stepped forward.

"You're my court witness on this. I know you don't file motions, but can you put that in your report and submit it to my clerk?"

"Yes, ma'am, I sure can." The older man didn't even bother to hide his grin.

"You're all crazy." Sylvie stomped her foot, the thick carpet stealing most of her thunder.

"You're right. The court will be looking more closely into this, if for no other reason than to settle custody of Brooke over the long haul."

Sylvie walked toward Morgan. "This isn't over."

Morgan sighed, but the look he gave her lacked any anger. Tara wondered what he was thinking, what he was looking for.

"Sylvie, get your act together. Figure *you* out. I won't take Brooke away from you. You're her mom, she loves you, but we have to do what's best for her right now."

Time ticked by as their gazes clashed. Sylvie's eyes shone, but whatever emotion she was feeling, whatever thoughts she'd let in, she quickly blinked away. Her eyes turned cold again and she stalked out of the room. The kitchen door slammed behind her.

Emily sighed, turning to Morgan. "She's probably right. This isn't over."

"I know." He smiled. "But it's better than it's been in ages. Thank you."

"Don't thank me. I'm just doing my job." She turned to Dutch. "Guess we'd better make sure she doesn't try to take Brooke again."

"Oh, I'm her ride. She ain't going nowhere." The older man nodded but headed to the door. "Besides, she'd have to get her away from Juanita."

"That's something I'd almost like to see." Emily laughed and smiled at Morgan. "Go get your daughter. I think she'll be happy."

"Thank you." Morgan's voice cracked. "Thank you all."

Tara watched him leave, watched the gratitude shine in his eyes. Wishing for so much more, she heard his silent goodbye.

CHAPTER TWENTY

TARA STOOD IN the parking lot of the Someday Café and stared at the disaster that had been her diner. It had taken two days to clear the roads of Haskins Corners so the town's inhabitants could return and begin picking up the pieces of their lives.

Roadblocks still limited who could enter this side of town. Today was Tara's first chance to see what was—and wasn't—left.

Mud and debris that looked like entire trees had wedged between the back door and the huge pine tree that had fallen from the creek bank. The familiar cab of Morgan's truck was nearly buried in the muck. She couldn't see through the branches well enough to know how badly damaged it was.

Wyatt, DJ and half the ranch crew had come with her. Wendy and Wade were meeting them here soon.

They couldn't get to the back door, much less through it. Walking slowly around the building, Tara went to the front door. She couldn't open it, either. It took DJ and Wyatt nearly ten minutes to clear enough mud from the doorway to open it.

Driving here, down the battered streets of town, she'd seen what had happened to the other businesses. She could tell who had worked to try to save their business, just as she could tell who hadn't been able to do anything. The swift current had swept so much away, had broken walls, damaged Sheetrock and stained everything.

At least here, the structure was still sound.

Just full of filth that she had no idea how to get rid of. One shovelful at a time, she guessed.

Finally, the guys shouldered the doors open, and Tara stepped inside. And gasped.

Mud lay nearly evenly over the wood floor she'd had refinished a few short weeks ago. A thick, gray-brown blanket. Just inches above the top, on the faint blue walls, an uneven brown line marked where the water had risen to.

But, other than the counter and the stools bolted to the floor, the room was empty. "Where's the furniture? My tables. My chairs!" It was all gone. She stared out the windows at the pile of sticks and twigs caught in the mud.

Her heart broke.

Even her chair from Mom's house. Gone.

She wanted to cry. She wanted to fall to her knees and wail. Not that it would do any good and not that she'd do that in the thick mud. But, oh, how she longed to release all her pent-up pain.

"Oh, no!" Wendy came through the front doors and froze. "It's awful." Carefully, she picked her way through the muck to come over to Tara. They hugged for a brief moment before surveying the mess again.

"It could be worse," Wyatt said.

Tara knew that. They'd all seen the house on Elm Street on the way here. The big Victorian that had sat at the creek bank for a century now sat precariously on the edge of…well, of nothing. A big gaping hole where the river bank had been last week.

"I guess." Wendy took a couple steps toward the kitchen. "How bad is it in there?"

Tara hadn't yet looked. The brand-new industrial stove wasn't something they'd even tried to move. It would have been foolish, but she wished they could have saved it. Her eyes burned. She had to look, but she didn't want to. Her imagination hurt too much.

Wendy lifted her chin and did the deed for her, shouldering open the swinging doors that were frozen in the mud. The sound of scraping between the door and the floor was loud. She stepped through and even from here Tara heard her gasp.

She couldn't look. She just couldn't. Her heart, what was left of it, was already broken.

"Come here," Wendy cried. "You have to see this."

She didn't want to. But she was the boss, the

owner, the person who would ultimately have to decide if they were going to work to reopen. Or give up. She'd have to look eventually.

Slowly, her steps heavy in the goop, she moved to the door. She didn't have to push against it as Wendy already had. The mud held it open.

Wendy was only a couple steps in front of her. Frozen. Staring.

Boxes. Dozens of them, every single one that had been in the pantry or the freezer, was stacked around the big stove. They were soaking wet, with mud climbing up their sides. But—moving closer, Tara squinted, not believing what she was seeing. Yes, there was dirt on the floor, but only about an inch deep. The stove was coated in grime, but not caked in mud like the rest of the diner.

Someone—most likely Wade and maybe Morgan helped—had created the barrier. They'd protected her livelihood.

Tears burned her eyes, blurring her vision as she stared at the stove, safe and salvageable. Beautiful. Blinking, she felt the damp spill over, sliding down her cheeks, probably leaving tracks in the dirt she felt on her face.

"They saved it," Wendy said unnecessarily. "We can reopen." Her excitement grew. "We can do this."

Tara felt some of Wendy's enthusiasm, which quickly faded as she looked around. It would take days...weeks to clean everything. How long would it take to get the necessary inspections done? She had to file an insurance claim. Mentally, she began making lists.

Voices and footsteps broke into her thoughts. *Wade must be here.* She needed to thank him.

Instead of her evening cook, half a dozen men she'd never met before came through the front doors. Jack led the way.

And Morgan pulled up the rear. Brooke was with him and wore a pair of bright purple rubber boots. She carried a toy shovel in one hand and a little bucket in the other.

Suddenly, Tara noticed everyone was carrying a grown-up version of Brooke's toy. What—?

"We're here to help," Jack said, smiling almost as brightly at Tara as he was at Wendy—almost. "These men work for us." He introduced everyone. "We hauled in supplies. Now we're here to help you."

"Oh, that's not necessary," Tara said.

"Don't turn down free help." Wendy nudged her. "It is free, right?"

Morgan nodded and approached Tara. "It's the least we can do for all you've done for us, right, Brooke?"

His gratitude rang true, so why did she feel disappointed? The shadows were gone from under his eyes, even though his face still sported pale versions of the bruises. He looked younger, too, from the happiness Tara knew he was feeling.

Brooke tilted her head and smiled at Tara. She looked happier, too, her hair now neatly combed and shiny. Two purple bows held her ponytails back.

"Did your dad do your hair?"

Brooke giggled. "No. He goofed it up. Uncle Jack did it."

Jack actually blushed. "Okay, people. We've got work to do."

The men who'd come with them set to work, scooping shovelfuls of dirt and mud into buckets and a lone wheelbarrow. Brooke took tiny scoops and with a determined look on her face, took each one to a bucket nearly as big as she was.

"Thank you," Tara said to Morgan as he worked and kept an eye on his daughter.

He stopped, crossing his big forearms atop the wooden handle of his shovel. "Like I said, it's the least we can do." He reached over and flipped one of Brooke's ponytails. "Right, honey?"

Brooke didn't stop scooping, carrying the little shovelful slowly, deliberately to the bucket. "Yep," she finally answered once she dumped the mud. "Daddy said he wouldn't've found me without you."

"Hey, that was all you." Tara forced herself to smile at Brooke.

"How long 'fore you can make more cookies?" Brooke looked up, hopeful.

Tara's heart sank. "I don't know." She tried to shake off the sadness that loomed over her. "You can have the first batch. Promise." She forced herself to smile at Brooke. The girl grinned back, and Tara's heart warmed.

Time passed as the truckers joined the men from the ranch in the cleanup. Taking turns shoveling, carrying full buckets to the creek bank.

Tara and Wendy worked on moving boxes away from the stove. "I—I can't believe it's all gone. All my furniture." Tara only realized she'd said it aloud when everyone fell silent.

Morgan stepped closer, frowning at her. "Wade didn't tell you?"

"Tell me what?"

"Come here." Morgan took Tara's hand in his, guiding her out the front door.

"What are you doing?"

He simply smiled and stopped when they reached the big trailer. He took a deep breath, and Tara wanted to know what he was doing. It distracted her from wanting so much more than gratitude and favors. So much of what she couldn't have.

"Let's see if my plan worked." With a series of clanks and thumps, Morgan unlocked the back doors. His burly arms flexed as he pulled the heavy metal doors. They thumped hard against the trailer's outer walls.

Tara could only stare. Her furniture. All of it—the chairs neatly stacked, the tables carefully placed on their sides, their legs safe and dry as they reached into the air. The buffet leaned against the sidewall as if it were meant to sit there instead of in her dining room.

And her chair from Mom's sat front and center—dry and as inviting as ever. Her vision blurred and she hastily blinked it clear. Morgan reached a hand out and slid his palm along the seat's edge. "When I walked into the diner and saw the meal you'd fixed Brooke on that table…" He swallowed hard. "I knew how special you were."

Everything looked clean and dry and safe. "Morgan?" She didn't know what else to say. "How did you do all this?"

"Wade helped." Morgan scrubbed his hand down his face. "Damn, I didn't realize until just now how worried I was that it wouldn't be okay." He took a deep breath and hung his head for an instant. "Thank God."

Tara could only stare. First, at the furniture that was safe and sound. Then at the big tree that was still wedged against the back door. Finally, at his once-beautiful truck, now mangled by the storm.

"If your truck hadn't been here—" She walked around to look closer at the damage. "The tree would have taken out the whole building," she whispered. "And what the tree didn't destroy—"

"The water would have," he finished for her.

How close she'd come, how close they'd both come to losing everything—she looked at Brooke diligently scooping the dirt—suddenly dawned on her. Despite the day's growing heat, she shivered. "Oh, Morgan." She went to him. "You saved everything."

"Tara," he whispered, a caress, and slowly walked to her. She expected him to pull her close and maybe even kiss her, but he didn't. Instead, he cupped her chin in his big, strong hand. "No, *you* saved everything." He cleared his throat. "You saved me."

"How—?"

"You gave me back my life, my daughter. More than that, you taught me how to live, to love." He softly kissed her lips. "I'm being honest when I say thank you." He paused, looking into her eyes with a depth of emotion, longing, happiness and desire like she'd never seen on his face before.

He moved in closer. "But that's only a small piece of what I feel for you." He paused and rubbed her cheekbones with his thumbs. "Long before we found Brooke, I was drawn to you. You, this place…it feels like home. No one's ever made me feel this belonging before."

Tara gasped, afraid to hope. Gratitude wasn't

the same as lasting, forever love. It wasn't the same as what she felt for him.

"From the first time I met you, I've loved your spunk, your determination, your kindness." He leaned in close, his warm breath fanning over her face, over her lips that wanted so badly to kiss him.

"Morgan." She wanted to beg him to kiss her, but the words were stuck in her throat.

"Your beautiful face and body." His voice lowered. "Your heart." He pulled back slightly, his gaze finding hers. "I fell in love with you."

Was this real? She met his gaze and saw more than gratitude there. Heat washed over her as he wrapped his arms around her and pulled her tight.

"Oh, Morgan. I—I was afraid to hope. You have so much in your life."

He laughed and pulled her close. "It doesn't mean a blessed thing without you."

Then he kissed her. Long and hard, as if he couldn't get enough and didn't plan to ever stop. His words echoed in her mind. The three important ones repeated over and over.

When he finally pulled away, he looked dazed. "I—I can't begin to hope you feel the same—"

Tara put her finger over his lips, enjoying the feel of his kiss, still soft and warm on her skin. "Don't you even think of doubting me." She smiled at him. "I love you, too," she blurted. Then, because she couldn't stand it anymore, she kissed him. Sweet and warm, she filled her kiss with every emotion she couldn't begin to put into words.

When they stepped apart several minutes later, Brooke was standing there, staring at them. Tara's cheeks warmed, not used to an audience. "Uh—"

"You need something, honey?" Morgan didn't move his arms from around Tara.

"I was thinkin'. When we go to Dallas, can Tara come with us?" Brooke smiled at Tara. Morgan followed his daughter's gaze with a look of his own.

"If she wants to." The hesitancy in his voice hit her hard, and Tara looked closer at him. Did he want her in his day-to-day life?

"Do you want to?" the girl asked Tara. She didn't answer, but the girl didn't seem to notice the loaded silence that followed her question.

Tara laughed. She wanted to be with him—them—more than she'd wanted pretty much anything else. She stared at the damaged building behind her. Stared at her damaged dream.

"I—"

"Hey." Morgan hesitantly pulled away from Tara. "Can I ask you something?" he said to Brooke, glancing only briefly at Tara.

Brooke nodded earnestly.

"What would you think about us moving to Haskins Corners?"

Brooke's eyes grew wide, and the smile that

broke over her face lit up the world. "Could we? My friend, Lisa, and me could go to school together?" The excitement in her voice was strong, like Morgan had said the right thing.

He met Tara's gaze. "What do you think?" He slowly returned to his full height, towering over them both, engulfing Tara with the warmth of his body and love.

A loud crash made them all jump. Tara turned to see a furry ball scurry out from between the tree branches. "Ricky!" she cried. The raccoon looked a little worse for wear, but he was alive and apparently hungry.

Tara stepped over to Morgan and slid her arms around his waist, loving the feel of his solid muscles beneath her hands, relishing the feel of those even stronger arms engulfing her.

"Looks like the customers are already coming back," she whispered. "There's a seat at the end of the counter that wouldn't be the same without you."

He laughed and hugged her tight. "I'll take it." His lips found hers then, and she kissed him back.

She'd worked so hard—at building the diner, at finally finding the right man, at finding herself. She'd nearly lost it all, but instead…she couldn't ask for anything more.

* * * * *

Get 2 Free Books,
Plus 2 Free Gifts—
just for trying the Reader Service!

Get 2 Free Books,
Plus 2 Free Gifts—

just for trying the
Reader Service!

HARLEQUIN *Presents*®

HP17R2

Get 2 Free Books,
Plus 2 Free Gifts—
just for trying the Reader Service!

HARLEQUIN SPECIAL EDITION